Five years after its initial publication, I had the rare opportunity to submit *The Grid* to a significant Hollywood film producer and director for his consideration. It was quite a thrill. Here was his response:

April 17, 2007

Dear Alden Studebaker,

Thank you very much for submitting your novel *THE GRID*. It's certainly a timely subject and one on everyone's mind these days. I congratulate you on the creation of it, but I don't feel that it's something for me, as either film or television material – which is not to say that you won't find enormous interest elsewhere.

I wish you all the best of success with it.

Sincerely,

Sydney Pollack

Other books by Alden Studebaker

Wisdom for a Lifetime in the 21st Century
How To Get the Bible Off the Shelf and Into Your Hands

Hoosieritis – The Contagious Condition That Is Indiana

The Fault

Not Just Any Bag of Bones (editor & publisher)

For more information:
https://aldenstudebaker.com

The Grid

Anne & David,
With love & blessings!

Alden Studebaker
October 2, 2020

ALDEN STUDEBAKER

For information, https://aldenstudebaker.com

ISBN: 9798689279114

Cover design: Chesapeake Group

This novel is fictional. Any references to actual events, businesses, organizations, government agencies and locations are only intended to give the story a sense of genuineness. Any resemblance to actual persons living or dead is entirely coincidental.

First Edition: Copyright © 2002 by Alden Studebaker.
Printed by Author House (previously 1st Books), Bloomington, Indiana
First published, 04/29/2002

ISBN: 1-4033-2282-1
ISBN: 1-4033-2281-3

Because of the dynamic nature of the Internet, any web addresses or links contained in this book may have changed since publication and may no longer be valid.

Dedication

This book is dedicated to my father, Henry "Hank" Studebaker, and to engineers everywhere.

Acknowledgements

Donna Studebaker, my wife, and chief editor, for her expert advice and loving inspiration.

Henry Studebaker, my father, and technical adviser.

Michael Maday, the editor of my first book, *Wisdom for a Lifetime*, for his steadfast encouragement of my continued writing work over my career.

Karen "Jake" Lindvig, for her belief in my potential as an author.

David LeBeau, my Bloomington, Indiana connection, for his enthusiasm and advice about submarines.

Verena Pickart-Demont, for her assistance with the German language.

Chapter 1

"WITH NEWS ON the half-hour, and breaking news at once, this is news radio 700, WLW, Cincinnati. At 6:30, our top story, Mayor Luken proposes meeting with residents of Over-the-Rhine to ease tensions after another police shooting…"

A hand shot out from under the sheets and landed on top of the clock radio silencing the recitation of the morning news. Through a hail of groans, grunts, and yawns Hank muttered to himself, "Damn it, why did I set that alarm?"

His arm, back under the covers, he laid in bed staring at the ceiling pondering what to do next. Today was the beginning of his vacation, and he wondered if he could bear the idea of being detached from his familiar work pattern. With a lurch, Hank sat up, as if someone had pressed a button on a control panel. The angle of the early morning sun through the bedroom window hit his face like a searchlight. Temporarily blinded, he stood up and trudged into the bathroom. The mirror revealed his tired, drained face. He closed his eyes and shook his head in an attempt to magically change his look. The movement caused his brown hair, once fuller, to shake about. Reopening his eyes he continued to see the face of a burned-out engineer.

"I've got to do something with myself other than sit around here all day," he thought. Immediately his autopilot took over as he showered, shaved, and dressed. Wearing a light blue dress shirt, red tie, and gray slacks, he grabbed his briefcase, and headed to his late model dark-green Chevy Malibu sedan.

As Hank drove out of the cul-de-sac neighborhood along his well-rutted route to work, his mind drifted off into the recent events of his life. For the first time in nearly a year he was officially released from the demands of his job. The mental pressure as chief engineering director for Ohio Valley Power had placed enormous stress on his psyche, especially the effort he had spearheaded to bring all of OVP's seventeen coal-fired power plants into Y2K compliance. This was no small task given the variety, and in some cases, the antiquity of the plant's computer controls. If it hadn't been for the unrelenting efforts of Hank and his staff much of, Indiana, Kentucky, and Ohio could have been cold, dark, and without a milliampere of power come January 1, 2000. This effort had stretched his body and mind to its breaking point.

While he made the series of right turns that plunged his car down the steep and winding Anderson Ferry Road he began to mull over the hundreds of "what if" scenarios he and his colleagues had entertained. These memories haunted him even on this fine, sunny June morning. Millions of people had unknowingly counted on him not only for their comfort, but some for their very existence. He had inwardly felt the tiny cries of premature babies holding on to their fragile lives cradled in the warmth of their incubators. Every critical hospital patient on a life-support machine needed electrical power to breathe, to live. Few others carried this awesome burden of responsibility. He had been puzzled and flabbergasted with those government officials and corporate CEO's who had been so cavalier and matter of the fact about the potential implications of Y2K. Their indifference had not only confused him, but had exacerbated the gravity of his task. Hank chose to isolate himself in the cocoon of his work, work that kept him going. Although he had been surrounded by his staff on that foreboding New Year's Eve, no one had felt more alone than Henry Charles Hudson, or felt more grateful when the lights stayed on. "A non-event they called it. Hell, it was a non-event because we made it one!" he thought to himself as he slipped into the left-turn lane and stopped for the traffic signal at US 50.

When the light turned green, Hank turned left onto River Road, the main artery along the banks of the Ohio River that eventually connected with the heart of Cincinnati's downtown business district. He quickly searched for his sunglasses now that he was heading east into the brilliance of the early morning sunrise. The OVP Building, a ten-story structure built in the 1960's stood alongside the other multi-story buildings lining Fourth Street. Hank parked the Malibu in his personal parking place in the underground garage and took the elevator to his office on the eighth floor. As he exited the elevator he saw a familiar figure perched on a ladder in the hallway.

"What's up, Gus?"

Looking down toward the direction of the voice came a response, "Well, Hank, you know, it's that time of year again when we replace all of these tubes, whether they're burned out or not."

"No kidding! What do you do with all them? Do you just throw them away?"

"Mostly. Sometimes I rescue the better ones and take them over to this old church in Camp Washington. They do a lot of good for the kids and families in the neighborhood on a shoestring budget. Not having to buy light bulbs makes a difference, I think. Could you hand me that one leaning against the wall?"

"Sure, no problem."

Hank lifted the new tube to Gus and exchanged it for the used one.

"Well, that's great. It's nice to know someone in our company isn't wasteful."

"Hey, aren't you on vacation? Somebody told me that you'd be gone until next week."

"Oh, I just have a few last-minute details to handle in the office. You know how it is?"

"Don't I! This place really sucks it out of you."

"Ain't that the truth? Take it easy, Gus."

Hank left the maintenance man and walked down the hallway to the Office of Engineering Services. Once in his office, he plopped down in his chair and booted up his desktop computer. Within minutes he was monitoring the power output of all of OVP's plants. His eye soon caught an irregularity at the Gallatin, Kentucky plant. Output was down to forty-five percent of capacity. He picked up the phone and called the manager on duty there.

"Hello, this is Hank Hudson at the Cincinnati office. May I speak with Keith Morgan, please?"

"Just a moment, Mr. Hudson, I will connect you."

Keith Morgan responded, "Hi Hank, I thought you were on vacation."

"I noticed that you're running a little low."

"We had to shut down Number Two. One of those new water purity indicators said the filters weren't working. We've got a crew looking into it right now. No sense mucking up one of the company's newest boilers."

"Just checking. Sounds like you've got a handle on it. Take it easy, Keith."

"You too, Hank."

Satisfied that everything was in order, Hank began fussing around with the papers on his desk, the very same ones he had stacked into priority piles the night before. After a few minutes, he walked out into the administrative area, made a pot of coffee, and returned to his office with the fresh brew. The sun was inching higher into the sky illuminating the hazy summer atmosphere that hung over the Tri-State area. It was just before eight o'clock when his administrative assistant, Janie Hausman, arrived. She saw his door open and leaned in.

"Hank, what are you doing here today? You're supposed to be home getting ready for your fishing trip!"

"There were a few things I had to check I couldn't get done last night," he lied.

Janie shook her head, "Nothing could be so important that you had to come back here today. Let the rest of us do a little work for a change, and go home. You need to relax."

"Maybe you're right," as Hank took the last sip of his coffee and tossed the styrofoam cup into the trash can, "I guess I didn't know what else to do except come to work. It's all I've done for the last several months."

With that insight, Hank picked up his briefcase and followed Janie out to her desk.

"That's why you need this vacation and the European power conference trip next month. The company won't fall apart while you're gone."

Hank smiled back at her, "Okay, I can take a hint. I'll see you next week, Janie."

"Good-bye, Hank."

Hank left the office and headed back toward the elevator.

"Janie, Hank is way too dedicated. This company works him like a slave," said Jennifer, the secretary to Hank's boss.

"You've got that right," fired back Janie, "David Banning is no Hank Hudson. You're lucky if he gets in here by ten."

Banished from his office by Janie, Hank descended to the garage level and was back in his car by 8:15. In an effort to get in the vacation spirit, he pulled off his tie and threw it in the passenger seat. Within a minute he was out of the parking garage and immersed in the downtown traffic full of commuters arriving for work. Back on River Road Hank felt a pang of hunger—the cup of coffee he had in the office had been insufficient to properly stoke his boiler. Hank pulled into UDF. After filling up the Malibu, he went inside the United Dairy Farmers store to have a look around and pay the bill.

"Can I help you with something?" asked Kellie, the young woman behind the counter.

"Do you make milk shakes this early in the day?"

"If you want one, it makes no difference to me. The company doesn't care when we sell the ice cream. What'll ya have?"

"Make me a large chocolate shake, and I'll have this bag of chili-flavored corn chips too."

"It'll be a couple of minutes on the shake; we make 'em from scratch, you know."

"That'll be fine. I'm in no hurry. I'm on vacation starting today."

"Really, are ya going anywhere special?"

"Yeah, tomorrow I'm driving down to Missouri to do some fishing. I haven't been there since I went with my brother a couple of years ago."

"I hear there's good fishin' down there. My Uncle Bud swears by it. He goes to tournaments there two or three times a year."

The shake machine whirred while the clerk waited on a couple of customers paying for gas.

"So, where do ya work?" she asked as she put a plastic lid on the freshly prepared shake.

"Oh, I'm with the power company."

"Really? You don't look like you're dressed to read meters."

"Actually I don't read meters. I work in the downtown office. I'm more in the production end of things. Boilers, turbines, that kind of stuff."

"I see," said the cashier with a raise of her eyebrows, "your total with the gas is $21.57."

"Here's my credit card. Just put everything on it."

Hank paid the bill, and was back on River Road sucking on his shake when he flipped on the radio to the classic rock station.

"...whatever it is, that girl put a spell on me...help me, help me..."

Hank began tapping his fingers on the steering wheel and started to relax—just a little. When he arrived back at his house there was a call on his answer machine from Darrell.

It had been months since Hank had last seen his old navy friend, Darrell LeBrec. Hank first met Darrell while they served as shipmates aboard the U.S.S. San Francisco, a Los Angeles class nuclear submarine based out of Pearl Harbor. Hank's B.S. degree in mechanical engineering from Purdue University had landed him a job as a junior engineering officer on the San Francisco. Darrell, on the other hand, was a Pork Chop, otherwise known as a supply officer. They had instantly hit it off after discovering they were each native Hoosiers, and had gone straight from NROTC programs at Indiana colleges to OCS, and then to Submarine School in Groton, Connecticut.

Hank had grown up along the shore of Lake Michigan in the small town of Dune Acres, halfway between Gary and Michigan City. The water and boating were in his blood. He and his brother, Lewis, could be found at the beach most days of the summer, especially in the cool of the evening when they were done working for their father's contracting business. It was no surprise to anyone that knew Hank when he opted for a tour of duty in the Navy.

Darrell came from the southern Indiana college town of Bloomington, where he had attended Indiana University. The only time Hank and Darrell were ever at odds was during the playing of the Oaken Bucket game, that one Saturday of the college football season when Purdue and Indiana would play against each other. Naturally, they could never agree on which team would win the bucket.

After their discharge from the Navy, within a year of each other, they went their separate ways. Hank returned to Indiana and Purdue University where he added an M.S.

degree in mechanical engineering. This subsequently led to his hiring by OVP.

Darrell moved to California and pursued a radically different path. He became active in environmental issues with the Sierra Club, studied parapsychology at the University of California at Berkeley, and was ordained as a metaphysical minister. After several years, Darrell received his Ph.D. from Berkeley, and returned to his hometown and alma mater, Indiana University, as an associate professor of psychology. One day, while visiting his Aunt Alla Morgan in Madison, Indiana, Hank ran into Darrell at an antique store. After a couple of cold beers at a nearby pub, they happily discovered they were living less than a three-hour drive from each other. Following their unexpected reunion, they met for lunch every few months, usually when Hank was visiting OVP power plants in southern Indiana.

The urgency and focus of the Y2K compliance effort had so utterly consumed Hank that he had had little time for social interaction. Hank had kept up with Darrell by e-mail, and the occasional phone call, but no more. Hank wasted no time picking up the phone and returning Darrell's call.

"Darrell, it's Hank. I got your message."

"Hank, it's great to hear your voice. What's it been, six…no, seven months since we had lunch over in Columbus?"

"I think you're right it's been seven months. It was right after Thanksgiving. Do you remember they were still serving turkey dinners at the Bob Evans restaurant there off of I-65? Hey, I was thinking about calling you myself. I've actually got some vacation time this coming week and I was considering stopping by your place on the backside of my fishing trip."

"That would be great, Hank. I have something I need to share with you in-person, something important."

"What is it, Darrell? You sound mysterious."

"It'll have to wait until I see you. When were you planning to come by?"

"How about lunch next Wednesday?"

"Wednesday is good for me. My classes will be done by noon. Meet me at the Pizza Hut near my house. You know the one. I'll look for you around 12:30."

"12:30 it is. I'll be there. See ya, Darrell."

Hank hung up the phone and flicked on the TV and began channel surfing.

"The A-6 Intruder, the ugly work-horse of the Vietnam War and Desert Storm coming up on the Discovery Channel "...click..."And now your local forecast, on the Weather Channel."

"All right, the A-6!" Hank thought to himself, "I remember seeing those on the carriers back at Pearl. That was a mean airplane if there ever was one."

He could hardly wait for the commercial to be over before switching back to the show. Any programs having to do with mechanical devices were his favorites, especially those about military aircraft.

While he watched the local weather forecast he noticed that temperatures would be rising into the nineties, a bit early for the second week of June. His mind snapped back into his job. Power demands would be the highest of the year, but his staff could handle it. After the scorching summers of the past several years, they were well versed in keeping the grid up. He tried to dismiss these workaholic thoughts, but they dogged him nonetheless.

All through the rest of Thursday, Hank pondered the enigmatic nature of his conversation with Darrell. His out-of-the-blue remark had piqued his interest. What could he possibly want to discuss with him that he wouldn't share over the phone? He would find out next Wednesday. In the meantime, he had a fishing trip ahead of him.

Chapter 2

FOR HOURS HANK sailed west through the green corn and soybean seas of southern Indiana and Illinois. Despite the fact that he was on vacation he felt incredibly restless. Every electric power line and mobile phone tower he passed reminded him that he was not on the job. Considering the proliferation of these phone towers in rural America during the past year, Hank had ample reminders of his self-induced truancy. Feelings of guilt started to creep into his consciousness.

"Do I really deserve this vacation when there are so many needs back at the office that demand my attention? I should be driving down to Gallatin to help sort out that filter problem Keith Morgan was having, not gallivanting across the countryside," he thought to himself.

Before long his sense of guilt was transformed into incompleteness. He felt unwanted, unneeded, and unproductive. What a strange feeling it was to be free from the weight of responsibility. The shock to his psyche was not what he had anticipated. Although he was away from the offices, control rooms, boilers, and computers, all he wanted to do was plan for the next disaster, the next calamity, for Y3K. He stopped in Effingham for gas.

Eventually the monotonously flat landscape of the farmer's fields gave way to the urban sprawl of the St. Louis metropolitan area. Traffic quickly slowed to a crawl as Hank inched his way past one freeway exit after another. "Damn it, I should've got going earlier!" he kicked himself for not having left at the crack of dawn to avoid the plethora of vehicles now smothering him.

Hank had driven through St. Louis many times on business, and nearly always ran into this kind of congestion. Today the roads were especially thick with people taking advantage of the early summer weather to travel out of town for a weekend on the rivers and lakes of the Missouri Ozarks. Nothing could be hotter and more uncomfortable than a hot, humid day in St. Louis. Thankfully, the air conditioning in his Malibu was blowing ice cold.

After he crossed the Missouri River into St. Charles the traffic thinned out and the pace picked up for the rest of his jaunt down I-70. A couple of hours later he pulled off the freeway at Kingdom City and went straight into McDonalds for a Big Mac, fries, and a large chocolate shake. Other than filling up his car in Illinois, this was his first stop in hours. He noticed the large fish tank in the middle of the restaurant, an unusual feature for a plastic, cookie-cutter establishment like McDonalds. Was the fish tank a sign of his future fishing luck? He could only hope. A seven-year old girl joined him at the aquarium.

"Aren't they beautiful?" she asked.

Surprised by her voice, Hank responded, "Why, yes, they are, aren't they? Which one do you like best?"

"I like the blue one with the black and yellow stripes. He's real handsome, like he's dressed up in a suit."

"Yeah, he's a nice one."

"Come on, Debbie, our food is ready," said the girl's mother ushering her toward an open table.

"OK, Mom. Good-bye," she said waving to Hank.

Hank lamented the fact that he would never likely have children of his own. He loved children, but his broken, childless marriage, and lack of suitable prospects, made that likelihood fairly certain. Talking with the girl reminded him of this probability.

After finishing his own meal, Hank headed south on US 54, a route that meandered through Jefferson City, Lake of the Ozarks, and eventually to the small town of Hermitage where he picked up State Route 254 into the even smaller Carsons Corner. Once across the dam, a left turn down a gravel access road led him to the Angler's Dream Resort, an odd assortment of bluish-green cabins on the shore of Lake Pomme de Terre. He had spotted the resort while surfing the internet one night, and thought that it would fit the bill for his fishing get-away. The cabins were simple, comfortable, and quite reasonable.

Shortly after checking in, Hank headed back across the dam into Carson's Corner to the Trading Post where he picked up some groceries, a fishing license, and a Kansas City Star. After a dinner of canned chili and beer, he turned on the early-80's vintage black and white television. Its prehistoric nature reminded him of the first TV his father brought home, a little twelve-inch model. By comparison, this set was practically state of the art. After fiddling with the rabbit ears for a minute he was rewarded with two watchable stations, NBC and PBS. He opted for PBS and a show on dinosaur digging in Argentina. After nodding off during the show several times he convinced himself to go to bed.

Hank awoke to the sound of a weed whacker outside his cabin window. He looked at his watch, 9:44. The day was already marching on. By now, Hank would have already have been at work, even on a Saturday morning. He sat up, feeling slightly disoriented, scratched his head, looked around at the imitation oak-paneled walls of the bedroom, and realized that he wasn't home. Today, tomorrow, and the next day were his to do as he wished. He could go fishing, hiking in the woods, read a book, or just do nothing. What was doing nothing like anyway? Maybe he would remember.

Saturday flew by him like an F-15 with its afterburners blasting. After devouring the newspaper from the day before, he showered and shaved and managed to drag himself into town for a meal of fried catfish and apple pie at the Carson's Corner Lodge and Restaurant, across from the Trading Post. Sunday like Saturday was a blur of nothing as he really began to relax and release the internal stress he'd been carrying for so long. By Monday Hank was beginning to feel like himself again. Why had he blown these last three days just loafing around? Had they been a waste, or had he needed time to decompress? "I came here to go fishing, I'd better get to it!" he chided himself.

Each cabin came with a boat. A motor was extra, but nothing Hank couldn't afford. The resort owner told him that the boat would be tied to the pier, a half-mile from the resort down the gravel access road. He decided to walk there rather than drive. Hank was getting up in years, forty-seven a year ago September, but he wasn't an invalid. Not yet anyway. The walk would do him good. The aluminum fishing boat was just where the owner said it would be. Due to an ongoing drought, the lake level was lower than normal. He had to be careful not to drag the bottom of the motor as he negotiated his way out of the landing area.

Lake Pomme de Terre was created in the early 1960's by the Army Corps of Engineers as a means of flood control. Its 7,800 acres and maximum water depth of eighty-five feet made it one of the best fishing lakes in the Missouri Ozarks. Fish of all kinds, including the mighty muskie, could be caught in the lake, hence its nickname, "Gem of the Ozarks." Hank was counting on hauling in some keepers. The 10-hp Evinrude quickly propelled the *S.S. Hudson* southeast to a small cove where its captain dropped anchor and began the task at hand. Hank had two poles, an old bait casting rod that he had inherited from his ex-father-in-law, and a newer spin cast outfit he bought on sale at Walmart. He decided to use the bait caster with night crawlers and a bobber for pan fish, and with the other pole he would cast lures for bigger fry. He retrieved a cold beer from the small cooler, cracked it open, took a quick drink, and began casting a lure into the lake. The image of the fish tank he had seen at the

McDonald's a few days before flashed in his mind's eye. He began to imagine his basket filling with fish, large fish like bass, catfish, walleye...suddenly the bobber dove on his bait casting rig. Hank grabbed the rod and began reeling in his catch. The fish fought valiantly, but to no avail. Within seconds Hank had landed his first fish of the day, a thirteen-inch crappie. He unhooked the fish, tossed it into the wire basket, and dropped the basket back into the lake. Now he had the beginnings of dinner. Not wanting to waste another fishing moment he re-baited the hook, and threw the line back into the same spot it had been. As Hank washed the worm mess from his hands in the lake, a familiar yet foreign sound pierced the air.

Before Hank left Cincinnati, his immediate supervisor, David Banning, had said to him, "Hank, we want you to have fun and enjoy your trip. If anyone deserves to kick back a little, it's you. Hell, I wish I was going with you. The best fishing is down there in Missouri. You don't have to take a cell phone with you, but could you take your pager, the satellite one, just in case we really need to talk with you. I mean, don't get me wrong, I know your staff is the best, but with these hot temperatures forecast for this next week, I'd feel safer knowing that we could get a hold of you if we had to."

Reluctantly, Hank had agreed. Now he regretted that decision with all of his being. The joy of landing his first fish was wrested from him by the shrill pulsations of the pager's sound system. Each relentless tone was like a jab from an ice pick being driven into his cerebral cortex. With the reflexes of Jesse James, his right hand grabbed the infernal device attached to his belt in one fluid, smooth motion, while his left hand, still dripping with lake water, pushed the off button. Immediately, the natural sound of waves dashing against the boat was all he could hear. Peace had returned to the S.S. Hudson, but its captain was perturbed. He pushed another button that brought up the phone number of the caller. It was Banning's number. "Damn! What could he possibly want now? And the fish are biting too!" Hank muttered to himself.

Grudgingly, Hank reeled in both poles, pulled up anchor, and was soon underway toward the northwest. Within ten minutes he pulled up to the dock, picked up his gear and catch of the day, and trudged back to his cabin. "This better be important," he mumbled.

Hank soon discovered that there were no phones in the cabins at the Angler's Paradise Resort; consequently, he had to drive into Carsons Corner to use a pay phone. Two pay phones stood like security guards on watch in front of a derelict gas station. Hank pulled the Malibu up in front of them, got out, and punched in the necessary numbers.

"Hello, Banning here."

"It's Hank Hudson, you paged me!"

"Hank, how's the fishing down there? Catch anything yet?"

"Yeah, I'd just caught my first one when you paged," replied Hank with full control of his emotions.

"Hey, I hope I'm not disturbing you."

"Not in the least. What's up?"

"I was talking with Janie here in the office about that big power conference in Europe next month. Are you still up for that after your fishing trip?"

"What kind of imbecile pages me in the middle of my vacation to ask a stupid question like that? Couldn't this wait a few days?" Hank stewed.

"Wasn't it was all arranged? On Wednesday, Janie said she was making the plane, car, and hotel reservations. I'm counting on going. It looked like real sport, and my mother's family is from that part of France. I was planning to take a few extra days after the convention and poke around a little."

"Hey, that's fine. We just wanted to make sure you were okay with it before we cut the tickets. We'll see you back in the office on Thursday. Take it easy, Hank. Bye."

"Bye."

Hank stood there in a state of utter bafflement. It was impractical to be angry. It was destructive to be furious. It was foolish to even think another thought about this phone conversation with Banning. He took a deep breath, let it out, and then another. He looked across the street at the Trading Post from the pay phone area. It was almost noon. Behind him was the restaurant. It was time for lunch and a restocking of his dwindling beer supply.

Chapter 3

IT WAS EARLY Wednesday afternoon when Hank pulled into the outskirts of Bloomington, Indiana. Hot, humid weather continued to plague the lower Midwest, with daytime temperatures hovering in the lower nineties. Hank momentarily tapped into the work part of his brain and wondered how OVP's end of the grid was holding up, if the capacity was sufficient for the demand of the day. The peaking plants would probably be brought on line. He knew he'd be back at work in the morning, and already his brain was entering the crank zone. He caught himself, and snapped his attention back to negotiating his way through the Indiana University campus. Hank found the Pizza Hut and pulled into the parking lot. It was 12:35. Darrell had arrived a few moments before, and greeted his old friend with a quick hug. Once inside, they opted for the lunch buffet and a couple of iced teas.

"How have you been, Hank? Y2K really whacked you out, didn't it?"

"You got that right. I don't think I could've stood another diagnostic test."

"When you told me that you had bought an electric generator for your house, I figured I'd better do the same. If the top engineer of Ohio Valley Power had one, everybody should. Of course nothing really happened, but I kind of like the peace of mind knowing that I've got options if the grid does go down some day. Heck, I didn't even have to buy gas for my lawn mower this spring with all that I stored for the generator."

"I just love your positive attitude, Darrell. Most of my other friends are cursing me now for having bought portable generators."

"I wouldn't curse you, Hank. You're too decent a man. It sure is good to see you."

"Same here, I don't know why I didn't just take a little more time off this past year. I guess I was too obsessed with the Y2K compliance job. After having lunch with you last November, I only saw my folks for Christmas."

"Hey, I'm not accusing you. I for one am glad you were obsessed. Better to err on the side of thoroughness."

The iced teas arrived just when they were most needed.

"So, what's going on Darrell? What do you have to tell me now that you couldn't on the phone? You're going to bet that Purdue will win this year?"

"It's about my recent conversations with Dr. Nicholas Spencer. Ever heard of him?"

"Can't say I have."

"He's an archaeology prof here at IU, kind of a nut, but well-meaning and tops in his field. 'Crazy Nick' they call him. Anyway, although he spent years studying ancient Mayan culture, he specializes in the study of mythological civilizations."

"So, this guy is into unicorns, centaurs, and mermaids?"

"Oh yes, but that's just a part of it. He says that they once existed thousands of years ago, but that nature and human evolution have advanced beyond those days."

"So, what does this have to do with me? I'm not exactly a mythology buff, you know, just another boring engineer."

"When I finish telling you of my last conversation with Nick, you won't feel like such an ignoramus anymore."

"Alright, keep going. But can we get a little food first? I'm starving. I've only had a couple of donuts and coffee since I started driving at five this morning."

"Sure, no sweat."

Hank and Darrell strolled over to the buffet tables and loaded up with Caesar salad and assorted slices of pizza. Once they each had a few bites the conversation resumed.

"OK, so fill me in on this Nick fellow of yours."

"Have you ever heard of Atlantis?"

"Yes, of course. Didn't Donavan sing a song about it back in the 60s? Something about it sinking into the Atlantic Ocean."

"The same. You always did know your songs, Hank. Well, Nick has done some research into their power generation system, and has discovered through psychic readings and on-site investigations in the Bahamas that the Atlanteans had developed the ability to generate power without burning fuel or creating toxic waste."

"Whoa, just a minute, Darrell! Am I on *Fantasy Island,* or have we utterly lost our senses? You're talking about a free energy device. Is this cold fusion? Hell, we've been talking about that for years, but no one has been able to get it to work."

"It's not cold fusion, and I'm not Ricardo Montalban. I'm serious about this! According to Nick, the Atlanteans were able to create and direct power through the use of a crystal aligned with the magnetic field of the earth."

Hank paused and looked out the window as he imagined what such a device would look like. A moment later he looked straight back at Darrell and responded.

"How could it have worked? Nothing in my engineering background speaks of magnetic fields of the earth, or crystals. However, when you take into account the first law of thermodynamics, the conservation of energy...hmm...the law clearly states that energy is never created nor destroyed. The earth has a very strong magnetic field. Well, who's to say, I could be blowing smoke here, but there is perhaps the remote possibility that a certain kind of conductor could access the magnetic field. If there were a way to tap into that field, the energy produced could be substantial to say the least. But, then you run into the second law of thermodynamics."

"Which is?"

"The degradation of energy. You see, energy is like water. It runs downhill. The trick is utilizing as much of it as you can before it all hits the bottom of the hill."

"Yes, but what about the first law of thermodynamics? You just said that energy is neither created nor destroyed."

"Maybe I should take you on a tour of one of my power plants and I'll show you how we deal with these two paradoxical laws every day."

"Some other time, Hank. Perhaps when you're dismantling one of them."

"Dismantling? I've spent most of my career keeping them going. Not to mention, the industry isn't building many more of them. We're strapped for development money and trying to get people to conserve electricity. My colleagues in California are pulling their hair out trying to keep up with consumer demand. I don't think tearing down plants is in the cards. You must be pulling my leg, Darrell!"

"Hank, I'm dead serious about what Crazy Nick has discovered. Someday in the future you will be razing your plants, or at least changing them over to this new technology. I can sense it."

"Darrell, I've never read anything about this so-called 'Atlantean' technology in any of my power rags, nor has it ever been mentioned at the conferences I've attended. A lot of progress has been made with fuel cells, but we still haven't figured out a way of producing hydrogen cheaply. Work with superconductivity has made advances in delivering and using power more efficiently. This is the cutting edge of power generation. Hey, it's my business to know."

"I know, I know," implored Darrell, "but hear me out on this one. It's because you're so good at what you do, and you're my friend, that I had to tell you all about it. Are you busy this afternoon?"

"No, just visiting with you."

"Good! We've got an appointment with Nick at 1:30. I've told him all about you. He's a bit eccentric, totally consumed with his work, but he grows on you. Let's get going, it's already a quarter after."

"I have a dinner date with my Aunt Alla down in Madison at 6:30, so I can't stay too long."

The Pizza Hut was located in a strip mall, so leaving Hank's car for a few hours wasn't a problem. They took Darrell's aging red Subaru wagon for the five-minute drive to the Indiana University campus. Professor Nicholas Spencer's office was on the second floor of a gray limestone building. The door to the office was wide open as they walked toward it. Crazy Nick was at his computer checking his e-mail. He was of average build, had a receding gray hairline, a day's stubble on his face, and was wearing an open collared denim shirt with navy slacks.

"Darrell, come on in," he motioned them in with his hand and went back to his computer screen. "I'm almost done with this message, give me a sec."

The walls of his office were covered with books on nearly every ancient civilization that had inhabited the earth and then some. Hank noticed the large collection of Roman books. He thought to himself, "Now those were some bona fide engineers, those Romans. They sure knew how to use an arch, channel water, and mix concrete. That's an ancient civilization I can relate to."

Nick looked up from his computer screen.

"That should take care of it. A colleague of mine in Turkey has been digging around in ancient Ephesus and wanted to pick my brain on a few things. I was at Ephesus back in my twenties, and would love to go back. It was once one of the largest cities in the Roman Empire, with over a million people. Now it's gone like so many great cities. In the future they'll be digging up New York, Paris, London, maybe even Bloomington."

Hank thought to himself again, "Ephesus is a Roman city. Maybe I'll have to go there sometime – on my next vacation."

"Nick, I want you to meet my old Navy buddy, Hank Hudson. We were shipmates aboard the San Francisco."

"Hank, it's really good to finally meet you. Darrell tells me you're a crackerjack engineer, and that you single-handedly saved the world from the Y2K bug."

"Darrell has been telling tall tales again."

"So, what tales has he been telling about Ole Crazy Nick?"

"I told Hank about your discovery of the Atlantean's energy generation system."

"That's pretty much all he told me, other than you're the best, and that I might be out of a job soon because of this amazing discovery of yours."

"Not out of a job, but working at a better one I believe," Nick corrected.

"How so? With the scenario Darrell's laid out before me I'll soon be tearing down all of my places of work."

"I actually envision you simply changing your existing plants over to this new, or should I say, *old* technology. There's no point in tearing down all of the transmission lines, not yet anyway. Would you like to know what I've found through all of my research on our Atlantean ancestors?"

"I'm all ears."

For the next couple of hours Crazy Nick told the two former submariners what seemed to be a fanciful tale of an ancient yet technologically advanced civilization that once ruled the earth over 13,000 years ago, but a civilization that destroyed itself through the misuse of its power.

"I'm not a highly technical person, Hank, so I can't explain precisely how the Atlanteans generated and directed their power. Darrell's told you about the crystal and its interaction with the magnetic fields. Suffice to say that they were able to heat and cool their homes, fly through the air, and enjoy a very high standard of living much as we do today, only without the harmful side effects of toxic pollution."

"At this point, Nick, all I can say about this is where is the evidence that the Atlantean civilization ever existed, let alone that they had technology more advanced than ours? I live in the world of facts, figures, and proof. Where's the proof of any of this? Artifacts should be on display in museums, and spread all over the cover of the *National Geographic*. I'd like to believe you, but my logical side isn't buying it. Nick, where's the proof?" Hank looked at Darrell for support.

Nick was ready. "Have you ever heard of the Bermuda Triangle, Hank?"

"Who hasn't? It's an area of the Atlantic Ocean between Florida, The Bahamas, and Bermuda. Unexplained disappearances of ships and aircraft have occurred in that vicinity for over 50 years. I saw a show on the Discovery Channel about it a couple of years ago. You're telling me that the ancient Atlanteans used their energy system to vaporize these craft?"

"I am Hank, more or less. But, not the Atlanteans directly, rather, their technology. Around 11,500 B.C., one of their main temples, or to put it in your language, power plants, was inundated with the sinking of Poseida, an island remnant of their once great continent. Obviously there is no one left to man the controls, but it is occasionally set off by fluctuations in the earth's magnetic field. Hence, the odd phenomena that have plagued humanity for millennia."

"Again, Nick, where's the proof of it? How is it that you are so certain that the Bermuda Triangle is related to an ancient power source gone wild?"

"Can you come up with a better explanation? I know you haven't put in the time on this like I have, but my instincts and experience in dealing with archaeology tells me it's true. I've also read all of the books available on ancient Atlantis, and visited the Bahamas, one of the few ancient Atlanteans lands still above water. I've even consulted psychics, who have added that the technology was given to the Atlanteans by visitors from another star system."

Hank glanced at Darrell with incredulity, "Darrell, I think you guys have been watching too many episodes of *Star Trek*."

Darrell joined in the conversation, "Hank, set aside your logical mind for a moment and open yourself up to the possibility of inexpensive, pollution-free energy. Consider for a moment the potential blessings such a system would bring to our planet."

"It would be revolutionary to say the least."

"Don't you think that this is the kind of revolution we need today? You told me at lunch how power companies are not building many more plants. Perhaps they shouldn't. Once this technology is discovered and developed there won't be any need to mine coal, drill for oil or gas, or decide where on earth to bury radioactive wastes."

"Hey, I am very cognizant of what comes out of my smokestacks. The EPA is constantly breathing down our necks with emissions regulations. It's a miracle we can produce a kilowatt of power with those guys after us. I know it ain't pretty, but it's the cleanest we can make it."

"Well, imagine no smoke, smokestacks, or EPA on your ass."

"This all still sounds like a fairy tale to me. Magic crystals, extraterrestrial benefactors, and this psychic thing. I've never called in a psychic to tell me what was wrong with one of my boilers. I can just see Banning's face looking at a bill from one of those 1-900 psychic phone lines."

"Hank, do you remember all of that parapsychology stuff I was into out at Berkeley? We were working to prove the existence of psychic phenomena. We tested hundreds of people and determined that everyone is a psychic to one degree or another. Every person has intuition, the ability to know the truth about something without any external input. It is my belief and understanding that all of the experiences of humankind are imprinted in kind of a data bank, or accumulated consciousness. Carl Jung called it the collective unconscious. Who's to say that someone living today through their intuitive abilities couldn't access the thoughts, impressions, and ideas of the ancient Atlanteans? I myself have caught glimpses, flashes of insight regarding their civilization. They did exist. They were real people not unlike us today. In fact, Hank, we were them. Millions of us living today were once Atlantean. We're just now discovering the truth about ourselves."

"So, I'm a reincarnated Atlantean! Why didn't you tell me before?"

"Would you have heard me before? You always say what a boring, stiff engineer you are. But, I don't believe you're as dull as you think you are. In my book, you're downright brilliant, but perhaps I'm a bit biased. Remember back on the San Francisco when we were on patrol out of Pearl running on the surface when the control room hatch status panel still showed a red circle for the after escape trunk hatch?"

"Who could forget that day? We were getting ready to dive and everyone was close to puking their guts after eight hours of rolling around on the surface."

"That's right. And do you remember that no matter how many times we tried to re-dog it the light stayed red? Then you went to the MPA and told him that if we opened and shut the hatch that the indicator light would read green. How did you know it would work?"

"I don't know. I just knew it would. Mechanical devices often seem to have a personality all their own."

"It's intuition, Hank. It's simply knowing something to be true without concrete evidence. We use it all of the time without knowing that we are. In a flash of insight you could see what needed to be done to get the light to read green. And, you were right."

"Yeah, yeah, I see your point. If only I'd known that a big wave was going to hit the hull just as I opened the hatch then I wouldn't have got the engine room all wet and set off the alarms to batten down the hatches. I mean, here I was, wetter than an otter in a stream in the escape trunk with all hell breaking loose in the rest of the boat."

"But, you were right about the hatch, and it all worked out OK. The crew got to go through an unscheduled drill, and did so in record time. Following your intuition is like that, Hank. When you're not afraid to follow it things work out for the best. Intuition and spiritual guidance are the only sure sources of information, especially in critical situations where rational thinking yields little in the way of positive answers. I'm sure you use your intuition all the time in solving problems at work."

"Power plant engineering is sometimes an art form, but also good, logical science."

Nick interjected, "Hank, Darrell and I wanted to have this talk with you because we believe that bringing this power generation system to the world is what humanity most needs right now. It could be our saving grace, if you will, our salvation. How long can the world continue to rely upon coal, gas, oil, and nuclear fuels to produce energy? Nuclear plants are being decommissioned right and left, and it is my understanding that very few new power plants are being built to take up the slack, let alone handle future power needs. You of all people should see the problem."

"Most of us in the power business are focusing on conservation and efficiency, you're right about that. You're only partly correct about new plants. There are some in the works that are pretty nifty in that they combine cycles of generation into one highly efficient plant. But, you're right about fuels, they haven't changed in years. I suppose most of us simply go about our business as best as we can and hope that the future will work itself out."

Hank looked at his watch. It was 4:44. Three hours had seemed to go by in a matter of minutes, and he was just beginning to enjoy the discussion after its initial, tense sell job atmosphere.

"I need to get going down the road. My Aunt Alla's got dinner cooking for me, and she likes to eat on time, if you know what I mean?"

Darrell stood up and began to move toward the door. Hank followed.

"Just think about what we've said," Nick added as they hovered near the doorway. "Ponder it for a month and let's talk again. I'll even spring for lunch."

"As much as I'd like to, I've got to go to this power conference over in France next month. But, when I get back I'll give Darrell a holler and we can get together. Maybe I'll have more to say about this Atlantean power technology of yours. I'm sure they'll have a workshop on it at the conference," Hank said jokingly.

Darrell drove Hank back to his car in front of the Pizza Hut. Soon Hank headed south to Madison and Aunt Alla's Victorian era house. All through the dinner of meatloaf and mashed potatoes Hank could think of nothing else but his mystical conversation with Darrell and Crazy Nick. As far-fetched as it seemed a part of him longed for the day of clean, inexpensive energy. But what could he possibly do to hasten that day?

It was after eight o'clock before he was back on the road heading for his home in Cincinnati. In his rearview mirror he could see the smokestack of OVP's Clifty Falls Power Station looming in the setting sun belching its plume of acid rain producing fumes skyward, adding to the glowing yellow haze of the Midwest sundown. "That's ugly, isn't it?" he thought to himself.

As he came upon the many coal fired power plants that littered the banks of the Ohio River each one seemed to speak to him of their impending obsolescence, like dinosaurs waiting for the primordial comet to whack them into extinction. His entire life's work felt like a dream, a mere series of incidental happenings in the passage of time, none of which seemed lasting or permanent. Had his career been a waste to this point? He resolved not to become a dinosaur and to adapt to whatever lay before him.

Chapter 4

THE MORNING FOG began to lift off the Volga River as the sun inched into the eastern sky above Nizhny Novgorod. Today would be warmer than normal with the temperature reaching about twenty-eight degrees Celsius. Even though it was Russia's third largest city, Nizhny Novgorod was not well known to western tourists who usually made the rounds of the more familiar urban centers of Moscow and St. Petersburg. Established as a fortress city in the thirteenth century at the junction of the Volga and Oka rivers by Yuri Vsevolodovich, Prince of Vladimir, for most of the twentieth century Nizhny Novgorod was known as Gorky. In the 1930's, the Soviet government changed its name to Gorky to honor its hometown writer and friend of the Bolshevik revolution, Maxim Gorky. Due to its industrial might and militarily sensitive activities, Gorky was off limits to foreign travelers. The famous physicist, dissident, and Nobel Laureate, Andrei Sakharov, was exiled to Gorky to keep him shut away from the world. With the fall of the Soviet Union in 1991, Nizhny Novgorod took back its ancestral name and placed its welcome mat out to the world.

Nizhny Novgorod was home to over a million people, including Natasha Shakhova. Although she no longer lived in the city, she still considered it her hometown, her cloister, her safe haven. Most of her family, including her mother, Olga, and her sister, Natalya, lived in Nizhny. Serendipity had opened the way for her to visit not only her hometown and family, but also her alma mater, Nizhny Novgorod State Technical University, formerly Gorky Polytechnical Institute. She had been granted special leave from her job as chief engineering director at the Baltic Regional Power Plant to lecture at the university. Her experience and family background made her expertly qualified to speak on the particular challenges of nuclear power generation.

Natasha's father, Dmitri Shakhov, had been on the engineering team that pioneered the Soviet Union's first attempts at harnessing nuclear energy as a source of electrical power. His example was an inspiration to his eldest son, Anatoly, and later his daughter, Natasha, to enter the engineering field. Tragically, as if some weird manifestation of karma had zeroed in on the Shakhov family, Dmitri and Anatoly each died within three years of each other.

Dmitri, like so many of his countrymen, passed away from the life-long effects of alcoholism. Officially, his death was listed as having been related to his exposure to nuclear radiation during his long years of service to the state, but everyone close to him knew the truth. Vodka and his propensity for perfectionism in his work had sucked away his vital force. Fortunately for Dmitri, he had lived long enough to see Anatoly receive his engineering degree from GPI, and begin his first job at the Chernobyl Power Plant in Ukraine. Fortuitously for Dmitri, he didn't witness his son's agonizing death in 1986 following the nuclear accident that made the word "Chernobyl" synonymous with "Death." If he had lived to see Anatoly die he surely would have died himself, for he would have felt personally responsible for having helped design such an environmentally faulty plant. The vodka saved him from such a fate. However, the Shakhov family women were less fortunate. The price of life for them was carrying the grief, anger, and sadness of their sudden losses. For Natasha, the weight of this underlying emotional trauma was heightened by the nature of her profession. She often felt responsible for their deaths, especially Anatoly's. Although she would consciously dismiss the illogic of these feelings, they haunted her nonetheless. Today was one of those days.

Oh, how she missed them both, especially this past week. They would have been so proud of her lecture series at the university. As she stood in front of the students she could inwardly see them in the back of the hall smiling and encouraging her every word. If only they could have been there in person rather than in her imagination. Her memories were all she had of them, images of a fuller and happier time. Although she was foremost in her field, at a high point professionally, Natasha felt hollow — like the inside of a birch log after its inner core had decayed. On the outside she was bright and focused, like the white, papery bark of the birch. Her insides were crumbled like rotting wood.

The hollowness of Natasha's psyche was also compounded by her mourning for a third man, her late husband, Nikolai. Two years after Anatoly's death she met a handsome, army lieutenant. Nikolai had filled in the void left by her father and brother's passing. His promotion to captain coincided with her hiring as an entry-level engineer at the Baltic Regional Power Plant at Sosnovy Bor near St. Petersburg. Certainly the fates, God, and a little bit of luck opened the way for him to be assigned as an artillery-training instructor at a garrison near the plant. Seeing this as a sign of good fortune, they married in 1989. In 1992, Katerina was born. Her arrival continued to affirm that better times lay ahead. However, with the demise of the Soviet Union came the deterioration of the Red Army. By 1995, Nikolai was reassigned to a regular artillery unit near Moscow. This changed their relationship forever. Nikolai had to live on the army base with his unit, and could only get home to Natasha and Katerina infrequently. Within the year their fortunes continued to fall as the first war in Chechnya erupted. Nikolai's unit was called up and headed south to the conflict. During the shelling of Islamic rebel forces near the Chechen capital of Grozny, Nikolai's unit was ambushed from the rear.

Two days later Natasha was visited by Nikolai's former supervisor at the training school, Colonel Alexandr Raskolnikov, who brought the news of Nikolai's valiant, untimely death. Her heart broken by the hammer of the colonel's words of condolence, she cried for days. Her supervisors at the power plant gave her a leave of absence to deal with the funeral arrangements and to spend time with her family in Nizhny. Her job at the plant would be waiting for her. She took full advantage of the time off to find the strength to continue.

Upon her return to Sosnovy Bor, Natasha put all her energy into performing her job well and creating a stable home for herself and Katerina. Although she longed for male companionship, she felt herself to be cursed with the touch of death. Many men courted her for she was an intelligent, attractive woman. However, few could penetrate the emotional barrier she had erected around herself. The forces of ill fate and the excessive self-responsibility she had unconsciously inherited from her father hampered her naturally warm and engaging personality. A brief fling with a local computer business entrepreneur from St. Petersburg, Alexei Pavlovich, ended in shambles when she discovered his close connection with the mafia. She vowed nothing would ever again ruin the tranquility of hers and Katerina's life. Numerous attempts by Alexei to renew their relationship were in vain. Eventually his fascination with Natasha waned when he found a new love interest. What had she gained from this relationship? The love and attention of a man, a man who would go on living, in spite of her curse. As yet she couldn't see the logical aspects of her love relationships. Vodka, Chernobyl, the Army, and the mafia were a potentially deadly mix for any who would partake of them, as her father, Anatoly, Nikolai, and Alexei had. She had been nothing less than a bright spot in their tragic lives, a blessing not a curse. But she couldn't see it. At least Alexei's future blood would not be on her hands, and the computer he gave her for her birthday was still powerful enough to surf "the Net."

Attrition in the management at the Baltic Regional Power Plant had hurt its staffing. This worked greatly to Natasha's professional advantage. Within a year after Nikolai's death, she was promoted to chief engineering director, and was sent to Vienna, Austria for a conference commemorating the tenth anniversary of the Chernobyl accident. This trip helped her get her mind off of Nikolai, and brought her some closure to Anatoly's sacrifice. The Vienna trip was also her first time outside Russia. Although she never bought the old communist propaganda about the decadence of the West, she was a bit apprehensive about going. Much to her surprise, she found Vienna to be a delightful city full of people much like herself trying to do the best they could at living a happy life. She vowed to return to Westernized Europe when and if the opportunity arose. That opportunity manifested itself at the beginning of the year when the invitation arrived from Energia, the giant German energy company, inviting one engineer from the plant to attend the "Energy for the New Millennium Conference" in Strasbourg, France, all expenses paid. Natasha's job put her in the enviable position of going to the conference. That pleasure was coming in only two weeks.

Today she was in her hometown with her younger sister, Natalya, at her side. The morning sun caressed her fair cheeks as she watched the swirls and curls of the Volga's mysteries flow by her perch on the Chkalov Staircase.

"What are you brooding about now?" Natalya asked her older sister for the thousandth time.

"I was just thinking about father and Anatoly. I could feel them in the lecture hall this week cheering me on."

"I'm sure they were watching you from heaven, but Natasha, is that all that's bothering you? You seem so distant. Your body is here but your mind is not," Natalya leaned forward toward her sister's face to catch her eyes still focused on the Volga.

Natasha looked up at Natalya and blurted out, "But they should have been here, alive, living their lives as we are! It should have been one of them giving the lectures and me sitting in the audience. It doesn't seem fair, does it? Why are we left? I'm sorry! There I go again as if you don't have any feelings about them."

"I miss them too, and so does mother, but we can't change anything. What's done is done and we must go on living and not look back wondering what if. We all have so much to look forward to. Yuri and I are getting married this fall. You have your work and Katerina. You're going to France soon. Try to be happy, Natasha."

Natasha looked back toward the river. Its waves and rivulets carried her away from her sister's well-intentioned words. She wished she could float downstream all the way to the Caspian Sea, free from all the heartache, hurt, and sorrow of her life upstream. Her momentary fantasy was interrupted by the electronic beep of her mobile phone. She quickly retrieved it from her purse.

"Hello, Natasha Shakhova."

"We have a minor crisis here, Natasha. That group of Swedish engineers and scientists who were scheduled to come and tour the plant next Thursday has asked to move up the time of their arrival to Monday," said Mariana Koroleva, Natasha's assistant.

Ever since Chernobyl, the Swedes and their other Nordic neighbors were especially concerned about the potential radioactive pollution from Russia's nuclear power plants. When waves of radioactive particles set off sensors at the Forsmark Nuclear Power Plant sixty miles north of Stockholm, Sweden on the morning of April 28, 1986, managers anxiously and immediately concluded that the readings must have come from a leak in their own plant. When none could be found, it was discovered that the trail of radioactivity led south to the Soviet Union. Soviet officials turned a deaf ear to the demands of the Swedish diplomats that an explanation be given for the abnormally high levels of radiation emanating from their country. After a day of stonewalling, the Soviet evening newscast reported that there had been an accident at the nuclear power plant at Chernobyl.

These watchdogs of the Baltic Sea would be none too pleased with what they would find in Natasha's backyard. It was bad enough that the reactors at the Baltic Regional Power Plant were identical to the ones at Chernobyl, old and in need of replacement. However, what she dreaded most was the possibility that they would discover that the storage of spent fuel rods from the plant's reactors lay a mere one hundred meters from the shore of the sea. No doubt the Swedes would be appalled at their sloppiness, but what could they do given the lack of funds available for proper removal and storage? She desperately needed money and lots of it to run her plant correctly, and money was a commodity that was in very short supply in Russia. People were even now paying for electric service with sausages not rubles! The Swedes held the key to a special grant from the European Union to upgrade plant safety. Although she wished she had more time to get ready for the Swedes, Natasha knew that her crew would be able to at least give the appearance that they were doing something about the plant's problems.

"I see. Did they give an explanation for the change?"

"The leader of the delegation, Dr. Anders Petersson, said that events beyond his control had forced him to make the request. He was very apologetic."

"All right, that will be fine. I'll take the overnight train to St. Petersburg tomorrow. We'll work through the weekend to get ready for their arrival. Tell the crew it will be worth it if we can get the Swedes to recommend funds from the EU to help us. Also, please double-check my plane reservations for the trip to Strasbourg."

"I'll meet you at the train."

"*Spasibo,*" Natasha said as she turned off the phone.

"What did your office want that was so urgent?"

"I have to go back to the plant tomorrow instead of Sunday. Can I leave Katerina with you and mother until I return from France? Something has come up at the plant that needs my personal attention."

Natalya frowned, "Nothing serious, I hope."

"Nothing mechanical engineering related, more public relations work. Do you know any Swedish?"

"*Nyet.* I thought you were going to France. I wish I could go with you. What a great time you'll have there, Natasha. Maybe you'll meet a good man."

"Stop that, Natalya! You're always trying to fix me up with somebody. I'm not interested in men right now, maybe someday, but I don't know why a man would be interested in me."

"You never know. You'll probably meet some handsome, rich American, fall in love, and move away from us. We'll never see you again!"

Natasha dismissed her sister's last remark with a shake of her head and a quick wave of her hand. They began walking up the stairs toward the top of the Verkhne-Volzhskaia Naberezhnaia, the Upper Embankment. The redbrick exterior of the Kremlin walls shone brightly in mid-morning sun, hovering above the Volga and Oka as they had done for centuries. Within minutes they reached the top of the staircase, and the small circular park with its imposing statue of Valerii Chkalov, the famous Soviet aviator who flew non-stop from Moscow to Vancouver, Canada in 1937.

"I have to go to work now, Natasha, but I should be home before you catch the train."

"*Da,* it doesn't leave until 21:00."

Natalya walked away down Bolshaia Pokrovskaia Street toward her job at the central post office. Natasha sat down on the terraced steps of the Chaklov statue and thought to herself, "Maybe it is time for a man in my life."

Chapter 5

Even though it was no longer the tallest building in Europe, the Messeturm certainly dominated the skyline of Frankfurt, Germany. At two hundred fifty-seven meters, its red granite-clad finish and pyramidal shaped peak gave it the appearance of a freshly sharpened giant pencil erupting out of the concrete laden urban landscape below. If one of the Titans of Greek mythology ever escaped their imprisonment from the underworld, the Messeturm, or "Trade Fair Tower," would be their choice of writing implement. Its imposing stature dwarfed all of the older and even the modern buildings on the west side of downtown, as if to say to all below, "Worship me!" Indeed, the Messeturm was worshipped by all aficionados of skyscrapers and was the most photographed building in all of Frankfurt.

Prior to World War II, Frankfurt, like many German cities, had a beautiful *Altstadt,* or inner city, which included the home of Germany's most famous writer, Johann Wolfgang Goethe. However, the historical significance of Goethe's birthplace was not enough to spare Frankfurt the wrath of war. Because of its importance as a key manufacturing center and supplier of Hitler's war machine, Frankfurt and the entire Rhein-Main area was continually pounded by Allied bombers between 1944-45. The bombing obliterated nearly all of downtown Frankfurt. In particular, on March 22, 1944, that shrine of literary inspiration, the Goethe-Haus, was reduced to rubble.

After the war, many older buildings were restored to their pre-war splendor, including the Goethe-Haus. The many that were not rebuilt became in essence the compost out of which the sprouts of a new, modern Frankfurt would emerge. These sprouts grew to fill the skies above the city as American style skyscrapers, or *Wolkenkratzer*, like the Messeturm. This upward growth accentuated Frankfurt's dominance as the economic capital of Central Europe.

The address of Friedrich-Ebert-Anlage in the boomtown of Frankfurt was the ideal location for the headquarters of the world's most powerful electrical energy company, Energia AG. Energia's multi-billion euro world-wide corporation employed over half a million people in more than a hundred countries—all of them engaged in the business of keeping up the grid. Energia either owned or controlled all the aspects of electrical energy production from power plants, distribution lines, substations, switchgear, and computer software to the fuels of electrical production including oil, natural gas, coal, nuclear, geothermal, solar, and hydroelectric. Through its countless subsidiary and partner companies, Energia dominated electrical energy production around the world.

From the lofty heights of the Messeturm's sixtieth story, Energia's CEO, Dieter Schmidt, lorded over his empire like Caesar himself. Although he was born in the former Soviet Union, he was at his core a German. Dieter Schmidt, like many of his countrymen, was a descendant of German immigrants who, in the aftermath of the Seven Years War, left the ravaged, impoverished, and politically unstable principalities of Central Germany for a better life elsewhere. That life was made possible through the invitation of the German born, Catherine the Great of Russia, who, in 1763, offered the deal of a lifetime to nearly all Europeans: free land, freedom of religion, freedom from taxation for thirty years, freedom from military service, and political autonomy. Beginning in 1764, tens of thousands of Germans found Catherine's offer irresistible and headed eastward to the lower Volga River region of Russia. For those who survived the year-long journey life was exceedingly difficult.

Upon their arrival in the Promised Land, colonists faced starvation and scant shelter. A lack of support from their Russian hosts, insufficient forests with which to build, and raids by Kirghiz tribesman further complicated their efforts to scratch a subsistence life out of the untamed Russian steppe. Yet in spite of these obstacles, over a hundred German villages sprang up in the countryside surrounding the Volga River cities of Samara and Saratov. In the years that followed, these industrious and motivated German colonists prospered, multiplied, and lived a peaceful life, for a while.

Dieter Schmidt's ancestors were originally farmers from the small town of Büdingen, and were among a huge wave of Germans who left Hessen in 1766. Hessen had been particularly hard hit during the Seven Years War by the military forces of France and Russia. By the spring of 1767, the Schmidt family arrived in Saratov by boat and settled down in the town of Graf on the eastern, or meadow side of the Volga.

In the 1870's, the Imperial Russian Government of Czar Alexander II revoked the Manifesto of Catherine the Great that guaranteed the German immigrants their special privileges. Military service became compulsory for the now well established Volga Germans. Thousands left for North and South America. Tensions mounted between ethnic Russians and their more prosperous German neighbors. Much of this animosity was self-induced by the Volga Germans because of their isolationism from Russian society. An upsurge of Russian nationalism further added to the erosion of relations.

By World War I, the situation deteriorated to the point that Germans living in western Ukrainian district of Volhynia were deported to the Volga region in advance of the battlefront. German businesses were looted and damaged. Speaking German in public was taboo. Shortly thereafter, a decree was issued to expel the Volga Germans, but the abdication of Czar Nicholas II, and the takeover of Russia by Lenin and the Bolsheviks temporarily halted this decision. Ironically, hundreds of thousands of *Russlanddeutschen* (Russian-Germans) served in the Russian Army against their fellow ethnic Germans.

Under Lenin, Germans living in the Volga region got a new lease on life. In 1924, the Autonomous Soviet Socialist Republic of the Volga Germans was established. However, this reprieve was short lived. The Communist Bolsheviks looked down upon religion in all forms. German clergy were sent to labor camps. More hardship soon followed under the oppressive rule of Joseph Stalin. The famines that devastated all of Russia during the 1920s and 1930s also wiped out hundreds of thousands in the A.S.S.R. of the Volga Germans. Beginning in 1928, prosperous, family-run German farms were confiscated by the government and turned into large collective farms. Many of these German farmers, branded as kulaks, were sent to the labor camps in Siberia, while others made their way to the cities in search of work.

In 1930, Dieter's parents, Friedrich and Anna Schmidt were in their early twenties when Stalin's men came to Graf, or Krutoyarovka as it was known in Russian. Freidrich's father, Georg, had been an enterprising businessman specializing in the sale of farm equipment. With the collectivization of farms, his business totally evaporated. Considered rich and bourgeois by the Soviet authorities, he, like the farmers he helped, was sent to the Siberian labor camps never to be seen again. Friedrich's mother, Hilde, her husband, home, and livelihood taken from her, was forced into serving as a domestic in nearby Saratov to make ends meet. Friedrich and Ana lived with her in a one-room apartment. Because of Friedrich's familiarity with farming equipment, he easily found work in a Saratov tractor factory. For a while, what was left of the Schmidt family survived. On the morning of January 13, 1936, Dieter Georg Schmidt was born.

Hitler's double-cross of Stalin and subsequent invasion of Russia in June of 1941 was the ultimate blow to the Volga Germans. Decades old hostility held by the native Russians toward their German colonist neighbors combined with Stalin's xenophobic mentality pushed the situation to the breaking point. Branded collaborators, fascists, and spies they instantly became persona non grata in their host country. On August 28, the Decree of Banishment was issued ordering that all Volga Germans and other ethnic groups such as the Crimean Tatars, and Chechens be deported to Siberia, Central Asia, and other desolate regions of the Soviet Union. The Volga Germans lost their citizenship, the Autonomous Soviet Socialist Republic of the Volga Germans was dissolved, and many able-bodied men were conscripted into the Red Army. On September 17, Hilde, Friedrich, Anna, and five-year old Dieter were rounded up, told to take a month's worth of provisions, and put onto cattle cars bound for Kazakhstan. Once in Kazakhstan, Friedrich was separated from the rest of the family, and sent to the Trudarmija, work army, in Siberia. Like his father Georg, Friedrich disappeared forever. In total, nearly a half-million Volga Germans were sent to the east in 1941. Most died in the process.

Like many of their fellow Volga Germans, the remaining Schmidts lasted out the war in a small settlement along the Kyrgyz-Kazakh border near the Kyrgyzstan city of Bishkek, known as Frunze during the Soviet era. They managed to eke out a minimalist living from the land. The end of the war brought little relief for Germans in Central Asia who continued to face discrimination, restrictions, and special supervision. However, with Stalin's death in 1953, amends for the ill done by the Soviet government toward the Russlanddeutschen began to trickle forth. In 1955, the Supreme Soviet of the USSR issued a decree granting amnesty and the removal of special supervision. A year later, Nikita Khrushchev declared that Stalin's 1941 deportation of non-Russians including the Germans was a violation of the Leninist principle of the equality of all ethnic groups. By 1964, decrees of rehabilitation included the freedom to use the German language, and full emancipation as citizens of the Soviet Union. All told, it took over 20 years before the Russians welcomed back into the fold their ethnic German neighbors, at least on paper.

Dieter was thirteen years old when he, his mother, and grandmother were permitted to leave the settlement along the Chuy River and move to the small village complex of Leninskoye near Uzgen in southern Kyrgyzstan. Leninskoye was the administrative center of a three-village cooperative called Vinsovhos that specialized in the production of wine. Vinsovhos wines were considered among the finest produced in the Soviet Union. The influx of Germans into the village and the winemaking enterprise helped to further the prosperity of the area. Hilde and Anna worked in the cooperative along with their fellow German and Russian neighbors. Soon afterward, a school was built that provided Dieter and other children with an education that included Math, Physics, History, Biology, Russian, Kyrgyz, German, and English. Dieter's natural intelligence shone in the school setting, particularly in the area of math and physics. This was no doubt the result of the homeschool lessons his mother, Anna, had given him since their deportation to Central Asia. After graduation, Dieter was the only German in his class to continue on to the university. The rest of his classmates remained behind to tend the vineyards.

In 1956, the closest university to Kyrgyzstan specializing in math and science was Rostov State University in the city of Rostov-on-Don in the northern Caucasus region of Russia. Dieter's high scores on aptitude tests and recommendations from faculty enabled him to enroll as a student that year. After receiving a mechanics and mathematics degree with honors in 1960, Dieter was immediately hired by the state and sent back to Central Asia to work on developing the

Soviet Union's vast natural gas resources. This job enabled him to frequently visit his family and friends in Leninskoye, much to the delight of Anna. When the effort was made to bring Soviet natural gas to an energy hungry Western Europe, Dieter's ability to speak fluent Russian, German and English, as well as Kyrgyz and Kazakh, plus his in-depth scientific acumen made him a natural choice to serve on the development team.

Regardless of his accomplishments, his Russian comrades constantly harassed Dieter because of his German heritage. Even though the official tone of the Soviet government was one of tolerance toward all ethnicities, including the once hated Germans, an intolerant attitude existed nonetheless. Dieter advanced in his career only on the basis of his merit and not because of any friends in high places. Propelled by his in-bred German work ethic, he attained every increase in his salary and level of responsibility by the sweat of his brow. This earned him the esteem of many of his less prejudicial colleagues and supervisors. However, no matter how much Dieter's contributions to the state were valued and honored he always felt like a foreigner in his home country. Deep at the core of his being he could never forgive the atrocities the state had done to his father and grandfather.

Then on a cold, wintery, February night in 1976, while helping to work out a contract with the West German government for natural gas deliveries, Dieter Schmidt slipped away from his KGB tail and presented himself for asylum at a West Berlin city police station. Within a matter of weeks Dieter became a West German citizen. His only wish was that he could have brought his mother, Anna, with him. Her repatriation to Germany and her family's hometown of Büdingen would come in 1991 after the fall of the Soviet Union.

Over two hundred years had elapsed since a member of the Schmidt family could honestly call Germany their home.

Because of his work on the Soviet natural gas project, Dieter had already made the acquaintance of many Germans involved in the energy business. By September, he was hired as an engineering specialist for Energia. Dieter's language, engineering, and political skills acquired in the Soviet Union, plus his penchant for hard work, not to mention his celebrity status as a repatriated German, positioned him perfectly for his ascent through the ranks of the company. In May 1993, the Board of Directors of Energia unanimously elected him CEO, a promotion that moved him to the sixtieth floor of the Messeturm.

Dieter Schmidt wasted no time in shedding his communist upbringing and diving into the capitalist realm of money, politics and greed, a world he absolutely reveled in. He was utterly and totally dominant within his company, and his company ruled the energy kingdom. It was as if the Creator had specially crafted and mated them to each other. No one would dare halt Dieter Schmidt from succeeding in his unrelenting quest to keep the river of power continuously flowing through Energia's domain.

As chief director of security for Energia, Klaus Vogel was officially in charge of protecting the company's prized secrets. In reality, he was the top gun in Dieter Schmidt's arsenal of dominance and intimidation. When the president of an electrical utility or alternative energy company refused to sell their operation to Energia, Klaus Vogel would be called into to apply the appropriate nudge. An attitude of compliance would soon be forthcoming once Klaus and his associates concentrated their unique talents of blackmail, coercion, and extortion on a victim. Klaus' success rate was impeccable, for his boss would tolerate nothing less than perfection, a record in which Klaus prided himself. His cadre of trained bullies was at his beck and call whenever a job was at hand.

The job of the week for Klaus and his gang was the successful functioning of the Energy for the "New

Millennium Conference" Energia was hosting at the convention center in Strasbourg, France. His office had received reports that a radical element of the Green Party was organizing a protest at the conference. This had Dieter Schmidt in a serious stew. As a member of the World Trade Organization, Dieter had personally witnessed the negative publicity created by the protests at the WTO Conference in Seattle, Washington last year. He had been especially perturbed about the lackadaisical attitude of government officials toward the protestors, particularly that of the President of the United States. He vowed that there would be no repeat of this experience in Strasbourg.

"Klaus, I want you to go and visit the mayor of Strasbourg, Pierre Schneider, about these *verdammten* Greens! I'll not have them mar our glorious conference," Dieter commanded, as he looked Klaus directly in the eye.

"That shouldn't be a problem. Günther and I will pay him a visit tomorrow. Is there anything special you want me to say to him?"

Dieter strolled over to a window that looked out over the city. There was just enough of the summer mixture of humidity and smog hanging in the air to obscure the finer details of the urban sprawl hundreds of meters below.

"Simply inform him that these protestors must not be allowed to demonstrate in front of the convention center at any time during our conference. If he balks, tell him that in spite of his French citizenship his German genes need to respond to my German genes."

With that instruction Klaus left Dieter's office for his own, one floor down, while Dieter continued to gaze out the window toward the southeast. From this height one could easily view the main train station, the Friedensbruecke across the Main River, and further in the distance the Offenbacher Kreutz. After a few minutes the sun managed to pierce through the perennial haze clarifying the smaller cars, trees, and people. Just then the intercom buzzed.

"Herr Schmidt, Angela Simulescu for you," chimed in Gretchen, his personal secretary.

Angela Simulescu came from the Romanian city of Timisoara. Her parents, Constantin and Valeria, had been respected members of the faculty in the chemistry department at the Polytechnical Institute of Timisoara. One night, in the fall of 1982 her father told Angela and her sister, Cristina, to pack their favorite clothes and things, and prepare to leave within the hour. Word had come from a reliable source that her parents were on a list to be rounded up by Ceauşescu's secret police for interrogation regarding anti-government activities. The next morning the family escaped across the border into Hungary.

By the time Angela was sixteen, the family had settled in Frankfurt. Constantin and Valeria soon found work as professors in the chemistry department at the Johann Wolfgang Goethe University. In 1990, Angela received her degree in German. She applied and was hired by Energia in the public relations department, a job few non-Germans could handle. Like her boss, Dieter, Angela was motivated and hard-working, and like her parents, she was gifted intellectually.

Working in the Messeturm was like a dream come true for Angela, for she had watched it being erected all through her college days just a few blocks away. At thirty-three years old, she was the youngest senior public relations director the company had ever had. Putting together the "Energy for a New Millennium Conference" was the World Cup of PR. Dieter had a special place in his heart for her, for like he, she too had managed to escape the oppression and confining nature of a Stalinesque country.

"How are the conference arrangements proceeding?"

"We are on schedule. My staff and I will be going to down to Strasbourg tomorrow to attend to the final details and will be there through the end of the conference."

"Good, excellent. I have the utmost confidence in your ability to make this conference successful for our company. Was there something you wanted from me since you called?"

"Yes, there is, sir. It has come to my attention that there may be protests against the conference by the Green Party outside the convention center. I heard about it on the radio driving to the office this morning. Would you like us to prepare a statement for the press?"

"Naturally. Good thinking. Keep it short, to the point, and non-inflammatory toward the protestors. Be sure to point out Energia's fine record in promoting environmentally friendly energy sources, such as solar, wind, and the use of energy efficient appliances. I'm sure you'll find the best words. Fax me a draft from Strasbourg before we issue it."

"We can do that, sir. I'll have it to you by tomorrow afternoon."

"Very good. I will be expecting it."

Dieter's confidence began to swell. Between Klaus' efforts behind the scenes, and Frau Simulescu's work with the public, Energia's image as the energy leader of the world would remain untarnished. Dieter's stature as the world's energy czar was safely intact. The feeling of being in total and absolute command of things rushed through his mind with hurricane force. His perch above the city added a physical effect to this feeling of dominance, one that coursed through every fiber of his being. Life couldn't be better than this. Again he gazed out the window as the sun's rays continued to burn through the clouds. The day was turning out to be a nice one.

Chapter 6

LATE SUNDAY AFTERNOON Hank packed his luggage in the trunk of his Malibu, as he had three weeks before, but this time he left his fishing poles in the garage of his Delhi Township home. He had bought the house three years earlier after he and his ex-wife, Nancy, had divorced. Nancy had been finishing up her Master's degree in education at Xavier University when Hank first met her at her cousin's wedding. After a short courtship they were married and moved into a house in suburban Montgomery near the elementary school where Nancy was the principal.

The stress and demands of their respective occupations consumed their fourteen-year marriage, including any prospects of having children. By the end of 1997 there was little left to hold them together. They parted as friends and continued on with their careers. Nancy kept the Montgomery house, and Hank, wanting to make a fresh start, began looking for a house on the other side of town. One day, while coming out of the IGA grocery near his apartment in Mt. Airy, he picked up a real estate brochure. This brochure led him to the perfect house, a three-bedroom brick ranch with an unobstructed view of the Ohio River. He was back on the water again.

Hank slammed the trunk of his car, double checked his pockets for his passport, locked up the house, and began the drive down the hill to US 50. From the west side of Cincinnati there was no easy way to drive to the airport. One either went by way of downtown and I-75 across the river, took the Anderson Ferry to the Kentucky side of the Ohio River, or swung around the I-275 loop through Indiana. Since traffic would be at a minimum on a Sunday afternoon, he opted for the downtown route to the Cincinnati-Northern Kentucky airport. Hank left his car in long-term parking and hopped a shuttle bus to Terminal Three. After checking in at the Delta Air Lines counter, he rode the underground subway to Concourse B. Once in the main lobby he grabbed an Americano at Starbucks, picked up a USA Today at Waterstone's Booksellers, changed some dollars for francs and marks at the Fifth Third Bank branch, and settled down in a chair at gate B9. It was an hour before takeoff—just enough time to finish his coffee, glance through the newspaper, and make one more stop in the men's room before boarding.

It had been ten years since Hank had been to Europe. OVP had sent him to the Ruhr Valley in Germany to tour power plants in the area. In advance of that trip, the company had sent him to a special German language class for executives, given by an elderly teacher from Germany by the name of Ingrid Schroeder. Although Hank never became fluent in German, at least he knew how to ask for a beer and the directions to the *Rathaus*. He had remembered to tuck the pocket English-German dictionary he had purchased for that trip into his briefcase. Certainly the German language had not changed significantly in the last ten years.

On his first trip, Hank had tried to get Nancy to go with him, but she couldn't get away from her responsibilities at school. This had been the story of their lives, busy, important people with no time for each other. He thought of her for a moment, and imagined what might have happened if she had been able to come with him. Perhaps things would have turned out differently. The reality of the present moment snapped him out of his reverie when the announcement came over the PA system:

"We will now begin boarding for Delta Flight 48, non-stop service to Frankfurt. All first-class and business class passengers and those traveling with small children may board at this time. We will begin general boarding by rows in just a few minutes."

Hank got up and quickly walked the hundred or so feet for a final pit stop. He'd be back to the gate in plenty of time. OVP, for all of its millions of dollars in profits, still sent its executives flying in economy class. Hank didn't relish the thought of sitting in its cramped confines for the next seven hours. Hopefully the movie would be interesting and the food tolerable. He was lucky on both accounts for the chicken wasn't too rubbery, nor the movie too dull—a Robert DeNiro flick. The sunset out of his left side window seat was simply spectacular as the Jet Stream pushed the plane eastward over the Canadian tundra toward the old country. Hank dozed off and on only to be awakened by the sunrise a couple of hours later.

The Delta Air Lines Boeing 767 had begun its decent from thirty-three thousand feet as it inched over the west coast of the Netherlands. From his window seat, Hank could see the sharply defined polders, or dikes that held back the constant pressure of the North Sea along the western Dutch shoreline. This engineering feat dazzled Hank's eyes and impressed his scientific mind. A few minutes later he could clearly see the industrial sprawl of Germany's Ruhr valley. He tried to pick out the power plants he had previously visited and thought perhaps he recognized one of them. As the plane continued its trek toward the Frankfurt area he could see the smokestacks of several other power plants sticking up out of the green foliage of the surrounding forests. They immediately reminded him of those he managed back in the Ohio Valley. Within a matter of minutes Flight 48 landed safely at Frankfurt's Rhein-Main Airport, 9:35 a.m. local time.

After disembarking, passengers headed up the escalators into the Crystal Cathedral of airports. Frankfurt's airport was a huge, ultra-modern looking mass of glass and metal—intimidating, yet spacious. This was Hank's first experience of it for on his previous trip he had flown in and out of Düsseldorf. Hank gaped at its impressive architecture as he made his way downstairs and into a large room to passport control. To the left, EU citizens breezed through the check without delay, and to the right those with non-EU passports, like Hank, waited longer. Customs was a much easier affair. Hank simply picked up his bags and walked through the door and into the main terminal with hardly a glance by the customs official.

"My God," he thought to himself, "you could bring anything into this country undetected."

As he walked through the terminal Hank was impressed by the airport's German and English signage that directed him to the elevator and the rental car desks located on the second level. Janie had reserved his rental car with Hertz. Hank stepped up to the counter with its familiar yellow and black logo. Within a few minutes the young bilingual Hertz representative handed him the car keys and directed him back to the elevator with instructions to take it to the garage level and Row 113. Awaiting Hank was a brand new dark blue Ford Mondeo station wagon. Although he had hoped for a Porsche or Audi, the Ford would suit his needs. He found the car to be a bit of a curiosity for it looked exactly like the Ford Contours back in the US. Hank had test driven a Contour when he was shopping for cars last year, but settled on the Malibu instead. What puzzled him is that he didn't remember there being any Contour station wagons on the dealer's lot. How curious to find one here.

Once out of the underground garage Hank slipped out of the airport and right onto the expressway. The rush of adrenaline to his nervous system was just what he needed given his lack of sleep on the plane and the fact that all of the other driver's on the road were past their second cup of coffee. Hank had heard stories from his colleagues about driving on the German *Autobahn,* but there was nothing like driving it himself. Unlike American freeways, the autobahn had fairly strict yet unofficial driving rules. The far-right lane was more or less owned by the trucks, most of which ambled along at about 100 km/h like a line of well-ordered shoeboxes with wheels. The next lane to the left was for the average driver yet not for one whom dragged their feet—120 km/h and more. Finally, the far-left lane seemed to be reserved for the Mercedes', Audi's, BMW's and everyone else who felt 200 km/h was simply a nice cruising speed.

Hank managed to get a grip on the flow of traffic that by now was well beyond rush hour. One thing he had to get used to was the Ford's 5-speed manual transmission. Every car he'd owned since he and Nancy had been married was an automatic. Guided by the map Hertz had given him, Hank's route took him south down the A5. He especially liked looking at the stands of Scotch Pine and Norway Spruce meticulously planted years before along the road. They looked healthy enough, much like the corn this time of year in his native Indiana.

Just below Darmstadt Hank began to get a little drowsy; the initial rush of adrenaline was wearing off. After a few more kilometers he pulled into a BP convenience store-gas station. While visiting the men's room he couldn't help but notice a man, possibly of Mediterranean origin, sitting on a chair collecting money. On his trip to the Ruhr Valley ten years ago, the German power company had handled all of the hotel, meal, and transportation arrangements. Seeing this young man essentially begging for money was something he'd never encountered before. He wondered about his story. After dropping a mark on his plate, he went into the convenience store and paid for a coffee and apple strudel. He thought to himself, "Apple strudel at a convenience store? Why did his ancestors ever leave this country?" It was just what he needed to stay awake.

The sun shone the entire drive south to Strasbourg. Hank was thankful he had remembered to bring along his sunglasses. He passed by the exits for Mannheim,

Heidelberg, and Karlsruhe until he saw sign for Strasbourg-Frankreich. Before he knew it he was across the Rhein River and into France just as easily as if he had driven from Ohio to Kentucky. However, unlike traveling from one US state to another, the language of the road signs suddenly changed from German to French. He followed all of the signs toward Strasbourg, its towering cathedral looming in the distance. As it grew closer the signs "Centre" and "Cathedrale" guided him through the tight city streets, across the Ill River into the center of the old city.

Hank parked the Ford in a public lot on the south side of the cathedral, and made his way across the cobblestone square to the entrance of the Hotel Cathedrale.

When the promotional packet for the "Energy for a New Millennium Conference" arrived at OVP from Energia it included several brochures on hotels that had been blocked out for conference attendees. Janie, who had put herself in charge of choosing Hank's accommodations, had settled on the Hotel Cathedrale. True to OVP's penchant for thriftiness, the hotel was modestly priced and yet managed a three-star ranking. If the hotel lived up to its brochure, photos showing the spire of the Notre-Dame Cathedral under the hotel's dark blue entry portico, Hank would have the best view in the house — provided he went outside. View rooms were one hundred forty francs more than those in the rear.

"Do you have a reservation for Hudson?" said Hank to the woman seated at the front desk.

"*Bonjour, Monsieur Hudson. Oui,* we have your reservation. Could you please fill out the registration card, *s'il vous plait?*" responded Madame Claudette Dietrich, front desk manager.

"Sure, *oui,* no problem," said Hank.

"Will you need a garage?" she asked.

"Excuse me?" Hank paused looking up from the registration card.

"Do you have a car, Monsieur?"

"Oh, yes, I'll need to park it somewhere. I have it over in parking lot by side of the cathedral."

"Jacque, please assist Monsieur Hudson with his *baggage et voiture*," she directed the young bellman.

"*Oui, Madame*. Will you show me to your car, Monsieur?"

"Thanks, I'd appreciate the help," said Hank genuinely. He never felt so out of his element as he did now in the middle of this foreign city.

After completing the registration, Hank led Jacque to the car for his luggage. Hank couldn't help but notice the sheer massiveness of the cathedral only a few feet in front of him. Although he was busy with the task at hand, he would steal a glance every few steps. He felt like the only one in the square captivated by its presence. Once his luggage was safely stowed in his room, he and Jacque returned to the car and drove it a few blocks to a special parking garage set up by the hotel. Once the car was secure, they returned to the hotel where Hank tipped Jacque a fifty-franc note, and headed for his room. The stimulating effect of the coffee and apple strudel was now wearing off. Once he closed the door of his narrow but adequate room he flopped on his bed for a much-needed nap. In the back of his mind he wanted to get out and enjoy the day. It was sunny, dry, and in the upper seventies, but he also knew that he'd have plenty of time later since the sun remained up well into the evening. Before he dozed off he checked his watch. 3:09 p.m. Janie would be in the office by now. He called Cincinnati to announce his safe arrival in Strasbourg.

"Office of Engineering Services, this is Janie Hausman speaking. May I help you?"

"Janie, it's Hank. Can you hear me okay?"

"Perfectly. How are you? Did you have a nice flight?"

"It was fine. I'm here in Strasbourg now."

"How is the room I booked for you? Does it have a view?"

"Oh, it's great, really wonderful. The view is marvelous," he lied.

"It's sure good to hear your voice, Hank."

"Likewise. Is there anything to report?"

"No, all the plants are functioning at capacity without any problems. It's still pretty hot here in Cincinnati. You know, typical July."

"What about the Gallatin plant?"

"The last report showed them back up to 850 megawatts."

"Okay, just checking. You remember the trouble we've been having with the water filters there?"

"Hank, stop working and enjoy yourself there. Please don't worry about anything here. That's an order!"

"Alright, you win!" Hank replied with a smile in his voice. "I'll see you when I get back home."

Hank put the receiver back on the phone and slid into bed dog-tired.

A few hours later, he woke with a start. It was a quarter to seven, and he was starving. He combed his hair, changed out of his traveling clothes and into a short-sleeved, black golf shirt and khaki slacks then headed out the door. His fascination with the cathedral returned full force as he stepped into the square. He squinted up at the four hundred fifty-six-foot tall spire glistening in the early evening sun. His stomach won out over architectural appreciation and he slipped into the Restaurant Dauphin for his first experience of Alsatian gastronomy.

Chapter 7

WHEN COMPARED WITH most cities in Russia, Sosnovy Bor was a mere infant. What began as a settlement in 1958 evolved into a small city of 60,000 in just fifteen years, all for the sole purpose of supporting its primary industry, the Baltic Regional Power Plant. Sosnovy Bor's close proximity to the urban centers of St. Petersburg and Helsinki, along with its Baltic Sea location, made it the ideal place for an electrical generating station. A closed city since its inception, Sosnovy Bor still carried with it a mystique of isolation into the post-Soviet era.

The Baltic Regional Power Plant was the largest of its kind in all of Europe. It employed over seven thousand workers, and was the only privately owned power plant in Russia. Its five RBMK-1000 reactors when functioning at full capacity produced five billion watts of energy, providing for over half of the electrical needs of the St. Petersburg Oblast, Novgorod, Kaliningrad, Pskov, and much of lower Finland. However, after many years of service, these potentially dangerous Chernobyl-like reactors were in need of replacement, or reconstruction. Although plans for newer reactors were in the works, the old reactors continued in service in spite of their age and unsafe design. Compounding the issue was the lack of money to upgrade and maintain them properly. The oldest reactor, Number One, that had been in use for twenty-seven years, had only three years of viable service left. The demise of the other three reactors was simply a function of time, time that was fast running out.

Natasha's return to Sosnovy Bor couldn't have been timelier. Hanging in the balance was a fifty million-euro grant, enough money to maintain all five of BRPP's reactors and improve safety measures. The delegation of Swedish engineers and scientists served on the committee that would hopefully recommend approval of the grant to the European Union banking interests. Linked to the grant was the possibility of further funds to totally upgrade all of the RBMK-1000 reactors, with many of the improvements to be carried out by none other than the energy giant, Energia. However, the International Atomic Energy Agency was at odds with this plan, asserting that all of LPP's aging Chernobyl-type reactors should be discarded. Billions of euros were at stake. For the city of Sosnovy Bor and its residents it meant long-term job security. For Energia and its CEO, Dieter Schmidt, it meant further dominance and control of the world's energy supply, not to mention corporate profits. For the average citizen of the Baltic Sea region, it meant the choice between the present electrical grid and the purity of the environment.

Natasha's train arrived in St. Petersburg at 5:30 a.m. Mariana met her at the station and they drove the eighty kilometers back to Sosnovy Bor. Natasha had managed to catch a few hours of sleep on the train, but she was still a bit fatigued. All through the night she kept thinking about Natalya's encouraging words. Maybe there was still hope for her when it came to finding a man. Perhaps her sister was right, she had to change herself, and let go of the dead to make room for the living. As they drove to the plant she quickly shifted into work mode when Mariana began to update her on the changes in the Swedish delegation's visit.

"Is everyone prepared to work today at one o'clock as I mentioned on the phone yesterday? I know it's Saturday, but our collective future is riding on making a favorable impression. If we show we're serious about safety, they'll be more inclined to recommend the grant."

"*Da!* All of the key managers, engineers, and operators will be there. I sent them all e-mails, and called those who didn't respond," replied Mariana.

"Good work. Thank you. Could you drop me off at my apartment? I need to change my clothes and freshen up before the meeting."

"I figured you'd need to. Were you able to sleep on the train?"

"A little, but not as much as I would have liked."

Natasha's one-bedroom apartment adjacent to the Andersengrad Park was better than most Russian citizens enjoyed. Electrical outages were rare, and all other utilities such as water and heat consistently worked. Andersengrad Park was a child's dream playground, built in the image of a fairy tale village. She and Katerina had spent hours playing, talking and daydreaming there.

Mariana pulled the white Lada sedan in front of Natasha's apartment.

"Come back for me around noon."

"I'll be here. Go take a nap, relax a little. Okay?"

Natasha got out of the car, pulled her bag from the backseat, and quickly strode through the entrance and up the flight of stairs to her second floor apartment. She lay down on the sofa and drifted off into a deep but restful sleep.

Later, back at the plant, refreshed by her mid-morning nap, Natasha explained the importance of the visit by the Swedish delegation. Everyone understood their role and purpose. She made it clear that any hint of being unconcerned about the environmental impact of the plant's safety practices and the care of the aging reactors was to be avoided. All sensitive or ambiguous questions were to be directed to her. As chief engineering director, she was responsible for every aspect of the plant.

Everyone was ready when Monday finally arrived. The delegation was headed up by Dr. Anders Petersson, the director of the International Energy Development, located at the IDEON Research Park in Lund, Sweden. Accompanying him were his IED colleagues, Sven Solberg and Bjorn Johansson. The tour of the plant began with an inspection of the control room.

"Mrs. Shakhova, I'm impressed with the effectiveness of your operation, especially given your meager operational funds. How do you do it?" asked Dr. Petersson.

"Our managers are committed to running the plant efficiently. We have had some challenges with the labor union demanding wage increases, and even threatening to strike."

"Is it legal for your workers to strike? How could you possibly manage one if it really happened?"

"A strike is very unlikely. Under Russian law it would be illegal unless our management approved of it -- which we obviously cannot do. The labor negotiations are mostly out of my hands."

"I sympathize with your plight in having to run a sophisticated operation, such as a nuclear power plant, with minimal financial help and labor problems. Could you show me the waste disposal buildings?"

"Da, it's just a short walk toward the sea. Please follow me outside."

Natasha's greatest fears were coming to pass. She knew that upon closer inspection that Dr. Petersson would notice the cracks in the waste disposal building walls, cracks that allowed radioactive materials to easily leach into the groundwater around the building.

"How many fuel assemblies are stored in this building?" he asked.

"Approximately twenty-thousand."

"And how much waste does the plant produce annually?"

"Two thousand tons."

As Dr. Petersson walked around the outside of the building he noticed the amateur anglers fishing along the Baltic shore. This scene painted a frightening environmental picture for anyone who had eyes to see.

"Do you eat fish from here?" he asked looking toward the fishermen.

Natasha shook her head, "No, I don't, and they shouldn't either," glancing toward the shore.

"Have you had the groundwater tested recently for contamination?"

"Yes, in April. Unfortunately, Cesium 137 and Plutonium 239 were above acceptable levels."

"How much higher?"

"I'm embarrassed to say."

"I see.

Anders Petersson knew that Russians were proud people, unaccustomed to taking advice from outsiders, but this situation was different. He thoroughly grasped the need for his Russian neighbors to get some help and quickly before conditions further deteriorated. With everyone's health and well-being at stake in the Baltic region, any monies given to BRPP had to be specifically earmarked for not only improving the safety features of the existing reactors, but also to develop a long-term solution for the processing of radioactive waste.

As they walked back toward the plant entrance with its colossal multi-colored mural facing them he gathered himself and said to her, "I can assure you that the grant will receive our highest recommendation."

Thank you, Dr. Petersson. We are most appreciative of the EU's support of the safety of our plant."

"Don't worry, the money will come in a few short months. In the meantime, if you have any questions about the progress of the grant, or anything else for that matter, please give me a call. Here's my card."

Sven Solberg and Bjorn Johansson, followed suit.

Natasha put the cards in her pocket.

Dr. Petersson and his team walked toward the waiting taxi that would take them back to St. Petersburg.

Although she could not discuss the details of her conversation with Dr. Petersson with her staff, she let them know how proud she was of their attentiveness to their jobs during the delegation's visit. She expressed her hope for a positive recommendation. Back at her apartment later that afternoon she called Natalya.

"I have some wonderful news, Natalya; the Swedes said that they are going to help us."

"Of course they are. How could they resist a beautiful woman?"

"Cut that out! You're just trying to bother me again."

"*Nyet.* I'm just preparing you for your trip to France. When do you leave?"

"Next Monday. How's Katerina doing? Can I talk with her now?"

"*Da,* she's right here. Hold on."

"Hi Momma, I wish you were here with Aunt Natalya and Grandma."

"Me too, Kat, but I've got work to do, and I'm going on a trip next week. Do you remember talking about it?"

"Yes, Momma I hope you have a nice time. Be sure to eat at a nice French restaurant. They have the best food in France. That's what Aunt Natalya says."

"What else has she told you?"

"Nothing...except that you're going to meet a rich, American man!"

Natasha laughed, "Don't believe everything Aunt Natalya says! You will be good, yes? She is in charge until I can come and take you back home."

"Okay, I will. I love you, Momma."

"I love you too. Let me talk with Aunt Natalya." Natasha heard her daughter call to her aunt, then burst into childish laughter in the background.

"I'll call you when I get back from the conference."

"Have a good time, Natasha, and don't work too hard. Be sure to check out all of the good-looking men at the conference."

"Good-bye."

When Monday morning arrived, Mariana picked up Natasha at her apartment and drove her to St. Petersburg's Pulkovo airport just south of the city.

"I want you to call me if anything irregular happens at the plant. My mobile phone will not work in Strasbourg, so you will have to leave messages for me at the hotel. Do you have the number?"

"*Da*, the Hotel Cathedrale. I have the number back at the office. Please, Natasha, don't worry about the plant. Everything will be all right while you're gone. After all, you'll only be gone one week."

"You're right, it's only one week. Certainly nothing much can happen in such a short time. I guess I feel as if I should be doing more about the EU grant application. We very much need the money."

"Didn't Dr. Petersson tell you to call him if you had questions?"

"I guess. I worry too much, don't I?"

"You do," said Mariana as she pulled the Lada up to the terminal.

"Yes, I'll try to enjoy the trip. Good-bye."

Mariana dropped Natasha off in front of the Lufthansa desk. After a change of planes in Frankfurt, she connected with a short flight to Strasbourg's Entzheim airport. Once she cleared customs, a limousine, compliments of Energia, chauffeured her from the airport to her accommodations at the Hotel Cathedrale.

En route, the driver handed her a package containing among others things, a generous per diem of francs to cover all of her meal expenses. Natasha was famished. After unpacking her bags and freshening up her makeup, she walked outside the hotel in search of the closest restaurant. Just to the left was the Dauphin. Perfect! After being seated at a table, she began to look over the menu searching for something to eat that would be quick and inexpensive. After deciding on the tarte flambé, she laid her menu down on the table and began looking for the waitress. Her eyes were instantly drawn to a handsome man seated just a few tables from hers. Who was he?

Chapter 8

HANK HAD BEEN studying his menu with engineer-like thoroughness. Although it was printed in three languages, French, German, and English, it still took him a while to decide what to order. The fare at the Dauphin hardly resembled Bob's Big Boy back home.

When he finally looked up from his menu he couldn't help but notice a very attractive woman in her thirties seated by herself across the aisle and two tables down from him. For a second they happened to catch each other's glance. In that brief moment Hank sensed an attraction, a curiosity, and a mysterious sense of recognition all at the same time. Who was she? Perhaps she was a local Strasbourg woman waiting for her husband or boyfriend to join her. From his angle of view she appeared to be on the tall side, maybe five-nine, a medium brunette, and nicely dressed in a black, fashionable dress with high-heeled shoes. It seemed odd to him that she was dressed to the nines just to eat dinner alone. Was she alone or by herself, he continued to wonder? He snuck a look at her every few seconds or so. Where else could he look?

Natasha felt a wave of self-consciousness sweep over her once she noticed this man looking back at her. Fortunately, her momentary attack of jitters subsided. Who was he? Perhaps he was a German tourist from across the border for a day of sightseeing? But his clothes seemed too…American, or possibly British. He had a kind face. She could hear Natalya egging her on in her head, as if she were sitting right next to her, "What about him? He's a handsome one, and he's not wearing any wedding rings. What are you waiting for? Don't let him walk out of here without getting him to introduce himself." "Shut up, Natalya, I'm just fine!" Her internal battle with her sister consumed her thoughts.

The waitress came to Hank's table.

"I'll try this," he said pointing to the local specialty, choucroute—a large helping of sauerkraut made with Riesling wine and various spices, surrounded by an assortment of sausages and meats.

"Excellent choice, and to drink, I recommend a glass of our Alsatian Gewürztraminer."

"That'll be fine," said Hank wondering what Gewürztraminer was. Shortly thereafter the waitress brought Hank his drink. To his delight, Gewürztraminer turned out to be a very pleasant white wine. After a few sips, Hank was back to figuring out who the mystery woman was. The more he looked at her the more curious he became about her true identity.

A few minutes later the waitress served Natasha her food. From his occasional observations Hank saw what looked like a pancake with cheese on it. When his order of choucroute arrived he asked the waitress about it.

"Oh, yes, that is tarte flambé. It is like pizza, but much better. You'll have to try it the next time you're here."

Hank dug into the mountain of choucroute. This was nothing like any sauerkraut he had eaten before—it was positively delicious.

Natasha finished her tarte flambé in short order. She could hear Natalya in her head telling her to order dessert and coffee just to delay her departure a little longer. She suppressed that thought and called the waitress, *"Madame, l'addition, s'il vous plaît."*

"Oui, Madame."

Once the bill arrived, Natasha fumbled around in her purse for the envelope full of money she had received upon arrival. The tarte flambé and eau mineral came to 95 francs. She gave the waitress a 100-franc bill. *"C'est pour vous."*

"Merci beaucoup, Madame."

Natasha got up from her seat and headed for the door. Out of the corner of her eye she glanced at her admirer and threw him a small smile of acknowledgement.

At that moment Hank was chewing a mouthful of choucroute, with little pieces of it hanging out of his mouth. He felt like an absolute idiot. Here was this attractive, French woman giving him a smile and he looked like a dog wolfing down its food. He managed a nod back toward his mystery woman. As she strolled by a wave of energy surged over him. And what was that perfume she was wearing? Jeezus!

Hank wasted no time finishing his meal. Within a few minutes he was out in the mid-evening air of the cathedral square. The sun was still up but shining at a steeper angle than when he entered the restaurant, and lit up the red sandstone surface of Notre-Dame with a pink glow. Many people were outside enjoying the warm summer temperatures. Maybe she wasn't far. He walked around the nearby streets hoping to find her. She must have gone home to her family or friend's house. But, why was she eating alone?

He checked his watch. It was after nine. He walked back across the square to the Hotel Cathedrale. Although his internal clock felt it was the middle of the afternoon, he thought he'd better try and get some sleep. The energy conference would be starting tomorrow, and he wanted to be sharp. Before entering the hotel Hank paused and looked back up at the cathedral. Its size and beauty mesmerized him. The single spire seemed to pierce the stratosphere. What genius created this engineering piece of artwork? Back in his room he pulled out the latest issue of *Power* magazine. This entertained him for an hour until he finally crawled into bed and tried to fall asleep. His mind was spinning from all he'd experienced today. The long plane ride, the drive on the autobahn, his first French meal, and a friendly smile from a woman. Hank blissfully drifted off to sleep in the very wee hours of the morning.

One floor above Natasha was fast asleep in her room.

Chapter 9

DIETER SCHMIDT WAS in no mood for the report his lieutenant had to share with him. At his suite in the Château de l'Ile he sat while Klaus recounted his meeting with Mayor Pierre Schneider of Strasbourg.

"When I told him that we didn't want any protestors in front of the convention center he just smiled. You wouldn't believe it!"

"And?"

Klaus continued, "He said, and I quote: 'Here in France we have a tradition of letting people express their views. Please tell Monsieur Schmidt that I cannot comply with his request.'"

"Did you appeal to his German roots, like I asked?

"*Ja,* he thought that was pretty funny. Then he said, 'Monsieur Schmidt is most welcome to bring his conference to our city. We appreciate the business, naturally. But, I'll not have you or him threaten or coerce me into violating the liberty of a citizen to have their say. The police will keep the protestors out of the convention center itself, but they may protest outside, within fifty meters of the front door. That is my final answer.'"

"Doesn't he know I could squash him like a little flea? I've helped elect mayors all over Germany. I could easily set my sights on France, beginning with Strasbourg."

"What do you want me to do next?"

"Get him on the phone and let me talk with him myself."

Klaus searched his left jacket pocket for a small piece of paper with the number of the *maire* written on it. From his right jacket pocket he retrieved his mobile, dialed the number, and handed it to Dieter.

"May I speak with Herr Schneider? Please tell him it's Dieter Schmidt of Energia. Yes, I'll hold."

"This is Claude Hirschberger, deputy mayor. Monsieur Schneider has asked that I handle all further communications with you, Monsieur Schmidt. Is there something I can do to help you?"

Fuming, Dieter snapped, "I insist on talking with Herr Schneider myself and not one of his underlings."

"Pardon, Monsieur. I regret to say that Monsieur Schneider was quite clear in his instructions to me that I receive all calls from you."

"Please inform him that for the safety of our conference delegates the police should increase the distance the protestors can demonstrate from fifty to one thousand meters from the convention center. This would be satisfactory to me," Dieter said in a diplomatic tone.

"*Oui*, Monsieur. I will pass along your suggestion when I meet with the mayor later."

"I will look forward to the good news that you've complied with my request. Good-bye."

Dieter turned off the phone and handed it back to Klaus. He was unaccustomed to feeling his control of a situation slip away without a good back up plan. How he wished he had some dirt on Pierre Schneider.

"I don't have a good feeling about this, Klaus. Why weren't you more convincing? I was counting on you to come through."

"Do you want me to go back and talk with him again?"

"Do you think you'll be more successful? Hmm? Let's see what our public relations staff can do instead. Maybe we can mitigate this situation."

Dieter retrieved his own mobile phone from his pocket and called Angela Simulescu. He had an idea.

"Angela, this is Dieter. I want you to know that I appreciate the excellent work you've done so far on the conference. The press release regarding the protest was outstanding. However, we need to take our case a step further. Call a press conference for nine o'clock tomorrow morning and prepare a statement like the press release touting Energia's service to humanity, and add something at the end asking the civil authorities to make the conference an orderly and safe one for all. Then take questions for fifteen minutes."

"Certainly, I can do that, sir," Angela replied from her room at the Hilton near the convention center.

"Good. I will see you inside after the press conference for my opening speech. Call me with any questions."

Dieter clicked off his phone. He felt more in control. He motioned to Klaus to follow him out of the suite for a stroll around the grounds before dinner. He had a few matters to discuss with him.

The Château de l'Ile, originally built in the seventeenth century, had undergone extensive renovations in the last century. It's half-timbered and heavily gabled Alsatian hotel surrounded a traditional sandstone turreted castle. Situated on ten acres of woods along the Ill River, it provided a peaceful environment for its guests just a few kilometers away from the busyness of urban Strasbourg. Its four-star rating, excellent cuisine, and available suites, amply suited Dieter and his top assistants.

"Klaus, I want you to keep a special eye on this conference, especially the protesters. Set up video cameras aimed at the crowd and review the tapes looking for the leaders. We need to know who's directing them. I have a feeling that there may be more setbacks before it's all over. This Pierre Schneider is an elusive man, someone we obviously cannot trust to keep things in order. I'll not have any funny business while our company is on public display."

"You can count on me, Herr Schmidt. Günther and I, and the rest of the security team will be ready. No one will make a fool of us!"

"That's what I want to hear. And see what you can dig up on the mayor. He must have a mistress somewhere, or be a part of an under the table business deal. I would like to look him in the face with the news of our findings."

"*Das ist kein Problem.* We've cornered the best of them."

"That you have, Klaus. You're the best. That's why you work for me."

Dieter and Klaus arrived at the hotel's restaurant. Klaus returned to his room to orchestrate his superior's wishes. Dieter dined alone on a meal of feuillantine of Scottish salmon, escalope of Alsatian foie gras of goose, and a bottle of Riesling.

Chapter 10

TUESDAY MORNING, NATASHA made her way down the hall to the breakfast room. Upon entering the room she marveled at the extent of the buffet presented by the hotel. This was not breakfast in Russia. The buffet tables were loaded with breads, croissants, butter, jellies, cheeses, meats, fruit juices, eggs, yogurt, and coffee. With all of her expenses paid by Energia, as they were for all conference delegates from Russia who could not have attended without financial assistance, Natasha felt the temptation to eat to overflowing. She resisted the impulse to stuff herself speculating as to whether or not she would continue to fit in her clothes once the conference ended. Judiciously, she filled her plate with bread, a piece of cheese, and yogurt.

The easterly orientation of the windows filled the room with bright sunlight, light that reflected off of Natasha's face. From her window seat she noticed the souvenir shop owners below moving their racks of postcards and other curios out the front doors of their businesses into the street. However, as she looked to her left, the utter size and loftiness of Notre Dame dominated the panorama. Although its monumental construction impressed the engineer in her, its majestic beauty stirred her soul. Russia had some of the most beautiful churches in the world, including the fairytale St. Basil's Cathedral in Moscow's Red Square. Yet, this one with its gothic architectural style and intricate exterior sculpture certainly held its own in her eyes. She made a mental note to see the inside before she returned to Russia.

Natasha retrieved her briefcase from her third-floor room and was downstairs in front of the hotel for the 8:45

pickup by the limousine service. While she waited her thoughts returned to Natalya and her matchmaking speech.

Why didn't she see any other engineers waiting for the ride to the convention? She began to wonder if she was the only delegate staying at the hotel. Within a couple of minutes a silver Renault Espace mini-van from the Alsace International Car Service arrived on schedule. Natasha quickly opted for a seat on the middle bench. As the driver was closing the side door, a man arrived huffing and puffing just in time to step up into the van and into the open seat next to Natasha. Both were startled to see each other, remembering one another's face from the restaurant the night before. The driver shut the door, returned to his seat, put the van in gear, and drove out of the cathedral plaza.

"Hello, I mean *bonjour, Madame,*" Hank mustered these words as he tried to clandestinely replenish his oxygen supply.

"*Bonjour,* hello, it is good to meet you."

Hank was dressed in his office best — a navy blue blazer, gray slacks, light-blue shirt, and a mostly red tie that had been hastily tied. He thought to himself for a moment, "That doesn't sound like a very French accent to me." Natasha, wearing her outfit from the day before, thought to herself, "An American for sure, definitely not British."

"I'm Hank Hudson, from Cincinnati. I overslept. The time change from the US has my internal clock all messed up. There's a six-hour time difference you know. Are you going to the power conference too?"

"I am Natasha Shakhova. Yes, I am attending as a representative from the Baltic Regional Power Plant," Natasha extended her right hand in greeting.

Hank suddenly realized she was Russian. After politely shaking her slim well-manicured hand, he said, "Oh, I see. I'm with OVP, that's Ohio Valley Power. I'm the chief engineering director."

The van took off on a circuitous route through the narrow streets of the old city before it stopped at the Hotel Maison Rouge to pick up two engineers from Italy. Both were men in their fifties, one of whom sat in the far back seat, the other opted for the front seat. The van continued on a couple of blocks to the Hotel de l'Europe to collect two more delegates from the Netherlands who filled the back seat. Now that the van was full and on its way to the convention, everyone's eyes focused on Natasha. As the sole woman passenger, she sensed their attention and turned to Hank.

"Does OVP have many plants?"

"We have seventeen baseload, plus five peaking plants with over seventeen thousand megawatts of capacity servicing over a million and a half customers in Indiana, Kentucky, and Ohio."

"I see. You have a great responsibility overseeing such a large network."

"You aren't kidding. Sometimes I wonder how we keep it all together. How about yourself? You said you were from the Baltic Regional Power Plant. Where is it located?"

"In Sosnovy Bor. It's not far from St. Petersburg. Like you, I am the chief engineering director. Our five reactors produce a total of five thousand megawatts for the entire St. Petersburg Oblast, including Finland."

"A nuclear plant?"

"*Da*, yes, that's correct. Does OVP have such plants?"

"No, not anymore. We actually converted one from nuclear into the most powerful coal plant in the world. It can crank out 1,400 megawatts. Almost all of our plants are coal fired, except for one that uses fuel oil. All of our peaking plants are natural gas. I used to work on a nuclear submarine when I was in the navy years ago, but nothing as big as your plant. Five thousand megawatts from one plant, that's enormous!"

"Yes, our plant is the largest nuclear electrical generating plant in the world," Natasha proudly stated.

The two Dutch engineers appeared interested in the discussion and leaned forward toward Hank and Natasha in the seat ahead of them.

"Are you also staying at the Hotel Cathedrale?"

"Yes, I am."

"I just wondered. I saw you last night in the restaurant. I had no idea you were an engineer, let alone from Russia."

"Yes, I remember you as well," Natasha nodded as she blushed.

Within a few minutes the van pulled up in front of the Strasbourg Convention Centre. Many other limousines, taxis, and vans were arriving at the same time delivering delegates to the conference. From across the street hundreds of protesters from the Green Party as well as a strong contingent of Strasbourg police in riot gear lined the sidewalks. Conference goers were greeted by repetitive shouts of: "STOP KILLING OUR FORESTS, STOP KILLING OUR FUTURE!" "NO NUKES, NO MORE!" along with placards and signs touting messages warning of global warming, environmental destruction, and corporate greed.

On the front steps of the conference center Angela Simulescu stood with her assistant while a crowd of reporters gathered for the press conference.

"Allow me to begin by thanking the members of the press for covering this important conference. Energia and all of the delegates of utilities from around the world are gathered here in Strasbourg to learn ways that we might more effectively deliver electricity to customers in the most environmentally friendly manner possible. We do not deny that the industry has had its darker moments in the past, but the future, the millennium, calls all of us to leave those days behind. With each year that passes technological advances will cause less pollution to enter the environment from electrical power plants...," Angela Simulescu continued to speak while the press took notes and videotaped.

Hank and Natasha walked side-by-side as they entered the registration area. The tables were arranged in alphabetical order. Each went to their respective check in areas, but kept an eye out for the other.

With the opening of the conference scheduled for ten o'clock, there was plenty of time to walk around and mingle. Complimentary refreshments were available to the left of the registration tables. Hank could hear his stomach rumble at the sight of food. His last-minute departure from the hotel had caused him to miss the buffet breakfast. He grabbed a cup of coffee and a croissant, which he promptly ate. While he sipped his coffee he scanned the lobby looking for anyone he might have known from previous conventions back in the US. As he took his second drink of coffee he felt a hand firmly on his back.

"Is that you, Hank?" a familiar voice spoke from behind him.

Hank turned around. Behind him was Jake Morelli from the Los Angeles Department of Water and Power, Paul McCurry from the Northern Indiana Public Service Company, and John Livingston from Chicago's Commonwealth Edison. He had attended the *Power Gen '99 Conference* in New Orleans last year, and hit it off with these guys. He still remembered the hangover from a night of partying down on Bourbon Street.

"Hi, Jake. Fancy meeting you here. I thought you didn't like flying over water."

"Hell, I couldn't resist not coming to this one with Y2K behind us, and the world not coming to an end. I figured if I downed a few glasses of wine I wouldn't know if I was flying over the land, or the ocean. Besides, the smog in L.A. was so thick I couldn't tell the difference. So, I decided to come here and give you a bad time!"

"I can see you're still the same old Jake. You can give me the business whenever you want. How are you two Chicagoland residents doing? Paul? John?

Paul spoke first, "Still keeping the lights on at your folk's place in Dune Acres. When are you going to get up for a visit again? What's it been, since last Christmas or something? You know I always keep a beer in the fridge for you."

"Paul and I thought the three of us might get together at the Berghoff next February, when the auto show is in town at McCormick Place," John added.

"Sounds like a plan. Paul and I could ride the South Shore into the city, get off at 31st street for the show, and then ride with you up to the loop and the Berghoff."

"You're on!"

"Enough of the Windy City talk guys, I say we get together tonight for dinner and drinks, just like back in New Orleans," Jake decreed.

Hank looked around the reception area for Natasha, but she had momentarily disappeared from his radar screen. As they entered the Erasme Auditorium for the opening keynote address he spotted her seated down toward the front in the center. He and his buddies found seats mid-way down on the right. While they plotted the evening campaign Hank continued to observe his first Russian acquaintance from a distance.

Offstage Dieter Schmidt sat in the ready room going over his speech notes. He wore a conservative black business suit with a starched white shirt and a blue tie. Although he continued to bitterly lament the fact that the protestors were just outside the convention center, he was confident that Klaus would soon produce the necessary ammunition to convert Mayor Schneider to his way of thinking. Fresh from the press conference, Angela arrived with sufficient time to go over Dieter's introduction with him.

"Was the press kind to you?"

"Oh, not too bad. They especially wanted to know what we thought about the protest across the street."

"And, what did you tell them?"

"Simply that Energia respects the views of all people, including those who disagree with our business. That our purpose is to bring the least expensive and most environmentally benevolent electricity to the world."

"*Ausgezeichnet,* Angela!"

At exactly ten o'clock, Angela Simulescu, came to the podium of the 2,000-seat Erasme Auditorium, now packed with engineers. Angela was of average height, slight of build, medium length wavy auburn hair, green-eyed, and very attractive. She wore a gray pin-striped business suit as she addressed the conference:

"*Guten Morgen meine Damen und Herren, Bonjour Madames et Messieurs,* Good morning ladies and gentlemen! On behalf of our sponsor, Energia, I am your host, Angela Simulescu. We wholeheartedly welcome you to the "Energy for the New Millennium Conference." We hope that you've been able to find the registration tables all right. If you haven't registered yet we encourage you to stop by the tables after the keynote speech. Your registration packet contains the conference schedule, tickets to Thursday night's banquet, as well as recreational information about Strasbourg and Alsace, including museums, wine tasting tours, boat rides, and other attractions. Also, there is a golf tournament scheduled for Thursday afternoon at the La Wantzenau Golf Club just north of Strasbourg. We need you to register for the tournament so that transportation can be arranged. If you have any questions about the conference, stop by the registration tables in the lobby. And, now, without further delay, I present to you the Chief Executive Officer and President of Energia, Dieter Schmidt."

A respectful ovation followed Dieter's walk from behind the curtain out onto the stage of the auditorium.

"*Vielen dank,* Frau Simulescu. Good morning fellow engineers! We are here today on the brink of a new millennium to usher in the third century of electrical power. What began as a mere scientific curiosity with Benjamin Franklin and his kite flying antics in a thunderstorm two hundred forty-eight years ago has developed into a lifestyle, an electrical way of life. Today, billions of people live a life of leisure because we bring electricity to them. Can we imagine a life without electric power? A life with no lights, telephones, televisions, computers, nor anything else that uses electricity to function. However, our efforts are not isolated to the present day. We do our work standing upon the shoulders of our electrical forefathers, including Alessandro Volta and the invention of the battery, Michael Faraday and the production of the generator, Thomas Edison and the light bulb, Nikola Tesla's discovery of alternating current, and many others that time prevents me from mentioning. Much has been accomplished, and, yet, much remains to be discovered. In this new millennium, this third century of electricity, we must find new, less costly and less polluting ways of generating electricity. We must develop appliances and other electrical devices that use less power, that are more efficient. Why must we do this? Because it is what our customers demand. It is what the world requires. Outside this convention hall are people demanding that we double our efforts. That is why we're holding this conference. We are here to support one another in bringing the combined genius of our industry to bear on this holiest of tasks."

Hank began to nod off at this point in Dieter Schmidt's speech. He liked the words. Who wouldn't? Every engineer wanted greater efficiency and cleaner burning power plants. However, he inwardly sensed that the speaker's words were pretentious, self-serving, and void of sincerity. How much more of this disingenuous crap could he put up with? Everyone knew that Dieter Schmidt's objectives were market share, creative domination, and making money, just like all company presidents. His mind wandered back to his conversation with Darrell and Crazy Nick about the ancient Atlantean energy technology. Could they actually be right about the future of power generation? The conference brochure didn't mention any seminars on crystals or magnetic fields. Again, his attention returned to his Natasha sitting further ahead looking attentively at the speaker. Could he ever have guessed that the beautiful woman who smiled at him last night in the restaurant would turn out to be an engineer like him?

Chapter 11

AFTER A REUNION lunch with his buddies in the convention center restaurant, Hank opted for an afternoon presentation for coal fired power plant engineers conducted by an engineer from the municipal utility department of the City of Kaiserslautern, Germany. Gutenberg Rooms I and II were packed for the lecture.

During the late 1980's and early 1990's, the anthracite coal industry in northeastern Pennsylvania needed a boost. The U.S. Congress responded by passing a resolution requiring each branch of the armed services to purchase 100,000 tons of the coal per year. Although this boondoggle cost the taxpayers millions of dollars, it kept the coal mining companies and their employees happy. As for the Army, Navy, and Air Force, they were faced with tons of coal that none of their boilers could use. The Navy sold theirs off at auction, but the Army and the Air Force shipped much of their allotment in freighters to their bases in Europe, with large quantities reaching the Ramstein Air Force Base next to Kaiserslautern. This shipment eventually became the property of the City of Kaiserslautern, or K-town as the American military called it. Their problem: How does one burn anthracite coal in stokers designed for bituminous coal?

Anthracite, the hardest and most BTU rich of the coals, was most often used in home heating applications. Bituminous and subbituminous coal, although softer and less potent, were commonly used in electrical powers plants and to make coke for steel factories. The City of Kaiserslautern's municipal heating plant engineers faced the opportunity and the challenge of figuring out how to make practical use of this free coal from the U.S. military. Cleverly, they contrived a system by which the anthracite coal was pulverized and blended with bituminous coal in a 10/90 mixture, and then carried by conveyer belt into the stoker. Modifications were made to the stoker's grates and airflow system to accommodate the unique mixture. The procedure was not without its flaws. Because the design of the stoker was made for larger bituminous coal, up to 10-12% percent of the pellet-like anthracite coal degraded, falling through some of the grates. However, what the U.S. military found to be a useless substance the Germans unleashed into useable energy to make steam for their topping cogeneration plant, thus providing electrical power and home heating for its residents at a lower cost.

While Hank sat in scientific fascination listening to this seminar, next door in the Kleber Rooms Natasha was with other fellow nuclear power plant engineers hearing a lecture by the French utility company, Electricite de France. Of all the countries of the world, France produced more of its electrical energy from nuclear fuel than any other did. Its fifty-four nuclear power plants produced in excess of sixty thousand megawatts of electricity supplying over seventy-five percent of France's electrical energy needs.

This monumental feat did not happen by accident. After the 1973 Arab oil embargo, French politicians made the decision to no longer be at the mercy of foreign powers for its energy needs. With few natural resources of its own, France turned to nuclear energy as its fuel of choice. Power plants were mass-produced throughout the country, especially up and down the Rhone River. For nearly twenty-five years, French utilities had amassed a spotless safety record in the handling of nuclear power and were on the cutting edge of innovations regarding the disposal of its wastes. The plant manager of the EDF's local power plant, located seventy kilometers south of Strasbourg, began the lecture.

"*Bon jour, bienvenue en Alsace!* Good afternoon, and welcome to Alsace! I am Philippe Stricker, plant manager at Electricite de France's plant here in eastern France. Our plant is located in Fessenheim along the Rhein River between Colmar and Mulhouse. Tomorrow afternoon we will be conducting a tour of the plant for anyone who is interested. Our convention hostess, Angela Simulescu, tells me that there is a sign-up sheet at the registration tables in the reception area. Buses will leave at 14:00 and return to the convention centre by 18:00. Our plant consists of two pressurized water reactors each producing 880 megawatts of electricity. Number One reactor came on line in January 1977, followed by Number Two in March 1978. Our particular plant supplies all of the electrical needs of Alsace, plus we sell surplus power to Switzerland. In the last twenty-two years we have not had a single accident or serious alarm at the plant, something for which we are all thankful. This safety record is due in part to the ongoing efforts of our parent company, Electricite de France, to make nuclear power safe for all people, both plant workers and citizens. We are here to share with you the latest innovations in the storage, transport, and disposal of spent nuclear fuel rods. Allow me to introduce, Monsieur Jean-Michel Bernard, the manager of our nuclear safety department, who will speak specifically to these new developments..."

Monsieur Stricker's words both buoyed Natasha's hope for the future of nuclear power plants, and yet at the same time cut her like a knife given the dreadful state of affairs at the Baltic Regional Power Plant and others in Russia. The visit by Anders Petersson and the rest of the Scandinavians lingered in the back of her mind. Their concern for the storage of the spent fuel rods so close to the sea, rather than in a proper storage facility, could not be denied. As her mind drifted through images of receiving the EU grant and modernizing her plant, and the face of her older brother, Anatoly. Again, she saw him lying in a hospital bed dying from radiation sickness, and recalled her prayerful promise that someday she would find a way to produce energy without someone having to die. If it was only possible! Russia needed energy, and nuclear energy was cheap, but at what a price to people and Mother Earth.

"In the past, once the spent fuel rods were removed from the reactor, they were placed in a storage area next to the plant, as happens at most nuclear power plants around the world. However, with this new system, the waste is transported almost immediately via a high security truck convoy to a centralized processing plant at the now resurrected Super-Phenix facility at Bouvesse east of Lyon, making long-term localized storage unnecessary," said Jean-Michel Bernard. Natasha snapped back into the reality of the present moment.

By 3:30 the lectures broke up for the day. Conference goers could check out the product booths in the tradeshow area, or catch a limousine back to their hotels, and enjoy the sites of old Strasbourg. Hank, Jake, Paul, and John decided to meet at seven o'clock in front of the cathedral. Hank suggested they might have dinner at the famous Maison Kammerzell, the renaissance era inn just across the street from his hotel.

Back at the hotel, Hank changed into more casual clothes, a light-blue golf shirt and light tan pants. Before meeting with his friends, he crossed the plaza to the Notre-Dame cathedral for a look inside. As impressive as the cathedral was on the outside, the inside was equally spectacular. Wow! The stain glass windows, especially the circular Rose Window at the cathedral's entrance, illuminated its spacious interior with a spiritual aura. After walking around, Hank sat down on a chair a few rows from the front to mentally take in all that he was seeing. He kept looking upward at the gothic arches, and the relatively thin outer walls. "How'd they build this?" he wondered to himself. "We surely couldn't do it today. No one knows how to cut stones like this anymore."

He got up from his chair and walked to the right toward the astronomical clock display. As he approached the alcove in front of him looking up at the clock was Natasha. As she looked down her gaze landed directly on Hank.

"Hello, Natasha!"

"It is nice to see you, Hank."

"Isn't this church just incredible? It's not like many we have back home. I grew up in the Lutheran church. My Swedish grandmother was going to be a missionary to China, until my grandfather swept her off her feet and married her. I don't think the Swedes ever forgave him. Do they build churches like this in Russia?"

"Not in this Gothic style, but they are just as grand and beautiful. I do love the light in this church. It feels so friendly, inviting and holy."

"I missed seeing you after we registered. I supposed you went to the lecture for nuclear engineers by EDF. What did you think of it?"

"Yes, I was in that lecture. It gives me great hope for our industry. The French appear to have good experience with handling the unique technology required to process waste. It's my goal to see that our plant can begin to use some of their ideas as soon as possible."

"That's great. My lecture was less practical, but interesting. We were learning about this German utility's challenges in using some of our American coal in their boilers. I've got to hand it to the Germans. They're pretty ingenious people. Our military engineers were stumped as to what to do with all of this hard coal the U.S. Congress dumped on them."

"Yes, I read the description of the lecture. I am sure it must have been quite interesting."

"Would you like to go out and get some fresh air?"

"I would, thank you."

"I noticed when I was outside walking around that it's possible to climb up to the mid-level of the cathedral tower. It looks to be at least two hundred feet high...not sure what that is in meters."

"That is a little over sixty meters."

"I see."

They walked around to the left side of the cathedral to a kiosk and entrance to the stairs. Hank shelled out forty francs so that they could enter the stairwell. Hank led the charge up the spiral staircase. Each turn of the red sandstone stairs brought them a little higher toward their goal and an increasingly spectacular view of the city below. After several turns Hank was huffing and puffing. "Am I really this out of shape?" he wondered to himself. On the other hand, Natasha seemed to be handling the climb with ease.

Once at the top, they emerged out of the upper room onto the roof. A dozen or so other tourists were milling around. The sun was shining brightly from the west revealing the outline of the Vosges Mountains in the distance. Metropolitan Strasbourg stretched out below with its sharply gabled rooftops filling the old city. To the north they could see the convention center, the European Parliament, and other church steeples. However, nothing could beat the steeple that towered above directly in front of them. From this middle section, nearly halfway up, the Notre-Dame's lone spire magnificently stretched up into the blue sky. At this close range the intricately carved sculpture stood out.

"I read that this spire was the tallest in all of Europe for over four hundred years."

"No kidding. Wow! Hmm, and to think that they must have built it without any modern tools, cranes, or electricity. It's incredible to think about, isn't it?"

Pulling his point-and-shoot camera out Hank aimed through the rope fence that had been erected surrounding the sides of the roof to deter jumpers. The fence proved to be almost as challenging to the photographer as to a jumper, but nonetheless Hank managed to get some good shots for his photo album.

"Perhaps I could take a photo of you in front of the spire."

"Would you? That would be great. Here, you push the gray button on the right," he handed the camera to her.

Natasha walked back toward the entrance to the roof and knelt down to get the best angle for the shot. She motioned Hank backward with her left hand. "Could move back just a little, please? That is good, right there. Smile, now!"

The camera reacted to the pressure of her right index finger on the shutter release with the familiar mechanical buzzing of a modern camera.

"Hey, why don't I take your picture? I could mail it to you in Russia."

"All right, why not." Natasha handed the camera back to Hank and walked over to the same spot where Hank had been standing while Hank assumed her former position and posture.

"Could you tilt your head just a little to the right? Oh, that's perfect. Here goes."

Click.

Through the viewfinder of his camera Hank couldn't help but make note of Natasha's natural beauty. Her face was fresh, friendly, with high cheekbones, fair skin, and well defined eyebrows. Her figure was tall, slender, and possessed a quality of elegance. He thought to himself, "She looks more like a fashion model than an engineer."

As Hank stood up from his crouching position, a short man in his forties approached him.

"Excuse me, my name is Steve Richardson. I heard you speaking English, and noticed you and your wife taking pictures of each other. It happens to me and my wife all the time on our vacations. We have tons of pictures of us standing all by ourselves, and only a few of us together. You know what I mean? And taking a tripod in your luggage all the way to Europe is so impractical. Anyway, I'd be happy to take your picture if you could take ours. Oh, I'm sorry, this my wife."

"Hi, I'm Laurie Richardson. It's nice to meet you."

"Hi, I'm Hank Hudson from Cincinnati. This is, uh, a colleague of mine from Russia, Natasha. We're attending a conference here in Strasbourg."

"Cincinnati! Get out, we're from Cincinnati too! East or west side?" Steve enthusiastically asked.

"I live in Delhi and yourselves?"

"We're just up from you in White Oak."

"Natasha, where are you from in Russia?" Laurie asked.

"I am from Sosnovy Bor, it is near St. Petersburg."

"Oh, that's very interesting. Steve and I haven't been to Russia, just here in France so far. We were in Paris last week, and saw all the sights there—the Eiffel Tower, the Louvre, and the Seine River. We're here in Strasbourg for a couple of days, and then we're off to Germany for a week. Isn't this cathedral just marvelous? I think it's a lot prettier than the Notre-Dame in Paris, don't you?"

"I would not know. I have not been to Paris,"

"You'd just love it there, I'm sure."

"Well, if you hand me your camera, I'll get a nice shot of you two," Steve interjected.

Hank and Natasha had their photo taken by the helpful American tourists, and Hank returned the favor by taking their photo, and they parted ways.

"That's pretty amazing running into people from your hometown in a place like this, don't you think?"

"I would agree. The probabilities are very unlikely. Even more so if your hometown is in Russia, like me. There are not many Russian tourists in France. We do not have money like you Americans."

"I can imagine."

Hank and Natasha leisurely strolled over to the western side of the roof, close to each other, but not touching. They lingered there for a minute or two looking out at the view of the city through the rope lattice. The afternoon sun seemed to illuminate the scene with life and energy.

"Look down there, would you. We're so high we can't even see the top of our hotel."

"You are right; the angle of view makes it impossible."

"Do you want go down now?"

"Yes, let us."

The walk down the spiral staircase was much faster and far less tiring. Natasha went first with Hank close behind. Occasionally they would have to scoot over to the inside while another person ascending passed on the outside wall.

"It sure is a lot easier going down, isn't it?"

"We have gravity on our side."

Once down on the street level, they walked around the narrow streets of the old city window-shopping. Natasha marveled at the selection of goods available for sale. Her eyes lit up at the sight of a patisserie, and the many fashion boutiques and specialty shops. She wished she could make purchases, but knew that her funds were limited to meals and incidentals.

On the other hand, Hank was less impressed by the assortment of merchandise, until he stumbled upon a store whose name grabbed him personally.

"Well, will you look at that, Natasha? A store with my name on it."

"Cafe Henri?

"Henri is French for Henry. My mother told me that when I was a young boy."

"Ah, I see. Maybe we should go inside," she urged.

Five minutes later, they each walked out of the store with a kilo of French Roast coffee to take home.

"That was very kind of you to buy me the coffee, Hank. Thank you, very much."

"It was my pleasure, and it really wasn't all that expensive. Only a hundred fifty francs for a kilo! That's cheaper than Starbucks."

"Starbucks?"

"It's a coffee store, kind of like this place, just trendier,"

"Trendy?"

"Popular, uh, in demand."

"*Da*. I understand."

Their path led them back to the entrance of the Hotel Cathedrale. It was already pushing seven.

"This has been a delightful afternoon. I'm so glad we ran into each other over at the cathedral."

"Ran into each other?"

"That means to discover each other at the same place and time," Hank translated his idiom.

"OK. Yes, it has been a very pleasant time for me too."

"I'd suggest that we dine together, but I promised some friends of mine from the US that we'd have dinner tonight. You could come along if you'd like."

"Thank you for the invitation, but I am feeling tired from the day. I will buy some food from one of the stores we passed and eat in my room tonight."

"It's just as well. These guys can get a bit wild once they've had a few beers."

"Yes, I understand"

"Perhaps we could have dinner tomorrow night instead, and sit at the same table too."

"Yes, I think I would like that."

With that, Natasha headed back down rue des Orfevres to the small *epicerie* she had seen earlier. Hank went back up to his room, tossed his coffee in his suitcase, and finished reading his two-day old USA Today in the bathroom. Later he found his friends down in front of his hotel buying postcards from the curio stands. The Maison Kammerzell and its culinary treasures awaited them just steps away.

Within minutes the beer was flowing. Tales of Y2K stories filled the table until the wee hours of the night.

For Natasha, the evening was filled with feelings, good feelings. As she sat in her room eating her dinner of quiche and pastry, it dawned on her that she hadn't been with a man quite like this in her entire life. He was kind, well mannered, generous, funny, and handsome. Was he real or an imaginary person? He seemed real enough, but where could this relationship ultimately go? Once the conference was over, they would go back to their homes and that would be the end of it. Maybe he would write her and send the photos from the top of the cathedral. Maybe it didn't really matter. She decided to enjoy the company of this Hank Hudson at least for the few days she could count on.

Chapter 12

BRIGHT RAYS OF the Wednesday morning sun were already streaming through the windows of the breakfast room when Natasha arrived for breakfast. After picking up a plate and loading it with croissants, butter, and jelly, she headed for the table nearest the window as she had the day before. She thought to herself, "I could get used to this kind of living."

Only three other people were in the room, an elderly German businessman reading a newspaper, and a young, newly married Swiss couple attached at the hip. Halfway into her croissant Hank dragged himself in ready for some strong coffee after his night out with the boys. Even considering his less than optimal state of alertness, he quickly spotted Natasha at her window side table. She was dressed in a stunning combination, a black and white patterned shirt with well-fitting black slacks. When Natasha saw Hank she motioned him to join her at the table. He willingly acceded.

"Good morning, Natasha, is this seat taken?"

"It is for you, Hank. Please join me."

"Thank you," said Hank as he scooted into the chair across from her.

"I have been wondering just what kind of name is Hank? That is not a familiar English name for me. And yesterday, you said your name was Henry, like the French, Henri."

"Oh, it's short for Henry, but hardly anyone calls me Henry anymore, except my mother."

"Short for Henry, I don't understand."

"Well, take you name, Natasha, for instance, you could shorten it to, Nat, Tasha, or something else I suppose."

"Oh, okay. I understand. We do that in Russia as well."

"It looks like it's going to be another great day outside,"

"Yes, it is. I love the way the sun shines here."

Hank excused himself and went to the buffet table for his breakfast selections. He returned with a plate piled high with three croissants, butter, jelly, yogurt, sliced meats, and an egg. After adorning the backside of a croissant with the butter and jelly, he proceeded to eat it washing it down with coffee at select intervals. Their eyes were drawn outside to the cathedral.

"Like I shared with you yesterday, churches back in America are nothing like this one. This church is both an engineering feat and a piece of artwork. Our churches are more functional and practical."

"You should come to Russia sometime and see our churches. We have some of the most beautiful in the world."

"I figured that you probably didn't have many of them, especially after being under communism for so long,"

"*Nyet*, we have churches everywhere. Almost every town has a church." We have very pretty churches in my hometown, Nizhny Novgorod."

"Where is that? I've never heard of it before. I've heard of Moscow, St. Petersburg, and Kiev."

"Kiev is in Ukraine, not Russia. Nizhny Novgorod is one of the largest cities in Russia. It used to be called Gorky."

"Oh, yeah, like Gorky Park, I've seen that movie before. It starred William Hurt, Lee Marvin, and Brian Dennehy."

"Not exactly. Gorky Park is in Moscow. Gorky was the name given to Nizhny Novgorod during Stalinist times."

"Interesting. I sometimes go to church with my parents when I'm back home visiting them."

"Yes, my mother still goes to church, and I have gone with her a few times when I have been home as well. My work at the power plant keeps me very busy with little time for church, but I believe in God."

"I know about some of your plants. I mean, who hasn't heard of Chernobyl? How's it all going? I read somewhere that they're shutting down that plant."

Natasha paused, looking out the window; Anatoly's face came to her mind for a moment. She held back the tears.

"Did I say something wrong?"

"Oh, I am fine, thank you, I was just thinking of my brother."

"Is he an engineer like you?"

"He was an engineer."

"I see. What does he do now? A career change or something?"

"He was at Chernobyl."

"Oh my, I apologize. I didn't know." Hank realized that he'd stepped into troubled waters. "You must miss him."

Tears now welled up ever so slightly in her eyes, *"Da,* yes, I carry him close to my heart. Please excuse my being so emotional."

Hank offered her his untouched napkin. She instinctively accepted it.

"His loss was such a waste, so unnecessary. Someday we engineers must find a better way of making electricity. We are killing ourselves. The workers at our plant are not healthy. We have radiation monitors all over the town. What is the point? Must people die just to keep the lights on?"

"I know what you mean. I'm not very proud of what my plants discharge into the air, but what can I do about it? We've installed all the latest scrubbers to keep the emissions down. Yet, there continues to be issues with acid rain in the Northeast and Canada from our plants."

Hank became quiet. Images of his plant's tailpipes now paraded through his mind. What a crazy, ridiculous thought to behold on such a beautiful morning. Here he was sitting with this gorgeous woman in front of him talking about power plant pollution of all things. Within a few minutes they finished their breakfast, and headed down the stairs to the front of the hotel for the morning limo transport to the convention centre. Neither spoke a word throughout the ride.

Upon arriving at the conference, protestors were vigilantly posted in front of the convention centre attempting to garner any attention they could from the conference goers. Hank noticed one sign that read, "ENERGY BELONGS TO THE PEOPLE, NOT DIETER SCHMIDT!" This surprisingly stunned him. What's with this guy Dieter Schmidt? He had read about him in Power magazine, the mogul of power generation and the conference's sponsor. Perhaps it was the intensity of the moment—Natasha's crying, the protestors, and his own thoughts about the power business that cut right through to the depths of his consciousness. Throughout his career he hadn't really considered the total impact of the work he did. He recalled his strange conversation with Darrel and Crazy Nick. If power was truly the people's, then he would have to start looking for a new job, and so would all the Dieter Schmidts of the world.

Natasha and Hank walked into the reception area together and straight into the Erasme auditorium for the morning presentation. They were a half-hour early, so they sat and talked together rather than hang out in the reception area. By now Natasha had recovered her composure.

"It was awful seeing my brother wither away in that hospital bed. There was nothing they could do for him except make him comfortable. Radiation poisoning is a horrific way to die. It was so needless."

"How old was he?"

"He had his thirty-first birthday only two days before the accident."

"He was very young."

"His death was unfair. He told me before he died that he had strongly recommended to his supervisors that they not conduct the test that led to the explosion. It was a breach of protocol, and look what happened."

"How old were you when he died?"

"Twenty-two. I was an engineering student at GPI when it happened."

"GPI?"

"Gorky Polytechnical Institute. There was a special program for nuclear engineers. Now it is called Nizhny Novgorod State Technical University."

"I see, you were following in your brother's footsteps, weren't you?"

"And my father's too."

"So, you come from a whole family of engineers!"

"Only the three of us. My mother and sister are not engineers. My mother is a pensioner, my sister, Natalya, works as a manager at the post office."

"And what about your dad, I mean, your father?"

"He died three years before Anatoly."

"I'm sorry to hear that. You're the only engineer left in your family.

"I wish that I was not the only one, and that my father and brother were still alive, but that is of course impossible."

The seats around them began to fill up with other conference delegates. Increased activity on stage signaled that the morning keynote address was soon to begin. Yasahara Shimabukuro, president and CEO of Turbidine Corporation, would be speaking about a subject common to nearly all power plants, whether they used gas or steam for propulsion—the latest in turbine technology.

Although they were miles apart culturally, Hank sensed that he and Natasha were kindred spirits. With each encounter he became more and more fascinated with her sense of purpose and being. Here was a woman, who, in spite of the fact that her brother was killed doing the same work as she, continued to persevere in that profession with passion, vision, and a determination to do the job better. Could a coal and a nuclear power plant engineer have a future together? Thank God she spoke such good English. He didn't dare try to utter a word of Russian.

Chapter 13

DIETER SCHMIDT POUNDED his fist on the desk in his bedroom at Château de l'Ile. He had finally made direct phone contact with Pierre Schneider, the Mayor of Strasbourg, and reiterated his demand that the Green Party protesters be dispersed to within one kilometer of the convention center. They were ruining his conference.

"I have spoken with your deputy mayor, what's his name, Claude something or other, more than once about the close proximity of the protesters to the convention hall. I can assure you that this kind of thing would never happen in Frankfurt."

"*Oui,* you spoke with my able friend and civil servant, Claude Hirschberger. He told me about your unhappiness with our policy regarding public displays of protest. We can certainly agree that we do not want any trouble. Let me assure you that our police force, like your own in Frankfurt, is very competent in handling this kind of situation. You needn't worry, Monsieur Schmidt. Everything will work out fine."

"I don't like the image the protest creates for my company. Look, Herr Schneider, certainly you, a politician, can appreciate the media aspects of this situation. Energia is too important a company to have our stock plunge because investors are unsure of the purity of our corporate intentions. These Green Party extremists make us look like a bunch of environmental killers, and nothing could be further from the truth," Dieter shot across Monsieur Schneider's bow.

"Excuse me for observing, but I do not think you help your cause by having the protest moved at this point in your conference. Trust me, in this, the media would see such a move as a treacherous and conniving conspiracy by the powerful corporate Energia and the City of Strasbourg to suppress the truth. You're better off just ignoring them and going about your business. Enjoy our fine city while you're here this week. You Germans need to, how do the Americans say it, to *chill out.*"

That last remark caused an uncontrolled cerebral nuclear chain reaction in Dieter. No one, but no one would ever get away with talking to him in such a condescending and prankish manner. No more warning shots. Dieter reloaded his verbal gun for a shot at point blank range.

"Allow me to make you a promise, Herr Schneider, that whoever runs against you in the next election will have my full and uncompromising financial support. *Vous comprenez?*"

"Spend your money as you choose, Monsieur Schmidt. After my discussion with your representative last week, Monsieur Klaus Vogel, it was my hope that you and I might be able to work this problem out amicably. He was crude and intimidating in his method with me. I had hoped that perhaps you would be different than he. Sadly, not. The lieutenant reflects his general very closely. I am confident that the citizens of Strasbourg will consider all of the good that my administration has done for them and will return me to office. Unless there is something else you would like to discuss with me, I need to turn my attention to other city business. Good-bye, Monsieur Schmidt."

The phone held in the hand of the president of Energia managed to remain intact in spite of the pressure being exerted on it by its owner. Dieter shoved the phone in his jacket pocket and turned to Klaus.

"When we return from the conference, Klaus, I want you to dig up every speck of dirt that exists on Herr Schneider. He's too shrewd and underhanded a bastard to not have cut a corner or two in his career. We're going to make him wish that he was the mayor of Antarctica."

"Consider it done."

"Let's get going. We're already late for the opening lecture. I want to hear what my friend, Herr Shimabukuro, is up to these days."

Dieter and Klaus left the room and made their way down the hall into the garden area pungent with the smell of flowers in bloom. A black Mercedes limousine waited for them in front of the Château de l'Ile. Klaus' personal assistant, Günther, was at the wheel. Once they were on their way into the city Klaus' mobile rang.

"*Hallo, Vogel. Ja, was gibts?*"

The call had come from Klaus' assistant director of security, Erich Koch, at the Frankfurt office. One of their top engineers, Franz Heidel, was reported missing from work for the third day in a row. He hadn't called in sick, nor did any of his co-workers know of his whereabouts. Ordinarily, this apparently minor personnel problem would not have drawn the attention of Energia's security department, except that Franz Heidel had been working on the company's most top-secret project.

Three years earlier, Energia had set up a special, covert project not even known to its own board of directors. The impetus for this project began when Dieter ran across an article in *Der Spiegel* about the famous American futurist and psychic, Lance Alan Morton. In the article, Morton had predicted that the future of energy generation was going to radically change from its present paradigm. The burning of fossil fuels and the splitting of the atom would forever be replaced by the manipulation of magnetic fields for the production of electrical energy. Paranoia had set into Dieter's mind. Could he idly sit by and watch his empire wiped out by one of his competitors, or worse, by some crackpot alternative energy tinkerer?

In August 1997, Project Atlantis was secretly birthed on the third floor of Energia's research and development laboratory at Höscht in suburban Frankfurt. A tightly knit group of engineers and technicians were selected from the company's vast human resource pool, particularly those who were considered to be expendable or of little political importance to Dieter's organization of company allies. The group was given a three-year deadline to produce a device that could utilize the earth's magnetic fields for the production of electrical energy. Secretly, Dieter's intention for the project was to prove that such a device was unworkable. However, in the unlikely event that the project even remotely succeeded, the knowledge and evidence of it could be easily and permanently suppressed by the personnel and security departments of Energia, in other words, by Klaus and company.

The research team was headed by electrical engineer, Franz Heidel, a graduate of the University of Technology in Darmstadt, and a veteran of Energia's R & D department. Heidel was a short, thin man, with thick, dark-rimmed glasses—the quintessential image of a research scientist. The cavalier intentions of Dieter Schmidt toward Project Atlantis were unbeknownst to Franz Heidel as he plowed away at fulfilling the mission of Project Atlantis: To produce an electrical energy generator using only the magnetic field of the earth.

Heidel's forty-year background in electrical engineering, along with his inquisitive nature made him an ideal project leader. He and his staff researched and analyzed every scrap of information available on magnetic fields. They hypothesized that a special conductor of some kind had to be developed that could interact with the magnetic fields sufficiently to direct the field's potential electrical energy. Where could such a conductor be found? What would it be comprised of? These questions haunted Heidel and his co-workers. Every possible hypothesis was considered without prejudice. No idea was excluded, including non-scientific information. Heidel even consulted with Lance Alan Morton himself, whose intuition guided him toward non-traditional informational resources. This input proved to be crucial, for it opened the doors to alternatives Heidel and his team probably wouldn't have likely considered. After nine months of tireless brainstorming, speculation, and exploration their investigation led them to a significant conclusion. They postulated that the energy of the earth's magnetic fields could be converted or tapped by a conductor of crystalline nature.

For the next two years the third floor Höscht laboratory was awash in crystal experts from around the world. Scientists from the Institute of Mineralogy at the University of Würzburg in Germany; the Department of Crystal and Structural Chemistry at Utrecht University in the Netherlands; the British Crystallographic Association; and the Crystallography Service at Michigan State University Department of Chemistry were consulted. Crystal making experts from Waterford, Ireland were hired to guide the team in the use of special synthetic crystal making equipment purchased from the Kabex Corporation. Lance Alan Morton had recommended that the preparation of crystals be supervised by Dr. William Donaldson, from the Department of Electrical and Computer Engineering at California State University in Northridge. Dr. Donaldson had been a close confidant of the late Dr. Marcel Vogel. Dr. Vogel, no relation to Klaus Vogel, had been a former IBM researcher, responsible for developing the coating for disc drives and LCD's, but later in life was an advocate of the use of crystals in healing. Dr. Donaldson's knowledge of Vogel's work and engineering background proved to be invaluable to Heidel. Although each party was paid for bits and pieces of information, and never given the whole picture and scope of Project Atlantis, Heidel had told Dr. Donaldson the whole scheme. They became good friends, and spent many a long lunch solving the world's problems.

With Dr. Donaldson's help, it was determined that a crystal of an elongated design and 21-sided shape would interact with the magnetic lay lines of the earth to cause an electric current to flow through connectors attached to each end of the crystal.

Then, in January of 2000, the improbable happened. Repeated trial and error of modifying the molecular quality of various crystals ultimately led to the production of a prototype generator dubbed E-6. What was different about E-6 compared with the five other prototypes before it was that it actually produced a measurable current. The euphoria of this breakthrough led to further experiments and refinements and the development of the E-7 model. Additionally, as was done with industrial lasers, the team discovered that passing a certain quantity of inert xenon gas through the crystal chamber had the effect of regulating and stabilizing the current flow, by removing impurities such as moisture, hydrocarbons, oxygen, and other contaminants. The results made the E-7 one hundred times more powerful than the E-6, with a whopping twenty kilowatts of output from a generator that weighed less than an average table-top television!

The fast pace of the E-7's development concerned Dieter Schmidt. What had begun as a fluke, an attempt to debunk Lance Allen Morton's prophecy, had become a serious problem for him. He quickly began to dismantle this success by moving personnel from Project Atlantis to other areas. One by one people began to disappear from the third floor of the Höscht lab, their personal items collected and sent to their new offices. Franz Heidel became suspicious of this abrupt reassigning of his staff and began to see the writing on the wall.

Because Franz Heidel had not shown up for work in the last three days, a search of his apartment in suburban

Höchst was conducted, but revealed nothing. One of his co-workers thought Heidel had said something about going down to Strasbourg. Heidel, brilliant but squirrely, was not someone to have milling around a convention full of engineers with all that he had locked up in his brain. Klaus alerted Dieter to the situation. A special security squad would be called in from Frankfurt to look for Heidel at the convention center. Klaus would head this team with help from Günther. As if things couldn't get worse for Dieter, now an AWOL engineer was on the loose with enough knowledge to possibly sink him and his company for good.

Chapter 14

THE MORNING LECTURE on state-of-the-art turbine technology by Yasahara Shimabukuro was well attended. For an hour and a half he expounded upon industry expectations for future improvements in turbine efficiency. Every extra tenth of percent in efficiency added up quickly considering the vast amounts of energy produced by each turbine. As the lecture ended, Dieter Schmidt came out on the stage to thank his friend for his enlightening and informative presentation.

Hank and Natasha made their way from the Erasme auditorium toward the convention centre restaurant. When they arrived the room was crowded with other conference goers trying to grab a quick bite to eat before the afternoon sessions. They each picked up a sandwich and drinks — coffee for Hank and mineral water for Natasha. After fumbling with their wallets at the cashier, they carried their trays out into the dining room. Just then, a familiar hand was waving at them from a large corner table.

"Over here, Hank!" yelled Jake Morelli.

Hank and Natasha's internal radar involuntarily zeroed in on the semaphore of Jake's waving arm and the sound of his booming voice, and walked in that direction. Paul McCurry and John Livingston were already making quick work of their luncheon selections of roast chicken.

"Hey Hank, have a seat. There's plenty of room for both of you. And who is this nice young lady?"

"Yeah, hold on a sec," Hank responded as he and Natasha put their trays of food down on the table and took their seats. "This is Natasha from Russia. We met yesterday on the limousine ride from our hotel."

"Same hotel, eh? Must be pretty cozy over there."

"Yes, I am Natasha Shakhova, and who do I have the pleasure of meeting?" Natasha interjected as she tilted her head toward Hank and lifted her eyebrows.

"Natasha, this is Jake Morelli from Los Angeles."

"I am pleased to meet you, Jake."

"And these fellows here are Paul McCurry from my hometown of Dune Acres, and John Livingston from Chicago. These are the guys I was telling you about yesterday, the ones I had dinner with."

"It is very nice to meet all of Hank's friends from America." Natasha managed a quick smile betwixt her genuine feelings of embarrassment from Jake's remarks about their *cozy hotel*.

For a few minutes everyone concentrated on eating. The room continued to fill with more patrons. As the lunch hour progressed so did the noise level.

"So, Natasha," Jake mumbled between bites of food, "how are you connected with this conference? Do you work for Energia in Russia or something? I just don't think I've ever seen you at any of the other power conferences before. I'm sure I would remember you."

Natasha finished her bite of food and responded in a very direct manner, "This is my first conference outside of Russia, except for when I attended the tenth anniversary of Chernobyl conference in Vienna four years ago. I am the chief engineering director of the Baltic Regional Power Plant in Sosnovy Bor. Are you familiar with our plant?"

Impressed with her assertiveness and confidence, Jake finished his meal, placed his napkin on the table in front of him and said, "I don't think I am. Honestly, it's all I can do to keep track of my own plants. I'll tell you, we could sure use some of your plants out in California. I mean, we're holding our own at the DWP, but my colleagues at Southern California Edison and Pacific Gas & Electric are really up a creek without a paddle, if you know what I mean?"

"Jake means, that there aren't enough plants in California to keep up with the demand for energy," Hank helped translate the idiom.

"Yes, I see. Well, I don't know if you really would want any of our plants in California considering the problems we have maintaining them properly. At our plant we are dealing with major problems with aging reactors and inadequate waste storage."

"You head up a nuke plant?"

"Yes, I am the manager of a *nuke* plant as you call it. We have them all over Russia, just like you have in America. My father, Dmitri Shakhov, helped to design and build many of them. Today, they account for nearly twelve percent of our country's electrical needs."

"I didn't realize that your father was so involved in the industry," Hank added.

"Well, I must say that I'm quite impressed by your work, Natasha. It's just that when Hank walked up with you a few moments ago I didn't figure you for a nuke plant engineer."

"Our company has several nuclear plants," John Livingston steered the conversation in a more professional direction. "For the first time in years we've finally got all ten reactors working at their optimal levels and without being under any special oversight by the NRC. It took a lot of teamwork to get us that far. I can surely appreciate the unique safety challenges you must be facing at your plant, Natasha."

"Yes, we have a very fine team at our plant too. We do the best we can with the resources available. However, there is so much more we must do to ensure the public's safety, do you agree?"

"I agree. We've just finished a program that focused completely upon safety measures, especially in the area of operator performance. A plant can only run as well as its staff can do the job right. I think that's what helped get us off the NRC's blacklist. Now, tell us about your plant. Is it a single or multi-reactor plant?"

"We have five reactors, each rated at one thousand megawatts. We supply power for the entire St. Petersburg region. You said there are ten reactors in your company?"

"Five thousand megawatts from one plant, my, that's tremendous! Our biggest one, the LaSalle plant in Marseilles, can crank out 2,150 megawatts. Yes, ComEd's group of ten reactors at five locations produce almost sixty percent of our company's capacity when running at full power, and is, to the best of my knowledge, the largest collection of nuclear plants in the nation. We supply electrical energy to all of Chicago and most of northern Illinois. That's somewhere around three and a half million households."

"Stop bragging, John. You're making Paul feel bad. Hell, you light up Chicago, all Paul has is Gary, Indiana and Hank's parent's house in Dune Acres," Jake chimed in.

"NIPSCO is just a little outfit next to these big city boys, Natasha. NIPSCO stands for Northern Indiana Public Service Company. However, if it wasn't for us Hank's parents would be in the dark," added Paul.

"Hell, if it wasn't for my company, all of Hollywood would be in the dark," Jake boasted. "The LA Department of Water and Power is the largest municipally owned utility in the nation. And, we've got a nuke plant out in the Arizona desert that's almost as big as Natasha's."

"Like I said, Natasha, Jake and John are the big boys here," said Paul. "I keep northern Indiana lit up, while Hank keeps the lights on down in Cincinnati,"

"I'm still impressed by your five thousand megawatt plant, Natasha," John butted back in. "Is it like the Chernobyl plant?"

"Yes, it is," Suddenly the conversation stopped for a moment. It was almost as if everyone was holding a moment of silence for the once deadly and now defunct power plant. Then everyone finished their meals.

"It's been a pleasure to meet you, Natasha," John broke the ice."

"Yes, it has. Thank you for gracing us old men with your presence," Paul added.

"Speak for yourself. I'm not old!" Jake reacted.

"See you guys later," Hank finally got a word in. Jake threw him a wink of approval. Hank and Natasha excused themselves and left the dining room for the convention center hallway.

"So, what did you think of my friends?" I hope they weren't too…ill-mannered."

"They were…fine."

"I'm sorry about John asking you about Chernobyl. He didn't know, of course."

"Of course, just as you did not know about my brother this morning when you asked me about Chernobyl."

"You're right. I walked into that minefield myself, didn't I?"

"It is okay, Hank. It has been fourteen years since Anatoly's death. I must learn to let go of my grief someday. Besides, I am a Russian, and a power plant engineer. It is reasonable that someone would ask me about Chernobyl."

"What are you doing this afternoon?"

"I was planning to go on the field trip to the Fessenheim plant. Why do you ask?"

"I don't know. What do you think of going for a ride in the country?"

Natasha blushed at his invitation. Again, as she had when she first saw Hank at the Restaurant Dauphin, Natasha could hear the encouraging words of Natalya echoing through her brain.

"You have a car?"

"Yes, I do. I drove down from the Frankfurt airport. I plan to do some sightseeing after the conference is over and thought that having a car would be handy. It's in a garage a few blocks from the hotel. The front desk can get it for me anytime I want it."

"Where would we go?"

"My mother's grandparents came from this area. I've heard that it's very pretty, especially the wine country. You know, I was looking at a map of where that Fessenheim plant is located. We could make that our destination if you'd like. You said that you wanted to take the tour. Heck, except for my tour of duty on the *San Francisco,* I've spent my whole life in coal fired plants. It's about time I saw a nuclear one. I'm sure we could arrive in time for the tour. Is it a deal?"

Natasha thought for a moment, and then the Natalya in her answered, "I would love to come!"

Hank and Natasha continued down the convention center hallway to the main entrance. Several taxis were available to convention goers. Within minutes they were back at the Hotel Cathedrale. Jacque, the bellman, retrieved Hank's Ford Mondeo station wagon from the garage and brought it to the parking lot on the south side of the Notre-Dame exactly where Hank had driven in days before. At this time in the afternoon the cathedral square was off limits to traffic. Hank negotiated the narrow streets of the old city and drove across the Ill River following the signs for the A35.

Once on the freeway Hank reached in his pocket for a local tourist map he had picked up at one of the curio shops in front of the hotel.

"How are you at reading a French map? I think it mentions that special scenic route through the wine country I mentioned before," Hank said as he handed the map to Natasha. After a minute of study she responded.

"Yes, *la Route du Vin d'Alsace.* It is mentioned right here in the legend. We just passed the exit for the airport. Coming up shortly follow the signs for A352, then in about ten kilometers there will be an exit for Molsheim. We get off there and follow a secondary road, D35."

"Are you always this efficient?"

"I run a *nuke* plant, remember?!"

Traffic was light coming out of the city. The ten-kilometer trek to the Molsheim exit went by in a flash. Signs seemed to be posted everywhere for *la Route du Vin d'Alsace*, as if to invite the entire world to sample its offerings. D35 proved to be one of the windiest and most twisted roads that Hank had ever come across. And yet, it was possibly among the most relaxing, enjoyable, and picturesque roads he had ever driven. The road snaked its way from one quaint village after another through a veritable ocean of green vineyards along the foothills of the Vosges Mountains. It was as if every square meter of space had been reserved for these sacred vines.

La Route du Vin d'Alsace meandered south from Molsheim through the towns of Obernai, Barr, Kintzheim, Ribeauville, Riquewihr, Kaysersberg, Winzenheim, and Eguisheim eventually shedding its D35 designation for other equally stimulating labels as it went along. The quaintness of each town begged stopping for a visit. However, the goal of the Fessenheim plant lurked in the back of each of their minds. At Eguisheim Natasha guided Hank off the wine route onto a series of roads that led to the power plant next to the Rhein River. It was 2:45 in the afternoon. Buses from the convention center were beginning to arrive in the plant parking lot. Hank and Natasha's timing couldn't have been better.

Nearly eighty engineers assembled in the plant's reception room for the tour. Philippe Stricker, plant manager, showed them to the control room, the brain and central nervous system of the plant.

"When the plant was first built in 1976 computers were not what they are today. Like the control rooms in your plants back home, we have had to upgrade our computers and sensors on an ongoing basis. I'm beginning to think I should've have become an electronic instead of an electrical engineer," Stricker joked. "But, we have some very smart young people employed by Electricite de France to keep us up to date."

The tour moved outside the main plant to the spent fuel rod storage area building nearby where they were met by Jean-Michel Bernard who continued the presentation.

"As you can see here, we have reduced the length of time spent fuel remains on-site. The large trucks you see at the rear of the building will soon be loaded with the rods for transport south to our reprocessing plant near Lyon. The trickiest part, of course, is the trip itself. The trucks are sent out two at a time with a special police escort, and cannot travel over 90 km/hr. This often plays havoc with other drivers who want to go faster, but once they discover who we are, they are most cooperative. Weather is also a factor in planning convoys. If heavy rain or snow is in the forecast, we wait until it passes. Additionally, convoys typically are conducted from mid-morning to mid-afternoon to avoid rush hour."

"How long does it take to drive to the reprocessing plant, especially at such a low speed?" asked a male engineer from Britain.

"Thank you for your question. The distance from Fessenheim to Bouvesse is four hundred sixty kilometers, which would usually take the average motorist about five hours to drive. With the convoy's reduced speed the trip runs about seven hours. Are there any other questions?"

"What about security? How do you prevent a terrorist, for instance, from threatening the convoy?" asked an engineer from the Czech Republic.

"Again, a vital question. Certainly, security is high at any power plant. It is even more important when transporting materials as toxic as spent nuclear fuel rods. Convoys are of course scheduled well in advance, but the knowledge of when they will be traveling is a guarded secret. Three days in advance of a convoy the police run a thorough security check of the route. Then once they depart, the convoy is monitored by plane, helicopter, and is, as I mentioned before, escorted by police cars. It is not a foolproof system, by any means, but everything has been, as you say in English, 'so far so good.'"

Hank turned to Natasha, "This spent fuel business is like handling glass with a sledgehammer. I don't know how you can do your job and not be afraid of screwing things up. A chunk of coal is pretty tame compared with this uranium and plutonium stuff."

"You must be so very careful, and follow safety procedures all of the time. The rest is a bit of luck and prayer."

The tour concluded at 4:30 back in the reception area where it began. The other engineers returned to the two buses that brought them down from Strasbourg. Hank and Natasha got back in the Ford and began retracing the way back to la Route du Vin d'Alsace. It was past five when they drifted into the hamlet of Eguisheim.

"What do you say we stop and check out this town?

"Sure, that would be fine with me."

Eguisheim was a perfectly preserved medieval village nestled in the vineyards of Alsace just a stone's throw from the larger city of Colmar. Laid out in a circular plan, Eguisheim's half-timbered houses, gabled roofs, and outer ramparts gave it plenty of charm and Old World atmosphere. This appeal was not bypassed by the tourist trade. Eguisheim, although only a town of 1,500 residents, contained an abundance of hotels, restaurants, shops, and interesting historical sites.

Hank parked the car in a public lot on the east end of town, which by this time of day was full of cars with German license plates like his. The sun, still fairly high in the sky, had warmed the pavement and buildings to a medium-hot temperature. Hank and Natasha ambled into the town along the Grand Rue toward the center of the town and the cobblestone Place du Chateau. The plaza was lined with Renaissance era houses and shops. At its center stood the Saint Leon fountain and statue of hometown son, Pope Leo IX, the only pope to come from Alsace. Behind the fountain were a small castle and the Chapelle Saint-Leon. Hank and Natasha gravitated to the fountain whose sides were adorned with bright pink flowers.

"I really love this town. The flowers are so beautiful."

"It's nice here. We don't have many towns like this back home. It seems that almost everything in the US is so modern. Whenever something gets old, we just tear it down and build something else. Back in Cincinnati, we have this sports stadium. It's called Riverfront Stadium, or, at least that's what we used to call it until OVP bought the rights to its name. Now it's called OVP Field. It doesn't have the same ring as Riverfront Stadium." Natasha listened patiently while Hank pontificated.

"Well, the Bengals football team demanded a new stadium, or they would leave town, so they passed a sales tax increase to build them their own stadium. It cost over half a billion dollars! Can you believe it? And the old stadium was just fine. Then, the Reds, that's the baseball team, decided they needed a new stadium too. They're going to build them a stadium and tear down Riverfront. I mean, why? It's only thirty years old. I think it's crazy spending all of our hard earned money on gladiator sports when there are many other worthy projects."

"You Americans have so much money to spend. You do not know how good you have it."

"You're probably right. You understand my point though? We Americans seem to care a lot less about our heritage." Hank paused for a moment in thought.

"My Aunt Alla lives in this town in Indiana down the river from Cincinnati called Madison. I think it was named after one of our earliest presidents. Madison has a charm sort of like this town. She lives in an old Victorian — a real nice looking house from the outside. It's a real bugger to heat and cool though. She's got the worst utility bills. But, the town is a real nice one to walk around. It has lots of antique stores and restaurants. They put the modern Madison up on the ridge above the old town. That's where the McDonald's and Wal-Mart are. I think that was real smart of the town fathers," Hank finished his dissertation.

Just then, a large, loud group of German tourists joined them at the fountain. Feeling the pressure of the crowd, Hank and Natasha lazily drifted slightly away from the fountain across the plaza to the front of a wine shop. On a table in front of the shop the owner had placed glasses and samples of their wares.

"Check this out! You'd never see this back home. Let's try some. I think that's the idea."

Hank poured a small amount of wine into the open glass and offered it to Natasha, and then poured himself one.

"This is excellent wine. It tastes just like the kind I had the other night at the restaurant. You remember when we first saw each other?"

Natasha took a sip from her glass.

"*C'est delicieux!*"

"Let's buy some!"

Hank and Natasha ascended the short stairway that led to the entrance of the wine shop. Once inside the clerk, a bearded man in his thirties looked up, "*Bonjour.*"

Natasha responded first, "*Bonjour.*"

"Yeah, *bonjour,*" followed Hank.

They browsed through the small shop filled with all of the wines of Alsace. Bottles of Pinot Noir, Riesling, Muscat, and Gewürztraminer were organized by year on the far shelf wall, and in separate displays around the shop. After a couple of minutes Hank broke the ice with the clerk.

"I would like to buy some wine, please. Like the kind you were serving outside."

"*Je suis disole, Monsieur. Je ne parlez pas l'anglais.*"

"What did he say?" Hank looked at Natasha.

"He doesn't speak English. Would you like me to help?

"If you don't mind. My French is about as good as his English."

"*Il voudrais acheter un bouteielle vin de Gewürztraminer, s'il vous plait.*" Natasha rattled off without missing a beat.

"*Quoi annee?*"

"He wants to know what vintage, what year you wish to buy."

"Whatever he had outside is fine with me."

"*Celui-la,*" Natasha pointed through the shop window at the bottle outside on the table.

"*Oui, Madame.*"

The clerk came around the cash register walked over to the wall rack and pulled down a green bottle with a gold label.

"Don't you want one too? I'd be happy to buy you one."

Caught off guard by his proposal, Natasha hesitated for a second, "Sure Hank, that is very kind of you."

"*Monsieur, pardon, on voudrais deux boutielles, s'il vous plais,*" Natasha amended the order.

"*Oui, Madame,*" the clerk affirmed the change in quantity.

The clerk packaged the two bottles of wine in a cardboard caddie.

"*Ça coûte combien?*"

"*Quatre-vingts six francs, s'il vous plait.*"

Natasha turned to Hank and said, "You must pay him eighty-six francs."

"OK, hold on a sec; let me get out my wallet. Here's a hundred-franc note. That ought to cover it."

With the wine transaction complete, Hank and Natasha walked outside and down the stairs into the plaza. The lure of the back streets of Eguisheim magnetically pulled them forward. Hank had asked Natasha to check with the wine store clerk about good restaurants in the town. He enthusiastically directed them up the rue d'Hopital, then left down the rue du Rempart Nord to the Caveau Bacchus. Since the restaurant would not be open for dinner for a half-hour, they made reservations for seven o'clock, and continued to stroll through the circular maze of cobblestone streets admiring the colorful houses. After a few minutes they arrived at the Place d'Eglise and the Eglise Saints Pierre et Paul. A hodge-podge of architectural eras and materials dating from Roman to Romanesque to modern times, this parish church with its yellow sandstone tower and gabled roof belfry dominated the entire town. Atop the tower perched the "official" bird of Alsace, the stork, blissfully watching over the town below.

"Check out the bird in the tower," Hank finally noticed the stork up above. He got out his camera, extended the zoom lens as far as it would go, and snapped a shot of the stork nest.

"Let me get your picture with the stork."

"What is this with you wanting pictures of me and church towers?"

"I don't know, call it a Kodak moment. I mean the tower certainly looks better with you in it than not."

Natasha rolled her eyes at his not so subtle flattery. "Okay, go ahead. But, I doubt you can get both me and the stork in the photo."

"This camera can also zoom out to twenty-eight millimeters, which is a pretty wide angle. Hold on, uh, stand over there just to the right of the tower, on the corner. That's it," Hank barked out his directions as Natasha heeded them.

Just then a boy, all of ten-years old, who had been playing soccer with a group of children in the plaza in front of the church, came up to Hank and offered to take his picture with Natasha. Hank didn't understand his words verbatim, but understood the offer. Once he backed up far enough toward the house in the back of the plaza, and adjusted the camera for wide-angle, he handed it off to the boy.

"You just push this button on the right."

"*Oui, Monsieur.*"

Hank joined Natasha under the church tower all the while praying that some of what he wanted in the photo succeeded making it on the film. The boy took two just to make sure, and then brought the camera back to Hank.

"*Merci,*" Hank managed.

"You're welcome, sir."

"You speak English? Here, hold on a moment."

Hank reached in his pocket and pulled out a ten-franc coin and handed it to the boy.

"Thank you," said the boy as he trotted back to the soccer game with his friends.

"Wasn't that just perfect him showing up like he did? I'll be sure to get double prints and send you a picture after I get back home. You're going to have to give me your address in Russia."

"Yes, I would like that. Thank you!"

They continued to wander around the western edge of the town, past the *ecole* where the young photographer probably learned his English, and back down rue Rempart du Nord to the restaurant, Caveau Bacchus, for dinner. They were seated at a corner table and given menus.

"Order whatever you want, my treat. I want to try some of that pizza looking stuff I saw you eating the other night. Do they have that here?"

"Tarte flambé. Yes, they have it on the menu, and you can get many toppings on it, just like pizza."

For the next two hours the two power plant engineers from two sides of the world dined on tarte flambé, toasted the wine of the region, and warmed to each other's mind and spirit. As the sun began to descend late in the evening, they returned to the car for the drive back to Strasbourg. Once the car was headed back to its garage cradle for the night with the bellman, each went to their rooms. By now Hank's room was filled with the aroma of his namesake's coffee; the kilo in his suitcase waiting to be taken home. He added the wine to his suitcase. Natasha returned back to her room energized by the day with a man who really seemed to understand her human side, her pain, and her life as an engineer. And he had a sense of humor. What would tomorrow bring?

Chapter 15

SINCE MONDAY, FRANZ HEIDEL had been holed up at his sister's home in Fischbach, about twenty kilometers northwest of Frankfurt. He and Gerta had always had a close sibling relationship. Whenever he had time off from the lab, Franz would often take the commuter train from Höchst to Kelkheim, where Gerta would pick him up and bring him over to her house. Gerta's husband, Werner, had died several years ago, so she welcomed Franz' frequent visits. This visit, however, had a less than jovial aura about it. Franz Heidel was on the run.

As he watched the subtle dismantling of Project Atlantis, both anger and fear welled up from within him. On one hand he was outraged to see the years of research, hard work, and success slipping away before his eyes. How could such a thing happen? Was this some kind of cruel joke? Was he a mere pawn in the hands of a corporate monster? Why kill the project? They had succeeded in their goal of making a pollution-free energy device. The possibilities for revolutionizing energy production were monumental. More research and development was needed, not less. What could possibly have possessed Dieter Schmidt? Scrapping Project Atlantis made no sense. Franz Heidel boiled with exasperation and confusion.

And yet, he had also heard the rumors about how employees would suddenly vanish for allegedly saying the wrong thing. Reassignments to other departments, unfounded terminations, and unexplainable disappearances were known to have happened. Franz Heidel felt the heat of Energia's security department, and perhaps for good reason. He knew too much. It was only a matter of time until something underhanded happened to him. Rather than wait for the inevitable to occur, he decided to take matters into his own hands. While visiting Gerta over the weekend, he conceived of a plan that just might save his own skin, and all of the research his team had done. Knowing that his absence from work would likely be investigated, he wisely chose not to return to his own apartment. He would have to launch his scheme from the relative safety of Gerta's humble abode.

Late on Wednesday afternoon, Franz Heidel slipped aboard the commuter train in Kelkheim bound for Frankfurt's Hauptbahnhof where he caught the 6:50 p.m. to Mannheim. After changing trains in Mannheim, and again in Offenburg, he arrived at the Strasbourg train station just after nine o'clock. As he walked from the train through the station his eyes nervously canvassed the terminal for inquisitive eyes. Relieved that no one seemed to take notice of his arrival, he proceeded directly to a taxi and asked the driver to take him to a modestly priced hotel in the old city. Within a few minutes he was delivered to the Hotel Suisse on the rue de la Rape, a short distance east of the cathedral.

Thankful that his arrival in Strasbourg appeared to go unnoticed by Energia's security personnel, Franz Heidel tossed his overnight bag and briefcase onto the gray carpeted floor, flopped down on the yellow patterned bedspread, and let out a sigh of relief. The gravity of what he was about to do was sinking in. His whole career as a research engineer with Energia flashed before him. Contained within his briefcase were all the key technical documents of Project Atlantis that he had smuggled out of the Höscht laboratory last Friday. His thievery seemed dwarfed by his company's apparent crime of industrial suppression. Determined to see that this crucial technology would continue to develop, he contemplated the possible ways he might reveal its truth. Would he find someone here in Strasbourg who would actually listen to him, or would

Energia's security eventually catch up with him? Regardless of the risks, he was ready to share his secrets.

Chapter 16

THE THURSDAY MORNING sun was beaming through the windows of the breakfast room at the Hotel Cathedrale when Natasha called out a cheerful greeting across the room, "Good morning, Hank."

As usual, Hank was running a little behind Natasha in his morning routine. His hair was still damp from the rushed shower he managed minutes before his arrival. They had agreed the night before to meet in the breakfast room by eight. It was now a quarter after.

"Hi Natasha, I'm sorry I'm late. Too many glasses of that incredible white wine last night, I'm afraid. What's it called again?"

"Gewürztraminer,"

"That's it. How are you this morning? Did you sleep well?" asked Hank as he took his seat at the table.

"I fell asleep right after we returned to the hotel."

"We sure had a long day yesterday, but it was perfect, wasn't it?"

"Yes, I had a wonderful time. I am glad I came along with you. Thank you for inviting me."

"Hey, it was my pleasure."

Hank got up from the table and returned shortly with his plate full of croissants and a cup of coffee in his hand.

"Doesn't it seem strange to come to a conference like this with our employers paying for everything and our having so much fun? It feels like we should be working on something," Hank thought out loud.

"I know what you mean. It all seems too good to be this way. I am sad that the convention will be ending tomorrow morning and that we will all be returning to our homes. I wish it could continue for another week,"

"Well, there's the big banquet tonight. Maybe we can sit together."

"I would like that, yes, Hank," Natasha accepted as she looked at him with a warm smile.

Hank returned Natasha's smile, and for the first time this morning, he noticed her stunning outfit—a white summer dress with gold piping around the cuffs and lapels, and matching white shoes. Her happy demeanor illumined her clothing, as if there were thousands of miniature light bulbs attached to her dress that glowed every time she smiled. He wondered to himself, "Why is a woman like her hanging out with a nearly fifty-year old guy like me? She must be crazy!" He shook off his momentary gaze and plowed into his mound of croissants.

"I really liked the tour of the nuke plant. I guess that was no biggie for you, you run one," Hank mumbled between bites.

Natasha had finished her breakfast and was sipping her coffee.

"That plant, I must tell you, is run much more efficiently than a Russian nuclear power plant. Although they produce about half of the power of my plant, they require only a fraction of the workers. They also have state-of-the-art computer controls and safety precautions in place that we can only pray that we will have someday. We are hoping that our grant application with the European Union will be approved and that we can begin the upgrading process."

"I just don't get how you can to work every day knowing that you've got the potential for 'China syndrome' burning away in that reactor."

"China syndrome?"

"It's an American movie with Jane Fonda, Michael Douglas, and Jack Lemmon about a near meltdown at a nuclear power plant in the US. It's quite an intense movie. I haven't seen it in years."

"I am still not sure why it is called, China syndrome."

"Oh, I think I see why you're puzzled. You see, in America, people say that if you dig all the way through the earth you'll come out the other side in China. I don't know if you really would surface in China, probably in the middle of the ocean."

"Okay, I understand what you mean. Was the theory of the movie that if the reactor core was breached, the fissionable material would melt its way through the earth? To China?"

"That's the gist of it. I'm not sure that you'd really enjoy that movie. It probably would hit too close to home with Chernobyl and all."

"Actually, Chernobyl was more of a *melt up* than a meltdown, a steam explosion caused by a power surge in the reactor initiated by some foolish plant workers. It was totally preventable and should not have happened. The Three Mile Island accident in 1979 in Pennsylvania had more of the potential of a meltdown. Stuck valves and operator error reduced water available for cooling the reactor core. The only thing available for cooling was steam, which is not good for that. The reactor core began to melt and puddle in the bottom of the containment area. Fortunately, the floor of the reactor building was not breached. Your country was spared a great catastrophe."

"I see what you mean. I have to admit, I still like making electricity the old fashioned way, with coal. At least it doesn't turn everything into a glowing, toxic, wasteland. I just don't see how you cope with the danger. I was always a little nervous about radiation during my stint on the *San Francisco.*"

"You have to put that possibility out of your mind, but also be prepared for it in case something goes wrong. It is crazy having to think that way all of the time, but I am used to it. However, a meltdown into and through the earth, this China syndrome, is not physically possible. For a nuclear reaction to continue and generate the heat needed to keep it going and melt the earth, the reactor core's shape must be maintained at a certain size. In the case of Chernobyl, the reactor's geometry was totally compromised. That does not mean that everything is okay just because the core cannot melt into the earth. At Chernobyl the explosion sent tons of radioactive fuel into the atmosphere. There are places in Belarus and Ukraine that are complete wastelands because of the accident."

"I guess we'd better get down to the front of the hotel for the limo pick-up, shouldn't we? What time is it?"

"It is 8:45. Yes, we should go now."

Hank finished the last bit of croissant and coffee, wiped his mouth off with the white linen napkin, and got up just as Natasha did. She led the way out of the room, down the stairs, and out into the cathedral square. A few minutes later the minivan from the Alsace International Car Service picked them up for the now familiar roundabout ride through the narrow streets of Strasbourg's old city. After retrieving the Italian and Dutch engineers the van arrived at the convention center.

Green Party and now Greenpeace protesters were vigilantly stationed at their posts across the street from the convention center, indicating that the stalemate between Dieter Schmidt and Pierre Schneider continued. By the third day of the convention conference goers were getting used to the litany of pro-environmental and anti-corporate slogans zealously displayed on placards and chanted by the faithful. "ENERGIA GO HOME!" "NO MORE CHERNOBYLS!" "THE EARTH CRIES FOR JUSTICE!" Vans and taxis poured into the loading zone.

Knowing that he dare not show his face in the convention center itself, Franz Heidel had taken cover behind a placard-waving protester. Here he was, less than one hundred meters from his fellow engineers, and he might as well have been on the moon. How could he possibly get the attention of one of his colleagues without alerting Dieter Schmidt's clearly visible henchmen pacing around in front of the convention center entrance? He had no desire to disappear like so many others, killed in a skiing accident while on a holiday in the Austrian Alps, or found drowned while swimming in the sea in the south of France. He had to be careful, but not too careful. How could he gain someone's attention?

Suddenly, he conceived of a plan. It just might work. He retrieved a note pad out of his coat pocket that he often carried for inspirations regarding the projects he worked on. Today's inspiration just might save one of those projects. He jotted down his message, and turned to the protester next to him for assistance. He handed him the note and pointed to the arriving vehicles. A nod of acceptance from the twentyish year old male protester ensued.

Seconds later, the protester broke through the police line dividing the sidewalk across from the convention center from the drop off area, and quickly ran up to a pair of arriving engineers.

"Désolé Monsieur et Madame, je dois vous transmettre ce message."

Hank took the note from the young man but could not understand his words.

"What did he say, Natasha?"

"He said that he must give us this message," she translated. Looking at the young man, "Qui vous a donné ce message?"

By now, two policemen approached the protester with the clear intent of escorting him back to the sidewalk. Seeing this, he began to walk away from Hank and Natasha, but managed to point toward the place in the crowd where he last saw Franz Heidel, "Il est la-bas."

However, Franz Heidel was nowhere to be seen. Grasping the note in his left hand, Hank and Natasha proceeded into the convention center's reception area just as they had the last two mornings. Curiosity was eating away at both of them. What did the note say? Why did this young man risk arrest by the police to deliver a note from a man who vanished into thin air? Instead of going straight into the Erasme Auditorium for the panel discussion on uses of the Internet in plant management, Hank and Natasha slipped away from the crowds to a quieter, less busy area. They happened upon a bench near some tall windows that looked out into the seven-hectare green belt that surrounded the complex.

Still holding the note in his hand, Hank unfolded it to reveal its mysterious contents. The note read as follows:

"Entschuldigen Sie mir, bitte, ich heiße Franz Heidel. Ich bin eine Ingenier von Energia AG. Es ist wichtig daß ich mit Ihnen bei der Gutenberg Platz neben der Statue an der 21:00 heute Abend sprechen muß. Bitte, komm alein. Ich habe die Information von das Projekt Atlantis, eine Verschmutzungfrei-Energievorrichtung. Energia wird dieses Projekt abbrechen. Bitte, hilfe mich! – Franz Heidel."

"I think it's in German. Can you read it?"

For the next minute, Natasha silently read the note a couple of times. She sat in stunned silence.

"What does it say, Natasha!"

"You are not going to believe it!"

"Sure I will, come on, tell me!"

"It says, 'Excuse me please, my name is Franz Heidel. I am an engineer from Energia AG. It is important that I meet with you this evening at nine o'clock at the Gutenberg Place near the statue. Please come alone! I have information about a Project Atlantis, a pollution-free energy device. Energia is going to dismantle the project. Please help me! —Franz Heidel.'"

"Project Atlantis! You've got to be kidding? Oh, I don't mean you, Natasha, I mean this guy, Franz."

"That is what the note says."

"Before I left for the convention, I stopped by to visit this old Navy friend of mine, Darrell LeBrec. He's a real great guy, an old Navy buddy. Anyway, he tells me about this ancient Atlantean technology that will someday revolutionize electrical power production around the world. Then he takes me to this wacky professor friend of his, Dr. Nick, who spent hours trying to convince me that the technology exists for utilizing the magnetic fields of the earth in producing energy. I'll tell ya, I thought these guys were nuts, and I told them so. I even said that I'd come back to see them and tell them about attending a lecture on Atlantean power systems at the convention. I was joking!"

"What if he is telling the truth, Hank? Maybe this man and your friends are correct. We have been talking about this kind of possibility almost since we first met. God has a way of bringing people together at the right way and at the right time. Perhaps we should meet with him as he asks. The Gutenberg Place is only two blocks from our hotel."

"Perhaps you're right. We ought to check it out. But, what about this Energia thing? Why do you think they are shutting down this project? Maybe we better just lay low for the day, go to all the sessions, come to the banquet for a while then go see this Franz guy."

"I agree."

Hank and Natasha returned to the Erasme Auditorium for the panel discussion on using the Internet. They even had lunch in the convention center restaurant with Jake, John, and Paul. However, they were so possessed by the contents of Franz Heidel's note, that the thought of staying for the afternoon session on water treatment, and coming back for the banquet seemed ridiculous. They returned to the hotel and later grabbed some dinner next door at the Dauphin.

Meanwhile, Klaus' men had been looking for Franz Heidel, and had made use of handheld camcorders to scan the crowds of conference goers, and occasionally the protesters across the street. Later that afternoon, after carefully reviewing each of the tapes, Klaus spotted Franz Heidel on one of the early morning ones. He called Dieter with the news.

"He is in the city, Herr Schmidt. I noticed his face behind one of the protesters outside the convention centre. The time on the tape was 8:58."

"Well then, don't waste another minute talking with me, find him!"

Chapter 17

K<small>LAUS</small> V<small>OGEL</small> A<small>ND</small> his crew of security personnel began frantically combing the old city in search of Franz Heidel. Photos from Heidel's personnel file had been e-mailed from Frankfurt and reproduced to aid in the search effort. Hotels, restaurants, and shops were all meticulously checked, so far without success. With so much riding on discovering the rogue engineer's whereabouts, the pressure was on. The warm, sticky evening had now begun to take its toll on Klaus' patience. From the front door of the Hotel Maison Rouge Klaus retrieved his mobile from inside his jacket pocket and punched in some well-memorized numbers.

"Günther, where are you now?"

From a few blocks away Günther responded, "Like you told me, we checked the Holiday Inn and the Hilton over by the convention center first, and now I am working on the hotels here by Petite France. I just finished up at the Hotel Hannong. I have the others working the train station area. They've finished at the Hotel St. Christophe, and are moving on to the Hotel du Rhin."

Klaus began to recover his equanimity, "Okay, tell them to keep working that group of hotels over by the train station, but when you are finished join me. My instincts are telling me that Heidel is somewhere closer to the cathedral, so let's focus our efforts over there. Meet me in front of the cathedral in ten minutes."

"*Ja, ich komme gleich.*"

After a light dinner of tarte flambé and a bottle of Riesling at the Dauphin, Hank and Natasha strolled down the rue Merciere from the Place de la Cathedrale a couple of short blocks toward the Place Gutenberg. The pedestrian zone street was full of people walking about the various curio shops and restaurants soaking in the last, leaning rays of sunshine bending in from the west.

"That dinner was pretty good, but not too filling. I think I could've eaten another one of those tarte flambés. How about you?"

"Oh, I'm just fine, thank you. It was delicious, Hank."

"Hey, will you look at that place, Haagen-Dazs Ice Cream. When I was younger, I used to be able to eat a whole pint of that stuff at one time. Chocolate Chocolate Chip was my favorite. You know, we didn't order dessert. Why don't we get some and eat out right here at these tables by the street? Do we have enough time?"

Natasha glanced at her watch. It was twenty minutes to nine.

"Alright, but just a small scoop for me."

"Chocolate Chocolate Chip?"

"*Da*, sure, why not."

Natasha sat down outside at an available table while Hank went inside the ice cream parlor. From her seat she could see the Place Gutenberg just a block away. Her eyes searched the people for their mystery colleague. She wondered whether or not he would actually come or if this some kind of practical joke? His note seemed believable enough. Instinctively, she took her lipstick out of her purse and touched up her lips with a bit more red. Shortly, Hank returned with dessert.

"They were all out of Chocolate Chocolate Chip, so I went for the Chocolate Swiss Almond. I hope that's okay."

Natasha smiled, "Hank, it will be fine."

"I really had my heart set on the Chocolate Chocolate Chip, but you're right, this'll be fine. At least it's chocolate."

Hank looked toward the Place Gutenberg with the same searching gaze that Natasha had just moments before, but was blinded by the brilliance of the setting sunlight. He dug into his ice cream and looked in the other direction toward the cathedral.

"I still can't get over this church. Especially right now with the sun shining all over its front. I mean, will you just look at it. It appears to be alive, although I know it's just an incredible arrangement of red sandstone blocks. The only thing that bothers me about it is I why they didn't finish it."

"I don't know if I understand."

"It only has one spire. Granted, it's one hell of a nice spire, high too. But, there's room on the right for another just like it. It would look more symmetrical, don't you think?"

"Maybe. I see your point, as an engineer. It would make sense to balance the top of the cathedral with another spire. Like the cathedral in Köln."

"Köln, where's that?"

"Cologne, north of here in Germany."

"Oh, yes, Cologne. I've been there, ten years ago on business. I've seen that cathedral. Our hosts took us there on an excursion. That was my first time visiting Europe. You know, you're right, it did have two spires, real tall ones. Maybe taller than this one."

"The Cologne cathedral is one hundred sixty meters high. This one is one hundred forty-two, but it is much more impressive when you take into account that it was built in the 1400's, hundreds of years before the spires in Cologne were finished."

"Where do you get all of that?"

"Reading."

"And you've got a memory to go with it," Hank quipped. "I guess since we don't have any more of that 1400's technology around, we'll just have to get used to the single spire. I still think it looks a little lonely up there all by itself."

Hank and Natasha sat in reverent admiration of the genius and skill of the cathedral's creators, moving between spoonfuls of Haagen-Dazs Chocolate Swiss Almond and upward glances at the spire. At the same time, Klaus Vogel hurriedly brushed by ignoring their presence, his eyes scanning the street for short, middle aged German men. Unfortunately for him, none of the candidates he spotted matched up with Heidel. "I know that little traitor is around here somewhere," he thought to himself.

"Are you finished yet?" asked Hank.

"Not quite. I have noticed that I eat more slowly than you do. It is better for the digestion."

"That's fine, we still have five more minutes before our meeting with this Franz guy. Do you think he's for real?"

"What, I don't understand, for real?"

"Well, do you think he was telling the truth about that Project Atlantis business and Energia's shutting it down?"

"I was thinking the same thing. It all seems so *neveroyatno!*"

"Excuse me, what was that word?"

"It is Russian. I am not sure of the English word, something like not believing."

"Unbelievable, perhaps?"

"That is what I mean, unbelievable. How could a big company like Energia allow this man to leave his office and come here to speak with us? In Russia he would have been put in jail."

"No kidding. You'd think they would want to keep him under wraps...I mean, prevent him from talking to others about it. I'll bet they're looking for him right now, provided this isn't a hoax to make fun of us, of course. Even if it is, I don't mind. This is a lot more fun than sitting around a banquet hall with a bunch of stuffy engineers."

Hank took Natasha's empty plastic ice cream cup and spoon, and tossed it along with his in a nearby trash can. A few moments later they sauntered up to the statue of Johann Gensfleisch Gutenberg in the middle of the plaza named for him. Under the statue were four bronze murals depicting the development of the printing press that Gutenberg is credited with inventing while he was a Strasbourg citizen.

"Did you know that Gutenberg was actually from Mainz, Germany?" Natasha quizzed Hank.

"I figured he must have been a German, with a name like Gutenberg. Besides, most of the great inventors and scientists of the world have been Germans."

"Yes, the Germans have done so much good, and at the same time, caused so much pain through the years. It is still difficult for us Russians to forget the Great Patriotic War."

"Which war was that?"

"You call it, World War Two, I believe."

"I know of it all too well, my grandfather was in the Army during it. He was thirty-six when he enlisted. He didn't have to enlist, but he did out of a sense of duty to his country. Well, the Army thought he was too old to serve on the front lines, so they assigned him to defend the country's gold."

"Defend the gold?"

"Fort Knox, Kentucky. Yep, that's where my grandfather rode out the war. The guys in his unit used to kid him about his Uncle Erich von Haiger, the German general. Imagine if they had confronted each other on the battlefield, cousins shooting at each other. I suppose there weren't too many American privates fighting German generals face to face. Anyway, so, Gutenberg lived here in Strasbourg?"

"Yes, during the time period when the cathedral spire was built, 1420's to 1440's. Many people think that your Bill Gates is the father of the information age, but if it hadn't been for Gutenberg, we would all still be working in the fields. Where there are no books, there is no education."

From around the corner of the rue des Serruriers, Franz Heidel watched them as they walked around the statue. He had effectively concealed his presence from Klaus' men by acting like an American tourist on vacation, wearing sunglasses, a Chicago Cubs baseball cap, and casual attire. Surprisingly, he hadn't been discovered. To make matters worse for Energia, he had registered at the hotel under the phony name, Fritz Heidenreich. Unassumingly, he walked up to Hank and Natasha and began to speak to them in German.

"*Guten Abend.*"

"*Guten Abend. Können wir Ihnen helfen?*" Natasha replied in perfect German.

"*Ich habe Sie beide an der Konferenz heute morgen gesehen. Ich bin die einzige, das Ihnen die Meldung geschickt habe,*" continued Heidel.

Natasha turned to Hank, "It is him," and then back to the stranger, "*Sind Sie Franz Heidel?*"

"*Ja ich heiße Franz Heidel. Erwarten Sie jemand anders?*"

"*Nein, niemand anders. Entschuldigen Sie mich, ich heiße Natasha Shakhova, und hier ist mein Kolleg, Hank Hudson.*"

Natasha held out her right hand and shook Franz Heidel's. Hank did likewise. He wondered when she had the time to learn all these languages, but also felt a little left out of the deal.

"Could you ask him if he knows English, I'm having a little trouble following the conversation," Hank quietly pleaded under his breath.

"*Ist es möglich, auf Englisch zu sprechen? Herr Hudson spricht nicht viel Deutsch,*" Natasha politely asked, explaining that Hank's German wasn't too good. Franz Heidel instantly switched into flawless English.

"Pardon me, I didn't mean to be so difficult. I speak pretty good English. It is good to meet the both of you. Is there someplace else we could go and talk? I fear that my employer's security department may be looking for me. We could easily be noticed in this open area."

"Why don't we head back to my room at the Hotel Cathedrale," suggested Hank.

In the meantime, Klaus and Günther had joined forces in front of the cathedral, and had begun a search of the nearby hotels. They first called at the Hotel Suisse. "Bonsoir, Madame, we are looking for a dear colleague of ours. We're all here for the Energia convention. He was supposed to have dinner with us, but didn't show up. Perhaps he is in his room?" asked Klaus.

The desk clerk, a redheaded woman in her fifties named Colette asked, "What is your friend's name? I could check and see if he is registered."

"Yes, that would be wonderful. His name is Franz Heidel. He's kind of short with graying hair. Perhaps you have met him yourself," Klaus charmed her.

"We don't have a Franz Heidel, but we have a Fritz Heidenreich in room twenty-two."

"That's right. Fritz Heidenreich from Wiesbaden. We met only yesterday. Franz Heidel, Fritz Heidenreich, I must have scrambled his name, don't you think so, Günther?"

"Oh, ja, that's right, Klaus. It was Fritz, not Franz."

"It says here that he's from Höchst in Hessen," she corrected.

"Well, that's not far from Wiesbaden, is it Günther?" Klaus continued the ruse.

"No, not far at all."

"Perhaps you could call on him and find out why he missed dinner with you. You both look like you're a lot of fun to be with," said the clerk with a wry smile.

"That's a good idea. Why don't we go and see old Fritz at his room, Günther? Thank you for your help," Klaus concluded the conversation as they walked away from the reception desk and up the staircase to the guestrooms Klaus whispered to Günther, "We've got him now!"

One block away, the three engineers took the elevator to the second floor of the Hotel Cathedrale and straight to Hank's room.

"Let me show you what I smuggled out of my office. I urge you to keep an open mind. Some of the ideas I will be sharing with you will seem far-fetched, but all of it is verifiable, I can assure you," Heidel said as he retrieved some papers from a plastic shopping bag.

For the next several hours, this unassuming looking yet brilliant man laid the key technical documents from Project Atlantis before their eyes. Included in these papers were test data from the E-6 and E-7 prototypes, data that confirmed that it was not only possible to create inexpensive, non-polluting electrical power in the laboratory, but that it was also feasible in an economic sense. Hank and Natasha sat in stunned silence as Franz Heidel painted a picture of the three-year project.

"You mean to tell me that Energia is dumping this rather than moving forward with its development? Why in the world would they do that?" asked Hank.

"I think I know why," Natasha answered, "they are just trying to protect their economic interest in the current system of energy production — of maintaining the status quo and controlling their customers. They are afraid of putting themselves out of business."

"That is precisely what I thought too," said Heidel. "If this information ever came to light it would change energy production forever. The disruption in Energia's domination of energy technology would be more than the company could bear. I'm sure it would put a lot of engineers and technicians out of work."

"You're starting to sound like a friend of mine back in the states. He said I would be out of a job soon because of a new technology precisely like you have described here with the crystal, the earth's magnetic fields, the whole nine yards. It just blows my mind that we've run into you like this. It's so, I don't know, uh...strange, a set up."

"It is God's will, the way things should be," added Natasha.

"But, you know, the more I think about it, you would expect the opposite reaction from them wouldn't you? Energia could dominate the market and bury all the other companies. Look at all the R&D money they sank into this project. If OVP had their hands on something like this they would milk it for all it's worth. What's this Dieter Schmidt been smoking?"

Natasha and Heidel momentarily mentally processed Hank's idiomatic speech about milk, smoking, and energy technology.

"The one at the top, Dieter Schmidt, has paranoia. *Er ist gefährlich und verrückt!*" Heidel blurted out.

Hank looked to Natasha for a translation.

"He means that Dieter Schmidt is dangerous and crazy."

"I apologize again for slipping into German like that. Force of habit."

"*Das ist kein Problem,*" said Hank.

"That's good. You are learning German well!"

"I've picked up a few phrases, like that one."

"Over the past few months, many of my colleagues on Project Atlantis were reassigned to other departments with no explanation. There are very few of us left in the lab. I fear that the project will soon be shutdown. I thought my only hope was to find someone who would be willing to listen and who had the technical know-how to understand these papers. What better place to find such people than at an energy conference? It seemed providential that the two events coincided with each other. So, what do you think? Are you willing to help me save Project Atlantis?"

Hank and Natasha looked at each other for a second, and then replied in unison, "Yes, we will!"

"Oh good, let me tell you, you're an answer to an old man's prayers!"

"But, what can we do to save the project? We're only a couple of power plant engineers far from home attending a conference. And it sounds like your boss is pulling the plug on the project. I mean, we can't exactly walk up to him and ask to have the generator as a souvenir. Where is it again?"

"The E-7 prototype is locked up on the third floor of Energia's Höscht laboratory near Frankfurt, at least it was when I left there last week."

"There's got to be a way of getting it out of there and to a safe place. But how? I don't have a clue."

After an eternal moment of silence they all knew what they had to do.

Hank looked at Natasha and back to Heidel and said, "You're not all thinking what I'm thinking, are you? No, we couldn't, could we? We couldn't just walk in there and take it and walk out. That'd be way too dangerous. The place is probably crawling with security guards with guns, and cameras. Wait a moment here!"

"Hank, we have to. Think of your friends back in the US who told you that this technology was coming someday, and that it could save the world from so much trouble. Think of the acidic fumes from your smokestacks, and the nuclear waste from my reactors. We both know that it is just a matter of time before our power plants will become obsolete. It would be worth the risk given the potential of bringing forth its environmental and economic blessings to the world. We cannot let this evil, stupid man delay what the world now needs," Natasha made her case.

"The laboratory is not so heavily guarded on the weekends. There are only two guards, and they spend most of their time at the front desk playing cards and talking about sports. I know. I've spent many a Saturday and Sunday working overtime. There is a good chance that my entry card still works, and there is a back door too. Saturday would be our first chance of getting it out."

It was now half past two in the morning and everyone was exhausted.

"You shouldn't go back to your hotel. I'm sure it isn't safe. Why don't you stay here tonight? I'm certain that no one has detected our meeting. Let's get some shut-eye, and wake up early and drive on up to Frankfurt."

"Thank you, Hank, you are most kind."

"Don't mention it. I still think we're all crazy for imagining we can do this," Hank said.

"Have faith, Hank, anything is possible," Natasha answered as she walked out the door toward her room, "Good night."

"Good night."

Natasha went back to her room. Franz Heidel curled up in the corner of Hank's narrow room, with an extra blanket and pillow. Back in room twenty-two at the Hotel Suisse, Klaus and Günther impatiently waited for Franz Heidel, a.k.a., Fritz Heidenreich, to return. Somewhere in the middle of the night they dozed off in the chairs with the overhead light burning brightly.

Chapter 18

Early Friday Morning, Klaus and Günther abruptly awoke from their naps in Franz Heidel's hotel room chairs. The pulse from Klaus' mobile phone served as their alarm clock. He snatched it out of his pocket and managed, *"Hallo."*

"Klaus, did Heidel come back to the room? What's going on over there? You haven't reported in for over four hours," Dieter's irritating voice brought him back to his full five senses.

"Nothing yet, unfortunately. Günther and I have been staked out here all night waiting for him to return. This is definitely his room. The ID tag on his overnight bag confirms it. Can you think of a better place for us to be?"

"Isn't it obvious that he's not coming back given the early hour. Who knows where he is? We can't waste another moment waiting for him to make a move. Put another team on his room and get back here to the hotel. We've got to figure out another way to find the little flea."

"Right away, sir. On it!" said Klaus as he clicked off the phone. "Damn it, Günther, what time is it already?"

Günther, still groggy from the wakeup call looked at his wristwatch, "It's 4:15."

"All right, call Stephan's team and get them over here right now. They're probably in their room in the Hilton. Let's get back to hotel and regroup. We're just wasting time sitting around here."

Back at the Château de l'Ile Dieter Schmidt couldn't sleep. He would've been basking in the glory of his successful conference if it weren't for that AWOL Franz Heidel. All through last night's banquet his eyes searched the room wondering if Heidel was lurking about behind a curtain, or posing as a member of the kitchen staff plotting some unsavory scheme to embarrass Energia. How dare this diminutive rat ruin a perfectly good time! The nerve of his disloyalty to the company! Why was Klaus unable to locate him? Finding his room at the Hotel Suisse was good security work, but not good enough. Where could that weasel be? The entire world's energy production structure would come unglued if any of the Project Atlantis material got out. He had to find Heidel! But where could he be hiding? Dieter's blood pressure rose with the morning sun.

Logic and worry began to replace his rage. Had he already made contact with the press, the protesters, or an eco-energy company? Maybe he had spoken to some of the conference delegates? He hadn't really considered that possibility. All along he had concluded that Heidel's presence in Strasbourg was to publicly embarrass him face to face. But, maybe not. Angela Simulescu had not called him from public relations. Maybe Heidel's strategy was along a different path. He certainly did not want him talking to anyone that could understand him. With all of these power engineers wandering about the convention...they just might be his targets! He had to know.

It was now five o'clock. He summoned Klaus on his mobile.

"Why aren't you back here already?"

"I'm pulling into the hotel parking lot as we speak," Klaus coolly responded.

"Good, get up here right away, I have an idea," with those words, Dieter clicked off his phone and sat back in his chair. Two minutes later Klaus and Günther knocked on his door.

"Komm rein!"

Klaus and Günther came in, their clothes and hair disheveled from their hotel room chair naps.

"Klaus, I think we've been looking for Heidel the wrong way. I don't think he's trying to make a big splash with the press, or harass us in a public manner. No, no, I think he's going after one or more of our conference delegates, to win them over to his side. Where else could he be than with one or more of them? I want you to check the convention records. Find out if any of the delegates missed the programs they signed up for, including the banquet. Get with it!"

A half-hour later Klaus returned with the news.

"Five delegates did not sign in for the afternoon session on water treatment systems, but three of them later showed up at the golf tournament. Four delegates did not attend the banquet. Two of them became ill and went back to their hotel rooms. Maybe they had too much good French food for lunch that day. The other two are the same two who missed the afternoon session."

"And, who are they?"

"*Ein Moment*...they are Henry Hudson from Ohio Valley Power Company in the US, and Natasha Shakhova from the Baltic Regional Power Plant in Russia."

"Yes, I know of her. She's one of the youngest plant managers in all of Russia. Her father, Dmitri Shahkov, was a pioneer in Soviet nuclear energy technology. His son, was also an engineer...Anatoly was his name. Poor bastard died at Chernobyl. Aren't we paying her way to the conference?"

"Yes, nearly all of the Russian delegates are here at our expense."

"So, these two engineers didn't use their banquet tickets, nor did they attend the water treatment session. You would think they would want to stay current with the latest information and not miss anything. Have they missed any other sessions this week?"

"Hold on a moment, let me check. Yes, they were also gone all Wednesday afternoon. Ah, but wait a minute. They didn't take the bus to Fessenheim, but they took the plant tour. So, they must be together. It's too much of a coincidence that they're missing and then showing up the same events. Certainly one of them has a car. My money is on Hudson."

Dieter slammed his hand on the desk, "That's it, Klaus! It's got to be them. What other explanation is there for their behavior?"

"Well, we can't rule out a convention romance. We've seen that happen before. A young, unmarried, female engineer surrounded by hundreds of male engineers. It's possible," Klaus played devil's advocate.

"It's possible, I'm sure. But we must investigate further, to make certain Heidel is not with them. Where are they staying?"

Klaus checked his records. "Both are registered at the Hotel Cathedrale."

"How convenient! I wonder if they're using just one room now. Maybe they decided to have dinner together and then who knows what they did afterward. Hopefully that little shit Heidel didn't stumble upon them. Klaus, do we know what their after convention plans happen to be?"

Klaus checked further, "Since Shakhova was staying at our expense, we arranged her travel. Here it is. She has a flight back to St. Petersburg this afternoon. As for the American, Hudson, I have no information."

"Don't let them leave Strasbourg without talking with them. We can't rule out the possibility that Heidel has corrupted them."

"Don't worry, we'll find Franz Heidel. Günther and will redouble our efforts."

Klaus and Günther quickly left the room and headed back to their car in the parking lot. En route to the Hotel Cathedrale Günther shot off a couple of calls to the rest of the security team to join them. It was now half past five.

Chapter 19

THE SUN HAD already risen by the time Hank Hudson was awakened by an inner impulse to go. It was just after five o'clock. Franz Heidel was curled up in the corner of the room just to the right of the bathroom snoring away. Hank tiptoed around him into the bathroom for a quick visit. There was no time for a shower this morning. He gave his guest a gentle pat on the shoulder, but was greeted with a deep grunting noise. With a stiffer tap, he stirred to consciousness.

"We better get Natasha and go."

"*Oh, ja, sicher.*"

Hank threw on a fresh golf shirt, and quickly packed up his clothes, the coffee still scenting the suitcase. After positioning it near the door, he scooted down the hall and up the elevator to Natasha's room and knocked. The door opened easily. Natasha was wide awake and packing herself. He hadn't seen her before without her makeup. She looked pretty even without it.

"Give me five more minutes."

"Okay, but hurry. I have this feeling that we'd better be going. I'll go check us out, give me your key."

Natasha retrieved her key from the top of the dresser and handed it to Hank, "Here it is. There should not be any money to pay on the room. Energia paid for it in advance."

"If they only knew what we were planning. Be right back."

Hank quickly walked to the elevator for the short trip down to the reception desk. Ten minutes later the car was brought around to the front of the hotel. Normally the cathedral plaza would be full of pedestrian traffic and no cars were allowed during the day. At this hour, service trucks were just beginning to arrive with supplies of food for the restaurants, and tourist items for the shops that encircled the cathedral square. Only a few people were around taking in the quietness of the morning. Car keys in hand, Hank was back at his room and knocked. Franz let him in.

"The car is downstairs, let's go," said Hank as he picked up his suitcase and briefcase. Franz followed with his plastic shopping bag full of documents. They met Natasha in the hallway, her makeup now properly in place, and headed down the narrow stairwell to the street and Hank's blue station wagon. After stowing the luggage in back, they got in the car, Natasha in the front passenger seat, and Franz stretched out in the back.

"This is a nice new car. It still has that fresh smell. Never lasts, though."

Hank pulled away from the front of the Hotel Cathedrale and drove through the back streets to the rue de la Division Leclerc and across the Ill River until he saw the signs for Kehl, Allemagne. This whisked them to the Route du Rhin in the direction of the Rhein River and into Germany. Within a matter of minutes they were through Kehl and on the A5 for the two hundred-kilometer drive north to Frankfurt.

There was a sleepy silence for the next twenty minutes as they drove through the early morning mist. Hank wisely didn't go any faster than 120 km/h given his severe fatigue factor. After Bühl, he spotted a sign for a gas station/rest area, the Tank & Rast, and pulled in. The fuel gauge was down to one quarter of a tank. He had avoided buying gas in France where the price was higher at well over four dollars per gallon. Hank soon discovered that German fuel was only a little cheaper, and still very high by US standards. While Hank was filling up the car, Franz and Natasha headed for the bathrooms. Natasha had begun to miss the breakfast buffet at the Hotel Cathedrale. There had been no time to eat, and the buffet was not ready when they left. Her stomach growled so loudly that she was sure someone heard it in Nizhny. She went into the convenience store and began to survey the offerings. Soon Hank came in and quietly approached her from the right side.

"Those are my favorites. I had some the other day when I drove down to Strasbourg. They're called apple strudel. Get a few. Whatever you want. We'll put it on my American corporate credit card."

A small smile emerged from Natasha's mouth. "Okay, we'll get some."

Franz was already back in the rear seat of the car with coffee and a sandwich. Hank and Natasha returned with coffee, apple strudel, and tomato juice. The caffeine in the coffee was good for starters, but when the fatigue kicked in nothing worked quite like tomato juice to keep one awake. Wakefulness was either achieved from the stimulation of one's saliva glands from the saltiness of the juice, or when mixed with a couple of apple strudels the resulting heartburn would do the trick. No one could fall asleep driving with a strong case of heartburn.

With the car fully fueled, and its occupants quickly fortifying themselves, they continued north at typical autobahn speed. They weren't the fastest car on the road. The BMW's, Audi's, Mercedes, and a lone yellow Lamborghini continued to make the left lane their personal dragstrip. Occasionally Hank would use the left lane to pass slower traffic, especially the many trucks that congregated in the far right lane. However, he always gave a long and thorough look in the side view and rearview mirrors before venturing left. The time passed quickly. By eight o'clock they were approaching the Frankfurt metro area. Franz expertly guided them through the big city's maze of roads to the suburban town of Kelkheim, then further north and west to the small village of Fischbach.

Franz' sister, Gerta Bauer, lived on Winkelgasse northwest of Highway 455. Her white two-story house in a quiet neighborhood was a perfect place to hide while they prepared their first ever foray into the world of industrial espionage. Hank parked the car in the driveway next to the stone façade of the first story wall. They all got out of the car and climbed the concrete stairs to the second floor entrance. Franz knocked on the door.

"Franz, what are you doing here, back so soon from Strasbourg?" said a startled Gerta. "And who are these people? Well, come on in!"

"Let me introduce you to my new friends, Hank Hudson from America, and Natasha Shakhova from Russia. Gerti, they're going to help me save Project Atlantis!"

"It is good to meet the both of you. Are you hungry? Can I get you some coffee?"

"I'm sure you're a wonderful cook, but I'm absolutely bushed, I mean, tired. We've been up most of the night with your brother listening to his story, and drive here really took it out of me. Is there somewhere I could lay down for an hour or so? How about you, Natasha?"

"I agree. I could benefit from some sleep as well."

"Okay, I'll feed you both later. Come with me, I have just the place for you."

She led them downstairs to a first floor bedroom, one with two small beds and an adjoining bathroom.

"I used to rent out this room years ago when we housed exchange students, mostly from America. There used to be a school up in the old castle near here, the Schloss Rettershof. That was before the Hare Krishna's made a mess of it. Now it's a fancy hotel and restaurant owned by the city."

"This is perfect, thank you," said Hank.

"Yes, thank you for your kind hospitality," Natasha added.

Within minutes both power plant engineers shut down their generators and crashed on their chosen beds for a long nap while Franz caught Gerta up on his adventure.

Chapter 20

MEANWHILE, BACK IN Strasbourg, two Energia security teams quietly descended on the cathedral plaza. Klaus and Günther, entered the Hotel Cathedrale and proceeded to the front desk while the second team canvassed the plaza.

"*Bonjour, Madame.* We wish to call on Madame Natasha Shakhova," Klaus politely inquired.

Claudette Dietrich, the second middle-aged receptionist that Klaus had encountered in so many hours looked at the clock on the wall and then back at him and said, "At 6:45 in the morning?"

"It is most urgent. I have news of a personal nature to share with her that cannot wait, if you would be so kind as to ring her room, *s'il vous plait*," Klaus turned up the charm.

She raised her eyebrows and delivered the bad news, "I am sorry, Monsieur, but she checked out a half-hour ago. You just missed her."

"I see. By chance, was she with anyone?"

Now, thoroughly enthralled with Klaus' friendly and pleasant demeanor, she filled in the blanks, "*Oui,* a Monsieur Henry Hudson actually checked her out. They met just a few days ago. What a nice couple of souls from such distant parts of our world. I'm so glad they found each other, aren't you Monsieur?"

"Yes, I am very happy for them. One never knows when love will happen. Did you see how they left, by taxi perhaps, or limousine?"

"No, Monsieur Hudson had a car. I believe they left together in the car. Just a minute," she turned to the bellboy sitting on a chair behind the desk. "Jacque, you retrieved Monsieur Hudson's car from the garage, *n'est-ce pas?*"

"*Oui, Madame,* the blue Ford."

"Was anyone with him when he left?"

"*Oui,* the nice looking woman from Russia, and a man, much older and shorter than Monsieur Hudson. He sat in the back."

Klaus' eyes nearly popped out of their sockets, but quickly returned to their normal places, "Did you possibly happen to catch the other man's name?"

"No, I am not familiar with the other man. He wasn't registered at our hotel, but he came down the stairs with Monsieur Hudson and Madame Shakhova."

"I see. Did you happen to overhear where they were going? I hate to pry, but the matter is urgent, you understand," Klaus turned up the heat a little.

"I am sorry, Monsieur, I did not hear of their destination. However, if it is of any help to you, the license plate of the car was from the State of Hessen in Germany, a Hertz car from the Frankfurt airport I would surmise. I see them all the time."

"Did he resemble the man in this photo?" Klaus held up a photo of Franz Heidel to the bellman.

"*Oui,* that is him!"

Klaus turned back to the receptionist, "*Merci, Madame* for all of your help. You've been most kind."

"You're welcome. Come back any time," she said in an inviting manner.

Klaus and Günther hurriedly left the hotel. Once in the cathedral square, Klaus looked up in frustration at the façade of the Hotel Cathedrale, its light blue letters against the white background now fully lit by the swiftly rising sun. Nothing pained him more than to lose the scent of someone he was tracking. Where could they possibly be now? Were they on their way to the airport for a flight to the US, or to Russia? Or, were they as the bellboy guessed, driving north to Frankfurt. His money was on the bellboy. With a quick hand motion summoned the rest of his team together in the middle of the square, the colossal spire of the Notre-Dame hovering above them.

"Get back and check out of your hotels and prepare to leave Strasbourg for Frankfurt. Our work is done here. We'll meet in my office at one o'clock."

It was time to report in. He pulled his mobile out of his jacket pocket and punched the speed dial button for Dieter.

"Hallo, Vogel. I have some good news and some bad news, sir."

"What the hell does that mean, good news and bad news?"

"We have determined with reasonable certainty that Heidel has made contact with Hudson and Shakhova, and is with them as we speak."

"And, what else?"

"They left here about an hour ago in Hudson's rental car, possibly toward Frankfurt. I cannot confirm that information, but it's the most likely conclusion from the tip the bellboy gave us," Klaus did his best to sugarcoat the bad news.

"The bellboy?"

"*Ja*, the bellboy. He saw Hudson, Shakhova, and a man meeting Heidel's description leave in a car. He recognized him from the personnel photo. The car was from the Frankfurt airport. We can assume they might be heading there."

"Don't waste another minute, Klaus, let's get back to Frankfurt and track down this traitor and his accomplices!"

"I've already directed our security teams to regroup at Energia headquarters at one this afternoon."

"You think you can stay one step ahead of me, don't you Klaus?"

"I'm just doing my job."

Chapter 21

IT WAS EARLY afternoon when Hank awoke from his nap. He felt a lot better, refreshed, but slightly disoriented. As his eyes focused he could see an "L" shaped room on the lower level of a house. In the bathroom immediately across from his bed he could hear the sound of running water and singing, Russian singing. He'd never heard her sing before. She was quite good.

"You are finally awake," she said as she came out of the bathroom.

"Yeah, I was pretty dead to the world."

Natasha paused for a moment after hearing his umpteenth figure of speech, and then responded, "Oh, I understand you. By the way, they could hear you snoring in Moscow."

"Oh, they could! I'm sorry. It's an inherited trait I'm told, from my Swedish side of the family. My Uncle Karl was the worst. My grandmother was Swedish, but my grandfather was German, French and English. We Americans are real mongrels, ethnically."

"It is what makes your country so strong, people from everywhere in the world, even Russians I am sure."

"Certainly none as nice as you."

Natasha's cheeks warmed with extra blood. She thought to herself, "How could this man be so good to her, so complimentary? He hasn't even made a pass at me! Oh, Natalya, what should I do?"

"Well, I think we had better go upstairs and talk with Franz and Gerta. I'm sure they are waiting for us after all of this time," she managed to say as she rubbed up against his legs trying to scoot by in the narrow space between the bed and the wall.

"Well, yeah, you're right. They're probably wondering what happened to us," Hank said as he noticed her confused emotions.

"Are you all right?"

"Yes, I am fine," she said as she brushed her hair and put in some clips to hold it in place.

Once upstairs, Gerta offered them a light lunch of sliced meats, cheeses, and breads.

Franz began the discussion, "I've been studying the security system of the Höscht laboratory, and there are no cameras at the rear entrance."

"Why do you think there aren't any?" Hank asked.

"They simply did not get around to putting them in, I surmise. Which is crazy, since they have cameras just about everywhere else, including the parking lot."

"So, we will have to be careful how we enter the parking lot and where we park the car," Natasha said.

"*Genau!* That will be the crucial piece of our plan, entering the parking lot and walking to the rear door undetected."

"And how will we do that?" asked Hank.

"By creating a small distraction for the guards. Right before we arrive, I will call them on the phone posing as a municipal director and ask them to check the building for a problem, some sort of story like that. I'll say enough to pull them both away from the front desk's video surveillance monitors."

"Do you think they'll buy it? Your story about being from the a city department?" Hank continued to play devil's advocate.

"Knowing these men, like I told you last night, they're not among Energia's smarter employees. They'll respond to an authoritative voice."

"Are you confident that your entry card is still valid?" quizzed Natasha.

"In the three years I have worked at the laboratory the codes were only changed twice. The last time was six months ago. I don't see any reason other than news of my recent absence that the card wouldn't work."

"Then it's got to work. When do we strike?" asked Hank.

"As I said before, the weekend is our only good opportunity. So, the sooner the better. I fear that they will move the E-7 prototype out of the laboratory very soon. How about tomorrow?"

"Natasha and I weren't doing anything tomorrow, were we?" Hank looked at her.

Natasha looked at her watch, "I would have been landing at the St. Petersburg airport about now, and returning to my job at the power plant." She looked up at Hank, "However, our fate is with you and bringing your Project Atlantis to the world!"

"Like I said, we didn't have any other plans for tomorrow."

"Then we're ready!" Franz said joyfully.

Friday afternoon, Dieter Schmidt, Klaus Vogel, and the rest of the security team had assembled back at Energia's central headquarters on the top floors of the Messeturm in downtown Frankfurt. Except for the annoyance of the environmentalist protesters, the "Energy for the New Millennium Conference" had been a resounding success. Dieter was pleased that he had been able to demonstrate his dominance in the energy production world and to showcase his company and its controlling interests around the world. The thousand plus attendees would go home sold on him and all that he represented. The flow of money into Energia would continue—and money was power. Nothing would dare cloud his vision, nothing except possibly that *verdammten* Franz Heidel!

Project Atlantis must never see the light of day. He had once thought he could control its production through patents and licensing agreements, but had decided against it. The simplicity of the technology could be too easily copied leading to a loss of direct control, not to mention the likely world opinion would be in favor of its quick proliferation. Now that its chief architect was missing he was genuinely worried. Heidel's abrupt and unannounced departure saved him from having to reassign him to another department, but what he had rolling around in his head could bury Energia and its global dominance in the energy field forever. What now worried him the most was that he had apparently teamed up with two power plant engineers who could understand his language, so to speak. But, would they actually believe him? Engineers are not known for stepping outside customary science and making the leap of faith required to understand something as fanciful as Project Atlantis. Hopefully they would conclude that Heidel was a crackpot and leave him behind to resume their romantic tryst. But, who were Henry Hudson and Natasha Shakhova? Were they a threat? He thought he'd better do some checking and called his head of security to his office. Within a couple of minutes Klaus popped up from his office one story below.

"Klaus, we need a quick and thorough investigation of these two engineers, Hudson and Shakhova. Find out more about their employers and their work history. We need information, and we need it immediately! Heidel has surely talked with them. Has anyone been by his apartment again?"

"We sent a team over there around noon, but nothing. We'll have some information on Hudson and Shakhova within an hour."

"Okay, see to it. And have someone working surveillance on Heidel's apartment."

There was nothing Dieter could do but wait. He didn't like waiting. After all, he didn't get as far as he had in his life by just sitting around waiting. His boyhood in Kyrgyzstan, rising up through the Soviet system, and then his move to Germany fifteen years ago, was all a process of moving forward. One had to grasp every opportunity to get ahead in this world. By God, Heidel and these two engineers better not be up to something! There was no sense sitting around the office anymore. Klaus could call him with an update. He reached for the intercom.

"Gretchen, call the Rettershof and see if they have a room available for tonight."

"Yes, sir, just a minute."

"Klaus, you know how important it is that we prevent Heidel taking any action with regard to Project Atlantis. Now that he has shown his disloyalty to the company, he cannot be trusted. That includes anyone with whom he has spoken. You know what needs to be done."

"Ja, klar, ich hab's kapiert!"

"Good, we have an understanding then,"

"Herr Schmidt?" said Gretchen through the intercom.

"Yes, Gretchen."

"Your room is reserved."

"Danke."

Dieter looked up from his desk at Klaus, "Walk with me to the elevator."

Dieter grabbed his briefcase and quickly headed from his office to the elevator for the trip down. Once inside, he continued, "Call me directly the minute you have more information on Hudson and Shakhova."

"We're already working on it," Klaus said as he exited the elevator at the fifty-ninth floor.

Dieter continued down to the parking garage beneath the Messeturm where his white Porsche Boxster convertible awaited him. The Schlosshotel Rettershof was just a half-hour drive northwest of Frankfurt. Located within the gentle Taunus Mountains, this former eighteenth century castle had been transformed into one of the many top-notch resorts and hotels where the rich of Frankfurt could relax and play. The weather was sunny and warm, perfect for a drive in the Porsche with the top down.

As Dieter pulled out of the subdued, cocooned darkness of the parking garage into the brilliant light and busy activity of urban Frankfurt, his mind suddenly began to unwind from the intensity of the past few days. After negotiating the circle around the Trade Fair complex he pointed the Porsche down the Theodore Heuss Allee which soon became Wiesbadener Strasse, a short piece of autobahn that soon carried him away from the city toward the mountains. He began to look forward to an afternoon and evening of relaxation away from the affairs of Energia. He would play some tennis, have dinner, and hopefully get his mind off of Heidel, Hudson, and Shakhova for a little while.

By mid-afternoon he was on the tennis courts playing with another hotel guest. After a dip in the pool he relaxed in the whirlpool trying to boil out all of his feelings of frustration, not to mention all the red clay dust he had picked up from his tennis game. He was back in his room for a quick shower before cocktails, when his mobile rang. It was Klaus.

"Have you found him, Klaus?"

"I wish I could say we have, but we have learned more about Heidel's possible accomplices. Henry Hudson, is the chief engineering director at Ohio Valley Power, Inc., based in Cincinnati, Ohio, USA. According to his secretary, a Frau Janie Hausman, he is the company's best engineer, and she hoped he was having a good visit to Europe. She remarked that Herr Hudson worked way too hard. Apparently he has added extra holiday time onto this conference trip and is not due back in Cincinnati for another week."

"And, what about Shakhova?"

"According to Lufthansa's records, she missed her flight back to St. Petersburg. I spoke with her assistant at the Baltic Regional Power Plant, a Frau Mariana Koroleva. She sounded very concerned about her delay in returning. Koroleva was to pick her up from the airport later this afternoon, and was thankful that we had alerted her to Shakhova's absence from the flight. She has a daughter staying with relatives who was to be reunited with her tomorrow evening. I also picked up from the tenor of her voice that the power plant needed her back right away. It had to do with some Swedish engineers who had visited the plant recently."

"Swedish engineers?" His mind roamed for answers. "What do you think, Klaus, are they going to be a problem for us?"

"*Ja, ich denke daß wir einen Problem haben.* These two engineers are tops in their field, and are probably smart enough to understand Project Atlantis, provided Heidel has had enough time to talk with them. That's what I think, since you're asking."

"Begin checking hotels, anywhere they could have registered for the night. And don't forget the train stations, airports, wherever. We've got to find them!"

"On it, sir."

Chapter 22

WITH THEIR PLANS to steal the prototype generator firmly in place, Hank, Natasha, Franz, and Gerta spent the rest of the afternoon getting acquainted. Thrust together by the influence of a common force, they each were crucial to the success of the mission. There wasn't a more unlikely group of spies.

"You have no idea what it is like to work for a man like Dieter Schmidt. On one hand he is a brilliant man. I have no doubts regarding his engineering acumen, or his ability to manage a huge company like Energia. His story about growing up in Stalinist Russia as a *Russlanddeutscher* and returning to Germany is positively fascinating. But, there is something not right about him."

"What do you mean by not right?" asked Hank.

"Why would the president of a company initiate a project that if proved to be successful, would make that company the darling of the world, throw that project and its people away like an old pair of shoes? Tell me, is that someone in their right mind?"

"I couldn't agree with you more. It makes no sense, especially if this prototype of yours actually does work like you say. You can't exactly argue with concrete results."

"I know it seems like a stretch of scientific faith that electrical power can be generated without turning a shaft on a turbine, or having the sun shine on a photovoltaic cell, or through some other chemical means. When we began Project Atlantis, hardly any of us thought we could actually achieve its aims. We felt like the three-year project term would simply be nothing more than a fun vacation from real science. However, once we got deeper into our work it was if a directive force took over. Call it God, or Providence, but we kept being led from one conclusion to another, one expert to another, each building on the other until, until to our amazement, the E-6 unit worked. When the current began to flow it was more than just electricity that passed through the wires, it was the very Spirit of God. You could feel that we had somehow divinely discovered what would become the method by which electricity would be produced everywhere in the world, from right here in Germany, to the darkest jungle on the planet. We would be putting an end to the craziness of drilling for more oil, digging for more coal, or playing Russian roulette with nuclear power. Oh, pardon me, Natasha, I did not mean to be insensitive."

"I am not offended. There is no need to apologize. In fact, I must completely agree with you, as a nuclear engineer, and as one who lost a family member at Chernobyl. We are all fortunate that so few accidents have happened. Perhaps the bullet will enter the chamber for yet another city. I pray not. The risk does not merit the rewards. I know it, but I am part of the problem with my job at BRPP. Perhaps I am, as you say, 'not right' myself!"

"Natasha, you are *wunderbar*," Gerta interjected, "and are a very brave and decent woman to risk so much to help my brother. We all have jobs we simply must do to survive. You too, Hank! It's as if God brought you together with Franz for this purpose."

"Well, we haven't really done anything yet. There's tomorrow to get through. I mean, industrial theft is not exactly on my resume.

"But, you will succeed. God wants Project Atlantis to live to bless the world. And God is working through us all to do it, especially through you two."

It was nearly six o'clock.

"Why don't we all go out for dinner, somewhere nice, on me?" Hank proposed.

"That's very generous of you, but why don't you and Natasha go, just the two of you? Gerta and I will stay here and visit."

"Are you sure about that, you've been so nice to us? I really wish that you'd come."

Gerta jumped in, "Franz and I can stay here and have some leftovers from lunch. We will be fine. Why don't you two have dinner at Le Duc? It's just up the road at the old castle, the Schlosshotel Rettershof. Let me call and make reservations for you. It's quite a good gourmet restaurant."

"Well, if you insist," Hank agreed. Natasha nodded her head in agreement.

"Then it's settled. The weather is nice, you might want to walk there, or ride the bicycles. I have a couple of good ones in my garage you can use. The path through the fields is well groomed and fairly level. My late husband, Werner, and I used to ride them all the time. I still keep them well maintained. The path is only two blocks away. What do you think?"

"I haven't ridden a bike in, well, uh, years! Can you ride one?" Hank looked at Natasha.

"Yes, of course I can," Natasha rolled her eyes and shook her head in response.

"Good, I'll go down and get them out of the garage right away."

A few minutes later Hank and Natasha were slowly pedaling on the path toward the castle. The sun's rays blazed through a grove of trees where two black horses were standing. They stopped for a minute to drink in the peaceful, pastoral scene that was unfolding before them. As they continued along the path the trees gave way to fields full of barley grain, green and growing taller with each minute of sunlight. Before they knew it they were pulling up to the entrance of the hotel. They leaned their bikes up against a short wall that enclosed a parking lot to the left, figuring that it was unlikely that the clientele of this establishment would steal them. They walked side by side up the driveway past a row of cherry trees full with fruit to the entrance of the hotel complex. A glass atrium separated the older castle on the left from the more modern hotel room building to the right. The registration desk was to the left. Natasha approached the young woman behind the desk and inquired.

"*Bitte, wo ist die Restaurant Le Duc? Wir haben eine Reservierung für 19:00 Uhr.*"

"It's right across the lobby over to the left."

"*Vielen dank,* thank you very much," Natasha replied bilingually.

Hank and Natasha entered the lobby of the beautifully restored former cloister, now owned by the nearby city of Kelkheim. A grand staircase led to a number of upper story rooms that were available for business conferences. To the left was Le Duc. They were seated near a window looking out into the garden area toward the tennis courts. The table was adorned with mauve tablecloths with a single lit candle in the middle. Hank ordered a bottle of white French wine, and they both opted for the sautéed salmon off the menu. After their first sips of wine conversation ensued.

"Do you think we're in over our heads, I mean, do you think we can really pull off this heist? It makes me feel more than a little nervous to think of the career change we're making—from power plant engineers to corporate thieves. They didn't exactly teach us how to do this in college," Hank fessed up to Natasha.

"I know how you feel. I am feeling, how do you say it, uneasy. Yes, Hank, we may be lunatics for even thinking about what we are about to do, but we must put that out of our minds and enjoy the moment we have right now here in this beautiful place," she looked at him with eyes of warmth and intensity.

Instinctively their hands met in the middle of the table. They both felt awkward yet comfortable with this first intimate touch as the warmth flowed between them, eye to eye, mind to mind, and heart to heart. For a brief yet endless moment their souls silently communed with each other on all levels of being, only to be disrupted by the arrival of their salads. They let go to pick up their forks. As they were about to take their first bites, Dieter Schmidt arrived at the restaurant and was seated in the back corner of the dining room within view of Hank.

"Speak of the devil, you're not going to believe this," Hank's eyes were riveted on the new restaurant guest. Natasha noticed his gaze and began to turn herself, "Don't look," Hank said in time.

Natasha refocused her head back toward Hank. "What do you mean by speak of the devil?"

"What I meant was that sitting right behind you is none other than our man, Dieter Schmidt."

"What?" she began to turn around again.

Hank cleared his throat, "Uh-uh!"

She quickly altered the course of her neck and glanced toward the painting on the wall. "What is going on Hank, have they discovered our intentions?"

"I don't think so. This could simply be a fluke, all of us eating here at the same time."

"What is he doing? Can he see us?"

"He's got his faced buried in the menu. Whoop! He just looked up and around the room. He might have seen us. Then again, he might be looking for a waiter. Even if it is just a strange coincidence, of all of the restaurants in the Frankfurt area he chose to eat at this one tonight. I still don't think I like the idea that he's sitting over there."

"What do we do, simply sit here and eat our meals as if he were not there?"

"That's ri-ight," Hank said in a low, controlled voice. "I suggest that we act normally, as if we have no clue who he is. Then let's get the hell out of here once we're done eating. Agreed?"

"*Da,* I agree."

Ten minutes passed before the salmon entrees arrived. Another ten minutes passed while they devoured the salmon. And still another ten minutes passed until the waiter recognized that they were finished with their salmon.

"Dessert, sir, madam?"

"*Nein, danke,* the check please?" Hank fumbled through his scant German.

"*Die Rechnung, bitte!*" Natasha rescued him.

"Thanks."

When the check arrived Hank didn't bother looking it over as he usually did, but plunked down his credit card on the plate in front of the waiter. Shortly thereafter the waiter returned with the charge receipt, Hank quickly signed it and dropped a twenty-mark bill on the plate that was graciously received by the waiter.

"Now, let's act as if we don't know that the president of Energia is sitting right over there," said Hank under his breath as they rose to leave.

Dieter looked up at them as they walked across the dining room toward the exit, making a simple note of them, especially Natasha and her naturally stunning looks. Once out of the dining room they quickly strode across the lobby, picking up their pace as they reached the registration desk and darted down the stairs into the atrium.

As they walked through the atrium they brushed by a well-dressed man in his thirties hurriedly heading up the stairs toward the dining room. When the man reached the top of the stairs he suddenly glanced back toward them with a momentary look of recognition. Hank and Natasha exited the atrium doors while the man continued his brisk gait through the lobby toward the dining room entrance until, in a nanosecond, a flash of realization filled his awareness. The photos he had illegally downloaded that evening from the personnel files of OVP and BRPP perfectly matched the couple he had just seen. Klaus Vogel had spotted his prey. However, incredulous to his newfound insight, he kept walking toward the dining room all the while his eyes focused behind him in the direction of the atrium. Once at Dieter's table, he yelled out, "It's them, Herr Schmidt!"

"What are you saying, Klaus? You're not making any sense."

"It's them! The engineers we've been tracking, Hudson and Shakhova. They just left the restaurant," said Klaus in an excited tone pointing toward the door."

"You mean to tell me that I've been sitting here all this time eating dinner with the very people we've been searching for? Why are you just standing here, Klaus, get after them! They must know where Heidel is!"

At once, Klaus ran out of the hotel in hot pursuit. The distance from the front of the hotel to the parking lot was almost a hundred meters. Trees and bushes on either side of the driveway hampered his view in that direction. As he rushed past the green and white hotel van parked directly in front of the hotel he muttered to himself, "*Scheiße!*" They couldn't have gone that distance so quickly."

While he ran toward the parking lot he yanked his mobile phone out of his pocket for a quick call.

"Günther, where are you?"

"I'm in Königstein on Highway 455 heading down toward the Rettershof. I'll be there pretty soon. What's the rush?"

"Hudson and Shakhova are here, at the Rettershof! You've got to get here quickly and help me corner them. They should be driving that blue Ford Mondeo station wagon. If you spot them, turn around and tail them. Call me, and I'll catch up with you," Klaus screamed as he entered the parking lot huffing and puffing.

He clicked off his phone and threw it in the passenger's seat. With the turn of the key, he blasted out of the parking lot, to the left and down the hill past the horse stables and through the woods toward Highway 455, all the while dodging hotels guests out for a walk in the warm summer evening light.

Upon hearing the squealing of tires, Hank and Natasha looked back from the dirt path up toward the castle to see a black Mercedes making the hairpin left from the outer entrance of the hotel complex and away from them. Instinctively, they kept pedaling hard crouching down as they rode hoping the tops of the barley would conceal their whereabouts. Within a matter of minutes they arrived back in Fischbach and the security of Gerta Bauer's home. Leaning the bicycles up against the garage doors, they scooted up the concrete steps to the front door and rang the bell. Gerta answered the door.

"Why are you home so early? Wasn't the food good? You look like you've seen a ghost, and you're all hot and sweaty. *Was ist los?*"

Hank caught his breath and said, "Can we come in, like, right now!"

Hank and Natasha rushed into the house and shut the door firmly behind them. Now safely inside, they began to tell their tale of adventure. Franz had just come out of the bathroom and joined them in the hallway.

"You are not going to believe this when I tell you who we saw, and what happened afterward," said Hank still breathing hard.

"Believe what, who?"

"Your *ex-boss*, Dieter Schmidt. He was having dinner at the same restaurant we were! There we were, sitting there minding our own business, eating our dinner, and pow! He walked in and sat down. Just like that!"

"That is unbelievable! You are certain it was him?"

"Yes, it was definitely him. I recognized him from the convention brochure and his opening lecture this past week. I am positive it was he. I got a good look at him when we left the restaurant," Natasha said with a tone of seriousness.

"Well, did he recognize you?"

"We don't think so. He hardly took notice of us. We tried hard not to stare at him. You weren't supposed to look at him, remember," Hank said looking at Natasha.

"He did look at me as I did at him, but it was only a quick look. He did not appear to know me," said Natasha shaking her head.

"That's good! What happened after you left the restaurant?"

"Well, we were about a half-mile down the path when we heard these tires squealing and saw a black car whipping out of the parking lot and down the hill on the right side of the hotel. That was enough of a signal to us that we needed to hightail it back here," Hank finished the saga.

Meanwhile, Klaus Vogel had not only reached the Highway 455, but also had driven south on it for a few kilometers and back to the Rettershof in search of Hank's blue Ford Mondeo station wagon. Günther had covered the highway to the north and had reported no sign of the car. Soon Günther arrived at the Rettershof in his own company issue black Mercedes sedan, and got out to speak with Klaus still sitting in his car by the side of the road.

"You are absolutely sure you didn't see them, Günther?"

"They didn't pass by me, I can assure you. I only saw one Ford Mondeo, but it was a white four-door sedan driven by an elderly couple."

"Damn it, Günther, this is not supposed to happen!" shrieked Klaus as he pounded on the steering wheel. "We should have easily caught up with them. They only had a one-minute head start at best. This makes no sense at all. I didn't become Dieter Schmidt's right hand man by not getting the job done."

"Maybe they didn't drive the car. Maybe they took a taxi, or someone in a different car picked them up. Maybe they're just hanging out around the hotel somewhere."

"You have a point there, Günther," He pulled out his mobile phone and contacted two other security teams to meet him at the hotel for a discreet but thorough search of the premises. Additionally, he called his security office at the Messeturm and asked them to check on taxi traffic in the area.

Back at Gerta's house in Fischbach, "We should avoid Rettershof from now on!" Franz said emphatically.

"That's all right by me," said Hank, "but I am kind of sorry we didn't get to order any dessert or finish that nice bottle of wine we started."

Gerta replied, "Let me tell you young man, you haven't lived until you've had my apple strudel. You just sit there and wait for me to get it."

"You have apple strudel?"

"You and your apple strudel," sighed Natasha shaking her head and laughing.

"I'll go get the apple strudel while you all go over again the plans for tomorrow."

"I am a welcome recipient!"

Back at the Schlosshotel Rettershof, Klaus and his teams found nothing. They scrutinized every couple staying at the hotel, but to no avail. Hesitantly, Klaus reported their findings to Dieter at his room. Dieter couldn't believe his own ears.

"Klaus, this is not acceptable! I won't be humiliated by a couple of second-rate engineers. Why are you letting them outwit you?"

"I don't know, sir. I'm really starting to hate these people."

"Go away, Klaus. Leave me alone. I'll call you in the morning."

Klaus left the room and returned to his car for the drive back to his apartment in central Frankfurt, leaving his boss in a state of helpless rage and frustration. Dieter fell asleep in his bed watching TV and nursing a bottle of vodka.

Chapter 23

ALTHOUGH CLOUDS HAD moved over central Europe overnight covering the earth with a blanket of gray, it didn't hamper the sunshiny greeting Frau Bauer delivered to her foreign houseguests.

"*Guten Morgen,* Hank, Natasha. It's nearly eight o'clock, and I knew you wanted to get an early start today."

Twist and turns, grunts and groans stirred from the two twin beds of the lower level guestroom. Groggy from all the wine and apple strudel from the night before, Hank and Natasha awoke from their slumber. While Hank continued to lie in his bed trying to build enough pressure to spin his turbine, Natasha's was already turning as she quickly rose out of bed. The sound of the water shooting out of the shower nozzle convinced Hank to resubmerge under his covers. He would wait for his turn in the bathroom.

An hour later they were both dressed and upstairs. To their delight, Gerta had pulled out all the stops by presenting them with a full blown German breakfast of fresh *Brötchen,* butter, jelly, yogurt, coffee, juice, and assorted *Wurst.* Franz soon joined them for the feast.

"Gerti, this is wonderful. But, you know I don't eat much for breakfast."

"You will need energy for your work today, besides, even if you don't need breakfast, our guests certainly do."

"This is a wonderful breakfast. Thank you so much for preparing it," said Natasha.

"This is real good," Hank managed between gulps of coffee and bites of butter and jelly-laden *Brötchen.*

Fortified by Gerta's culinary hospitality, Hank, Natasha, and Franz carefully packed the car and negotiated their way through the narrow streets of Fischbach toward the main road to Frankfurt. The Energia Laboratory, located in an industrial section of Höchst near the Main River, was less than a twenty-minute drive. Traffic was particularly light on this dreary Saturday morning.

"Continue down Schmalkalderner Strasse a few more blocks under the autobahn, and then left on Hunsrück Strasse, and then turn right at Liederbacher Strasse," Franz expertly guided Hank through the back streets.

"You'll let me know when I need to do all of that, won't you?

"Of course!"

After they passed under the S-Bahn tracks and around the circle onto Höschter Farben Strasse, Franz pulled out a mobile and dialed a number he had written down on a piece of paper.

"*Hallo,* this is Fritz Heidenreich from the City of Höscht Water Department, may I speak with someone in charge, please?" Franz spoke with authority.

"*Ja,* I can help you," said the security guard that answered the phone.

"We are having some trouble with the water pressure, and we're checking with the businesses in the area to see if the pressure is okay," Franz continued the ruse.

"The pressure is good here. Come back on Monday when the manager is in his office."

"Excuse me, this problem cannot wait until Monday to be resolved. If you would be so kind as to check the pressure in both the men's and women's bathrooms on your floor."

"*Ach so,* I guess we could do that. What do we have to do?"

Franz covered the receiver with his right hand and leaned forward toward Hank as he said, "Turn left here, the laboratory is just ahead on the right. See that silver and blue building with all of the tinted windows?"

"Got it. Should I slow down or pull over?"

"Yes, pull over to the right and park there," he motioned with his hand, "about fifty meters from the entrance."

Franz returned to the phone, "I need for at least two people to flush the toilets in both bathrooms twenty times, both at the same time, on my signal. That way we can properly test the pressure coming into your building. Is that clear?"

"Okay."

"Go into the bathrooms, now and begin flushing!"

At that moment, both security guards stationed at the front desk of the laboratory went to the bathrooms to carry out the testing for whom they thought was the municipal water company.

"Let's go, Hank."

"Roger that."

He drove ahead and then right into the parking lot behind the building and around to a wall next to the rear door. Hank pulled up the parking brake and turned off the engine.

"So far, so good."

"*Ja*, you are right about that. They would be back here with their guns drawn by now if it weren't for the fact that they're on about their second test flush," Franz joked.

"We'd better not waste any more flushes, shall we?"

All three engineers got out of the car and headed for the rear door of the five-story, ultra-modern, office building. Franz tried his entry card along with the code. The security light turned green. They were in.

"That was way too easy," remarked Hank.

"We are not finished," replied Natasha.

"We must keep our voices down until we're up to the correct floor. The elevator is on the right," Franz whispered.

Once on the elevator, they took it to the third floor. To this point they had encountered no one. However, once they began to walk down the hall, they heard a noise. Franz looked around the corner. He turned to Hank and Natasha.

"It's the cleaning service, a nice, old Turkish lady. I know her from my many weekends working here. Let's go around the corner and keep on walking nonchalantly down the hall as if there were no problem."

As they approached the lady Franz let out an upbeat, "*Guten Tag!*"

"*Guten Tag, Herr Heidel*" she replied smiling at them as they walked by, then returned to her mopping.

Franz put his special card key into the lock for the Atlantis Project door. It worked. Once they were in, he flicked on the lights, and wasted no time in moving into the second room where on a large metal table sat a cylindrically shaped device, no more than half-meter tall, and about thirty centimeters in diameter.

"That it?" asked Hank.

"Yes."

"It is so small," Natasha noticed.

"It's only the prototype, but that little can is capable of producing twenty kilowatts of electricity from thin air. I regret that we have no time to demonstrate. Wrap it up in these coats."

With those words, Hank and Natasha wrapped the generator in a couple of white lab coats and picked it up, each on one end of it.

"It's kind of heavy for its size, isn't it?"

"Yes, it weighs twenty-five kilograms. It's the crystal that weighs so much. Come on, let's go. The security guards will be getting back to their station soon."

They turned off the lights and headed out the laboratory door. By now the cleaning woman was further down the hall. She didn't bother to look up as they made the bend to the left to go to the elevator. Once on the ground floor, they walked briskly toward the rear door and outside toward the car. They carefully lowered the generator on the ground behind the car. Hank searched for the car keys deep in his left front pocket until he was able to press the remote control button to release the rear door of the station wagon. In one fluid motion, they gingerly placed the generator amidst their luggage, the softer pieces cradling this newborn babe in swaddling clothes.

"That was way too easy," beamed Hank at his two accomplices. Just as they all climbed in, the two security guards, fresh from testing the building's water pressure, came running out the back door with their guns drawn.

"I think the easy part is over. Hold on!" yelled Hank.

Natasha and Franz ducked down in their seats as Hank started the engine, put the car in gear, and floored it, whipping right past the security guards around the far side of the building and through the nearly empty parking lot. Shaken from their narrow miss with the front of the car, the guards recovered, ran around the building and immediately opened fire toward the back of the car as it pulled left onto the street in front of the laboratory.

"What was that popping noise back there, we didn't blow a tire, did we?"

"No, your tires are fine, it was just the two guards engaging in a little target practice on your nice new rental car," Franz answered looking back toward the building over the rear seat of the car.

"No way, they wouldn't actually shoot at us."

"Do not worry, Hank. They missed," Natasha breathed out a sigh of relief.

Franz turned around toward the front of the car and said, "Turn right up ahead back onto Höschter Farben Strasse."

"No problem, chief."

As they barreled down Höschter Farben Strasse, Hank spotted three black Mercedes sedans speedily approaching and then zooming past them. Through his side-view mirror, he observed the lead car making a sudden 180-degree turn back toward them, its rear end accidentally smashing into the front end of a parked car. The other two cars followed suit and reversed their direction without mishap.

"Uh-oh, I think we have visitors."

Natasha and Franz instinctively turned their heads backward in response to Hank's warning.

"Got any ideas? I didn't exactly grow up in this neighborhood."

Who were in the three dark, sinister cars now racing after them? That morning, Dieter Schmidt had been pacing the floor of his hotel room racking his brain trying to figure out why these two engineers were hanging around Frankfurt of all places. Why weren't they on their way home? After all, if Franz Heidel had told them what he knew of Project Atlantis wouldn't they want to communicate this information to their companies, or governments? Then the truth of the matter was revealed to him like a ton of bricks dropped from the top of the Messeturm onto his head. They were here to steal the E-7 prototype generator!

A quick call to Klaus Vogel at Energia headquarters was all it took for a security team to be dispatched and the laboratory to be alerted. Klaus and his best teams made haste to the Höscht lab, while the two security guards in the middle of their thirteenth flush were paged on their mobile phones and told to head immediately to the third floor lab. Once they discovered that the generator was gone, they rushed downstairs and out the back door just as the thieves were making their getaway. Now Klaus' eyes were riveted on the license plate from Hessen attached to the rear of Hank's blue Ford Mondeo station wagon.

"I feel just like James Bond."

Natasha replied, "If you are James Bond, then where is the secret escape route, or helicopter waiting for us around the corner?"

"Hey Franz, like I said, any suggestions as to where I need to drive this car would be much appreciated!"

"Okay, this is my neighborhood, so listen carefully. Go into the circle up ahead and take the second right turn on to Liederbacher Strasse and go back under the S-Bahn tracks. Then take a right on to Gebeschus Strasse."

"You're the man, Franz."

Hank complied with the driving instructions, but noticed that the lead Mercedes was making up the distance.

"I think we're being out horsepowered back there."

"Now, go a couple of blocks ahead until you come to Goten Strasse, and turn left. This will take you in the direction of the A66."

"What do you mean by you?"

"When you make the left turn, go into the far left lane and drive for about two blocks, it's a one-way street. Pull over and let me out. I have an idea about how to slow down our Energia pursuers."

"Then what do we do after that?"

"When you get to Bergunder Weg, turn left and go one block to Königsteiner Strasse, and then a right. You'll be in position to get on the autobahn and out of Frankfurt. Don't worry about me, I'll be all right. Remember, this is my neighborhood,"

Once onto Goten Strasse, Hank pulled the car over after the first intersection. Franz slipped out of the left rear door and said in impassioned haste, "Good luck, my friends. Get Project Atlantis to safety!"

Franz shut the door, ran behind the Ford and across the street toward the hospital. Parked in the front was an unattended ambulance with its keys lingering in the ignition switch.

"What's he doing?" Hank asked as they sped away toward the next intersection.

Now looking back Natasha reported, "He is getting in an ambulance."

"He's doing what?"

"The lights are on and he is driving away from the hospital right into the street."

"And?"

"That is all. He is getting out of the ambulance and running away toward some buildings."

Hank glanced in his rearview mirror just long enough to capture a glimpse of the hospital ambulance parked across the lanes of traffic effectively blocking the passage of all vehicles including the three black Mercedes sedans that had just turned the corner onto Goten Strasse.

"Oh shit, what the hell is this!" Klaus blurted out.

"It looks like some kind of problem with the hospital ambulance. Maybe they are backing it up into a parking space."

"*Nein,* Günther! This was done deliberately. I know it. And look ahead, will you. They are getting away," Klaus yelled as he could see the blue Ford several blocks ahead making a left turn onto Bergunder Weg. "*Schnell,* back up the car and get around this mess. They're heading for the autobahn. We can't lose them. *Schnell!* Get on Königsteiner Strasse!

"*Aber, das ist eine Einbahnstrasse,*" Günther pointed out.

"I don't give a crap if it is a one-way street, take it. It's the only way we'll catch up to them." Klaus stared down Günther.

Within seconds, the drivers on Königsteiner Strasse were suddenly greeted by two speeding cars using them as slalom practice for the next Höchst Grand Prix. The cacophonous sounds of car horns, scraped fenders, and verbal obscenities erupted from the street. In the meantime, the object of the pursuit, the blue Ford station wagon, was gaining speed up the on-ramp of the A66.

Chapter 24

"WE AREN'T ONE hundred percent sure if Heidel is still with them, but I doubt it. According to our third team back at the hospital, a man matching his description was the one who blocked the street with the ambulance. We have to assume that Hudson and Shakhova are now on their own and have the E-7 device with them," Klaus stated the facts to Dieter on his mobile phone as they raced the short few kilometers back to the Messeturm.

"Forget Heidel for now, we need to get Hudson and Shakhova and our property! What do you propose we do?"

"I'm thinking about it as we speak."

"Where do you think they are?

"Assuming they got on the A66, they could be going west toward Wiesbaden, or, east toward Frankfurt and the A5. The easiest, quickest direction would be east. Yes, east bound on the A66," Klaus logically deduced.

"And, so what do we do? Search all of Frankfurt for their car?"

"Not before we try this. We have to assume that they are trying to flee to Germany to a place of safety. We'll put teams at the airport and train stations in case they try to fly or ride the E-7 out of Germany. I will alert our security command center to tap into the autobahn cameras in the entire Rhein-Main area to look for their car. We now have the license plate number of the car from the video log tapes of the laboratory, so we can monitor the rental car agency for its return. We will also utilize our ability to monitor credit card transactions in case either of them tries to use plastic. We will flush them out, I can assure you. There won't be anywhere in Germany they will be able to hide for very long."

"Why are you so confident after so many recent failures, Klaus?"

"Because it's all that I can do."

"How soon will you start this plan?"

"Right now, we just pulled into the parking garage."

Chapter 25

Hank and Natasha's anxious mindset gave them little opportunity to notice the lush gentle green Taunus Mountains on the left nor the rolling fields and cities of Hessen on the right as they sped north on the A5. Every thirty seconds one of them would look back either by the turn of the head or a glance in the rearview mirror to see if the menacingly dark cars were still in hot pursuit. On one such perusal of the traffic…

"I think we've lost them."

"It looks like it. I have not seen them since we entered the autobahn."

"Jeez, I sure hope Franz is okay. If it wasn't for him blocking the street back there, those cars would've caught us for sure."

Natasha nodded in agreement.

"Where do we go now? I'm not even sure where this road leads," Hank said as they passed a line of slow moving trucks.

Just then, Hank spotted a sign for the *Raststätte Wetterau Ost* only a thousand meters ahead. "Why don't we stop here and figure out what we're doing and quickly. I have a feeling these Energia guys won't be scarce for long."

"Yes, please, let's stop, Hank. I need to stop."

The car's fuel gauge was now under a half, so Hank pulled the into the DEA gas station rest area for a fill up. The gas station was divided by a line of large boulders separating the cars on the left from the trucks on the right. The cashier and bathrooms were located in the middle. Natasha went straight to the restroom, while Hank saw to the refueling. They met back together at the cashier.

"Do you want anything to eat? We could go over to the restaurant," Hank pointed to a separate red-trim white building to the right of the gas station.

"*Da,* I am starting to feel hungry."

After paying for the gas, Hank pulled the car forward into the general parking lot. Natasha waited for him in front of the restaurant. They were seated at a table by the windows facing the gas station.

"*Was möchten Sie trinken, bitte?*" came the voice of a young, friendly waiter by the name of Moritz.

"I'll have a...no, I better not drink a beer, as much as I'd like one. I'll have a Coke, please, *bitte,*"

"Oh, you're an American! Yes, one Coke. And, for you?" he said turning to Natasha.

"A Fanta Orange, please."

"One Coke, one Fanta. I'll be right back with your drinks."

The restaurant was buzzing with activity. Waiters were scurrying about filling the orders of the traveling patrons who poured in from the busy autobahn. Even with the friendliness of the waiter, and people all around them, Hank and Natasha felt alone and isolated. To the casual observer, they looked like anyone else, typical travelers on vacation — their car had the usual assortment of suitcases, bags, coats, and other objects a tourist would bring. No one knew that they were now industrial thieves, probably wanted by the police, not to mention the mighty corporate giant, Energia. What lay in the back of their car was not your everyday, run-of-the-mill portable five-kilowatt gasoline-fired electrical generator, but a device of revolutionary importance to the world — a generator that wasn't dependent on fossil fuels, or anything else other than the magnetic field of the earth. The thought of it weighed heavily on the minds of the two hungry engineers.

"Here are your drinks. Are you ready to order, or would you like some more time, perhaps?"

Hank and Natasha had hardly looked at the menu; both lost in their thoughts.

"Let's see, uh, I'll have the, uh, goulash soup and a salad."

"*Bitte bringen Sie mir die Bauernomelette.*"

"Very good. It will take only a few minutes."

Hank began fiddling with the drink coasters, many of which were available in a small, green holder in the middle of the table. After several attempts to construct a cube out of six coasters, Natasha joined in the effort. They soon succeeded.

"What do we do Natasha? We can't stay here in this restaurant forever. Should we drive to the nearest airport and hop a plane back to Cincinnati? I'll bet you that they'll be looking for us."

"I have been thinking about that very thing since we sat down."

"And?"

"We have to go to Sweden."

"What? I mean, I've always wanted to go there. My maternal grandmother's family came to America from Goteburg. But, why Sweden?"

"We have to go there. They will know what to do."

"Who are they, and how can they help us?"

"Do you remember my telling you about the Swedish engineers who visited the power plant before I left for the convention?"

"Yeah."

"They said to me that if I ever needed any help to call them. They even gave me their business cards."

Natasha reached in her purse for the cards. "Right here, Dr. Anders Petersson, International Energy Development AB, Lund, Sweden. I have two other cards for Sven Solberg and Bjorn Johansson. Anders Petersson was the leader of the delegation."

"You really think they could help us?"

"*Da*, yes, I am sure of it. They are experts in power generation, especially alternative fuels. We must go there. There was indeed a reason they came and saw me, and I know it was more than just to help my company. Project Atlantis must be the reason."

"Okay, I believe you, I do, really, but Sweden is a hell of a long way from here. I'm not even sure we're heading the right way. I mean, you can't drive to Sweden. Don't you have to fly or take a boat or something?"

"When I was looking at the map of Germany provided by the rental car agency, I noticed that the A5 runs north - south. We are on the A5 heading north. I would think that it is the right direction toward Sweden. We can check the map when we go back to the car."

The food arrived quickly as promised. Hank and Natasha both dug in. The salad was much larger than Hank had anticipated.

"If you'd like some of this salad, you're welcome to it. It's more than I can eat."

"I don't know if I can finish my omelette either. I am not as hungry as I thought I was. My stomach feels..."

"Tight? I understand. My stomach is tied in knots too. Let's just eat what we can and go. I'm not even up for the apple strudel."

"What, no apple strudel?" prodded Natasha as she tilted her head upward toward Hank.

"Don't push me, now. I'm doing all I can here with the soup and salad."

After a few more minutes, Moritz brought the bill.

"Do I pay you?" asked Hank.

"No. You pay at the cashier. Thank you for coming, and please come again when you're back this way."

As they walked toward the cashier, Hank said to Natasha, "That fellow, Moritz, has to be the friendliest waiter I've ever met, don't you think?"

"He loves his work."

"There's something to be said for that, isn't there? I'll settle the bill and meet you out at the car."

Hank paid for the lunch, and they both visited the restrooms. Back at the car the plan for their escape from Germany was hatched.

"Okay, why don't you give this Anders Petersson a call. Here's my credit card. I'll wait here and study the map."

Natasha took Hank's credit card and walked to the pink and silver Deutsche Telecom phone booths right behind them.

"International Energy Development," a pleasant female voice came over the line.

"Excuse me please, I do not speak Swedish very well, I must speak with Dr. Anders Petersson."

"Certainly, we speak English here. Dr. Petersson is not here today. Perhaps I can help you."

"It is most urgent that I speak with him. My name is Natasha Shakhova. I am from Russia. Dr. Petersson came to visit my company recently," Natasha no sooner finished when the receptionist abruptly yet helpfully began to speak.

"Hold on, Mrs. Shakhova, let me call him at his home." After a thirty-second silence, a familiar voice came over the line.

"Hello, Natasha, how are you? How are things in Russia? Did you enjoy the conference in Strasbourg?"

"No, I am not in Russia, but Germany. It is a very long story, and we have little time to explain," Natasha was breathless with anxious energy.

"Calm down, what's the matter? Just one thing at a time."

Natasha explained the entire scenario, first with the contact by Franz Heidel, and ending with their snatching the E-7 generator from the Höchst laboratory that morning.

"All right. That is truly an amazing story, and I believe you. Dieter Schmidt is a paradox of a man, brilliant yet seriously flawed. The generator you have must be saved, and we will help you," Anders affirmed to Natasha.

"Thank you!"

"First, I would not underestimate the power of Energia and their ability to find you. They will do everything within their capacity to prevent you from leaving Germany. Discontinue the use of all credit cards or any other card that can be traced electronically. Go on a cash basis."

"I made this calling using Hank Hudson's VISA card, should I hang up?"

"No, what's done is done, but make future calls collect or with coins. How is your cash situation?"

"I don't know. We will have to check."

"I would avoid the airports and train stations. They would be too easy for them to spot you, especially a couple traveling with a strange object like the crystal generator. It would be best if you could drive here."

"It is possible to drive to Sweden?"

"Yes, since the Oresund Bridge was opened this month, you can now drive from Copenhagen to Malmo in just minutes. Our complex here in Lund is only thirty kilometers north of the bridge. You might pick up a map of Denmark at the rest area."

"This is great news. We are in your debt,"

"No, Natasha, the whole world will be in your debt. We'll see you here soon."

"Good-bye."

She returned to the car as Hank was pouring over the map from the rental car agency.

"What did he say?" Hank asked excitedly

"We are going to need better maps. He said for us to come, to drive to Sweden."

"You can drive to Sweden from here?"

"Da, there is this new bridge between Denmark and Sweden. We can drive there. But, he cautioned against our using credit cards. Energia can probably trace them. We should only use cash from now on."

They immediately began checking their wallets.

"What've you got?"

"Two hundred French francs, and a few German coins is all," Natasha showed the money to Hank.

"I've only got a little more than you, a hundred francs and three hundred twenty marks. Those francs aren't going to help us much. What are these marks worth?"

"The last exchange rate in US dollars, forty-five cents per mark."

"So, we've got about a hundred fifty bucks between us, and hundreds of miles to go. We're going to need some money, and quickly, and we can't use my credit card to get more cash. There's just got to be a way to get some more money, but how? Wait a minute!"

"You have an idea?"

"Yes, he'd do it for me. After all, he kind of got me into this mess. You remember my telling you about my old Navy friend, Darrell LeBrec. I'll call him and he can wire us the money. He still owes me from our last bet on the Oaken Bucket Game,"

"Oaken Bucket Game?" Natasha looked dumbfounded.

"It would take too long to explain right now. Let's go give him a call. What time is it back there?"

He looked at his watch. It was 2:36 p.m.

"It would be 8:36 in the morning back in Bloomington. Darrell has always been an early riser. He'd be up by now, even on a Saturday morning."

After locking the car, Hank and Natasha walked over to the same phone booths where Natasha had spoken with Anders Petersson.

"He's just going to love this, you watch."

Hank put in the necessary twenty-pfennig coin to make a call and asked for the long distance operator.

"I'd like to make a collect call to the US, the number is 812-555-0958."

"Your name, please," asked the operator.

"Henry Hudson."

"One moment, please."

On the other end of the line was heard, "Hello."

"Will you accept a collect call from a Henry Hudson?"

"Henry Hudson, uh, sure, I'll accept the charges."

"Darrell, can you hear me?"

"Loud and clear, Hank. What's up? I'm kind of surprised to get a collect call from you. Are you out of money?" Darrell jokingly asked.

"Now that you mention it, yes! I'm out of money, and I want you to wire a thousand dollars to me here in Germany."

For the next several minutes it was Hank's turn to tell someone their tale of industrial espionage.

"You mean to say that Energia was going to shit-can the generator because it actually worked. That's just wild!"

"I kid you not, Darrell. They were ready to dump it in a landfill and forget it until Franz, Natasha, and I stole it this morning."

"And it's just sitting in the back of your car with the rest of your luggage?"

"Yes, it's buried under our luggage wrapped up in some white lab coats."

"You've got to get out of there. Sweden, eh? Why not come home with it? All right, I'll go down to the bank and wire you the money. Where should I send it?"

"I was studying the map, how about at a bank in Hannover. It's on the way to Sweden. The banks won't be open until Monday, so we'll have to wait until then to get the money. I'll call you tomorrow to find out which bank you've picked."

"Got it, Hannover. Call me when you can, collect I'm sure," Darrell said with humor.

"Thanks, Darrell. You're a great friend. Talk to you soon. Bye."

"I think we had better be going, Hank."

"You got that right. We're fed, we've got a full tank of gas, and money's on the way. Let's drive as far as we can and then find some place to stay the night, some place cheap. Then on Sunday we'll stay in Hannover, get the money, and hightail it up to Sweden."

Hank eased the car onto the A5 north eventually merging onto the A7 past the cities of Kassel and Göttingen. Heavy traffic and road construction slowed their pace. The sun was beginning to dip toward the western horizon as they exited off the autobahn onto Highway 82. After several kilometers they arrived in the small village of Langelsheim.

"There's got to be a hotel in this town. What about that place over there, the Gästehaus Müller? They have a restaurant too," Hank glanced toward a three-story gray brick house.

"That looks good, Hank. I am very tired."

Hank parked the car around the back of the house. They got out of the car and walked around to the entrance. The restaurant was on the first floor, and had only a few patrons at this hour. A cheerful sixtyish year old woman wearing an apron soon greeted them.

"*Guten Abend, kann ich Ihnen helfen?*"

Hank looked at Natasha, "I think I'm in over my head here."

"*Bitte, wir wollen ein Doppelzimmer für übernachten,*" Natasha inquired about a room for the night.

"*Ja, wir haben ein Zimmer frei*, come with me upstairs," replied Frau Getrude Müller.

They walked up the old wooden stairs of the eighteenth century house to the next floor and the first room on the left.

"How will this room do? It's ninety marks per night, and it includes breakfast."

"Ninety marks per night," said Natasha tilting her head at Hank.

"That'll do fine. Do we pay in advance?"

"No, you can settle with me later. Are you hungry?"

"Famished," said Natasha.

"Me too," said Hank.

"After you get settled in, come on down to sign the register and then have some dinner in the restaurant. My husband, Wolfgang, is an excellent cook. You must try his sauerbraten."

After carrying their luggage upstairs, they found a quiet table in the restaurant for a meal of sauerbraten, potatoes, salad, and, of course, apple strudel. Their mood was subdued and low key. Although nourished by the food, the adrenaline of the day had begun to wear off. They trudged upstairs to their room, changed into their nightclothes, and fell fast asleep on their sides of the one bed. Tomorrow would come very soon. Outside in the parking lot behind the hotel sat Hank's Ford Mondeo station wagon, and safely sleeping in the back of it under a blanket of lab coats was the E-7 generator.

Chapter 26

AT PRECISELY 4:43 P.M. on Saturday afternoon Klaus jubilantly entered Dieter's office. Back from his short-lived holiday, Dieter was ready to oversee Klaus' dragnet.

"I have excellent news, sir. Through our connections at Eurocard and Deutsche Telecom, we have detected the whereabouts of our engineer thieves. They not only had lunch, but made at least one phone call from a pay phone at the *Raststätte Wetterau Ost* on the A5 using a credit card under the name of Henry Hudson. Shortly thereafter they made a seventeen-minute call to Sweden using the same credit card. Another call was made just five minutes later from the same telephone, an eight-minute collect call from a Henry Hudson to a residence in the US. We're still checking on the identity of these numbers."

"Where is the rest area? When were these calls made?"

"The trail is only about two hours old. We can surmise that they must have left the rest area shortly after the second call. It's only twenty kilometers north of Frankfurt."

"Isn't it obvious to you, Klaus, they are going north?"

"We have already alerted our security teams from the Kassel, Hannover, and Braunschweig offices to move south to observe the autobahns in all northerly directions. The fact that they are sticking to the autobahn will make our job of finding them much easier," said Klaus with confidence.

"Something is definitely going on here, Klaus. But, what are they up to? Are they going to fly to America or to Sweden? Sweden is much closer. We must find out who they called in Sweden."

In walked Günther with that very information and handed a piece of paper to Klaus.

"The number belongs to IED, International Energy Development, an R&D firm headed up by Dr. Anders Petersson."

"Anders Petersson! IED! Isn't that is one of those alternative energy companies we tried to buy? Of course, they must be in cahoots with him. I'll bet on it. Keep checking on the American phone number. It must be significant. And start canvassing the airports, train stations, and boat companies up north for anyone going to Sweden, or the US. And get some men out there looking for these people. How hard could it be to find a couple of amateurs like Hudson and Shakhova? Find them! I need that generator back, now!"

Chapter 27

THE CLOUDS OF the previous day gave way to the sunny warmth of a Sunday morning in the foothills of the Harz Mountains. Even though it was early, the sun streaked through the white sheer curtains of room number seven at the Gästehaus Müller. Hank and Natasha lay cuddled up next to each other fully adorned in their nightclothes. The sun's rays illumined Natasha's face sufficiently to awaken her from her slumber. Strands of her fine dark brown hair drooped across her face, glancing against Hank's forehead. She pushed them back to clear her view of Hank. He was sawing logs next to her just like back at Gerta Bauer's house. She smiled at him snoring away, and gave him a gentle shake.

"Wake up, Hank, it is morning!"

Slightly startled from the shaking, yet deep in a reverie of dreamland, Hank pushed himself to consciousness.

"What?"

"It is morning, time to get up!"

"Morning, Natasha, what happened?"

"Nothing, now let us get up and get going, shall we?"

She was in charge.

"If you say so," he sheepishly replied.

Natasha got up and attended to her bathroom routine. Eventually the sun drifted further toward Hank's face, forcing him to cover his face with his pillow. A few minutes later Natasha was done in the bathroom.

"The bathroom is free, come on Hank, get up!

"Okay, you win."

"Are you always so slow in the morning?"

"Awhhh, most of the time," he confessed through a yawn.

Hank hauled himself into the bathroom with the force of a flea attempting to move a large boulder. He showered and shaved while Natasha put on her makeup using a small mirror from her purse. Once dressed, they went downstairs for breakfast and a good dose of Frau Müller's hospitality. Just like at Gerta Bauer's house, the Gästehaus Müller put out a breakfast that would satisfy a hunger the size of Texas, or Russia for that matter. Laid before them were Brötchen, eggs, yogurt, sliced meats, coffee, assorted juices, jams and jellies.

"What shall we do today, Natasha? We have the whole day to kill. Oops, there I go again with another figure of speech."

"It is okay, I know what you mean," placing her hand on his. "Whatever we do, we must stay within our budget until we pick up the money tomorrow. We could ask Frau Müller what tourist sites there are around here?"

"Perhaps you could ask her. My German is still not up to par."

Natasha, the resident linguist, asked Frau Mueller's about sightseeing in the area.

"There are many lovely towns in the mountains, and the new Harz National Park is a beautiful place to wander around in nature. The weather today is going to be just perfect, very sunny and up to twenty-five degrees."

"*Mögen Sie Züge?* Herr Müller entered the conversation.

"He wants to know if we like trains," Natasha translated.

What engineer worth their salt didn't like trains?

"Oh, yes, *ja,* we love trains."

"There is a train yard in Wernigerode. It's not usually open on Sundays, except for prearranged tours. You might still be able to get in, especially in the summer. You could even ride the old steam train to the top of der Brocken. It's the highest point in the Harz Mountains."

The Harz was a small mountain range that erupted from the plains of central Germany. Divided for decades by the West-East German border, these heavily wooded, mystically revered mountains hovered to their right as they headed out of Langelsheim through the towns of Goslar and Bad Harzburg until they reached Wernigerode.

Wernigerode was a storybook, half-timbered town popular with tourists because of its nice shops, good restaurants, and five hundred-year-old city hall. However, its centerpiece was a magnificent castle set on a hill above the town at its southern perimeter. The town was already alive with people taking in its quaint charms when Hank and Natasha arrived for a day of guarded relaxation. After parking in one of the parking lots on the edge of the old town, they soon joined the rest of the tourist flock strolling about.

"What do you think of this place?" he asked her as they entered the *Marktplatz*.

"It is beautiful," she reached for Hank's hand. "Oh Natalya, maybe I'm being ridiculous to think that this man could like me, let alone love me some day. But, maybe you've been right from the beginning and knew I would find someone on this trip," she thought in her mind as she contemplated the wisdom of her move toward Hank.

Hank accepted her grasp naturally, without hesitation, sensing her desire to deepen their communion, "This place is a lot bigger than that town back in France, what was it called?"

"Eguisheim."

"Eguisheim. That was it. With the wine shop and the great restaurant," he responded noticing her smiling face. "God, she's so pretty when she smiles," he thought to himself. "She needs to smile more than she does."

Within a few minutes they crossed onto Unter den Zindeln and the train yard Herr Müller had spoken of. They were in luck; a large group of children and adults had just arrived for a tour. They tagged along, fitting right into the crowd. At only five marks each, they could splurge. The tour was a train aficionado's dream. Numerous working steam and diesel locomotives, rail cars, and passenger and freight carriages were maintained in the yard for the HSB, Harzer Schmalspurbahnen. For two power plant engineers, this tour was stimulating to say the least, a veritable thermodynamic delicatessen. A locomotive was in essence a power plant on wheels, whether steam or diesel powered it. The same principles and technology applied. The tour helped them get their focus. What belched out of a locomotive were smoke, steam, and pollutants. As romantic as these trains were, they were also a reminder of the power plants they hoped to replace. After talking extensively with the tour guide, they left the train yard and began walking back toward the center of town onto Breite Strasse until they found the Cafe Ahrends.

After a light lunch of bratwurst, salad, goulash soup, beer, and of course, apple strudel, Hank said to Natasha, "Why don't we go find out about taking a ride on the train they mentioned. The one that goes to the top of the big mountain," proposed Hank.

"To der Brocken?"

"Yeah, der Brocken," he said with his engineering juices overflowing. "Don't you want to ride on a steam locomotive?"

"Do we have enough money?"

"I think so," Hank surveyed the money in his wallet, "I still have two hundred eighty marks. That should be enough to cover everything until we pick up the money Darrell's sending us tomorrow."

Confident that the E-7 generator lay safely cradled in the trunk of the car, they walked back toward the train station.

Chapter 28

I̶T WAS LATE on Sunday morning when Klaus and his caravan of four black Mercedes sedans were speeding up the A7 north of Göttingen at a brisk 200 km/h. With Günther at the helm, Klaus was busy in the passenger's seat directing his subordinates on his mobile phone.

"You have been covering the Kreuzgrenze of the A7 and A39 south of Hannover with no sign of the blue Ford? Okay, good, they must be south of there, maybe in the Harz Mountains, or nearby. Put a camera there with satellite hookup to the Frankfurt office, and take the area west and south immediately along the A7. Investigate Bockenem, Bad Gandersheim, Einbeck and report back when you're finished," said Klaus as he reset his phone and punched in some more numbers.

"Energia Four, can you hear me?"

Klaus had called one of the company's helicopters searching for the car. Once he established contact, he continued the litany of pursuit, "Focus your efforts to the east along the north face of the Harz Mountains where there are numerous towns they could have gone to. We don't believe that they have gone further north than this area. Go above the A395 toward Bad Harzburg, and report in for further instructions when you've reached that position."

"You think we'll really find them?" Günther voiced the unthinkable question.

"They're here, Günther. I can feel it in my bones. They will be spotted by one of our people. You can count on it. They will not slip through our grasp this time. We've got three helicopters and ten cars turning over every stone looking for them. Remember, we're the professionals.

They're just two unsuspecting engineers who are in way over their heads. Even though they're trying to not use their credit cards, they are going to run out of money. They'll eventually slip up and use the card, and we'll be there to catch them when they do."

The four sedans broke up their column and joined the other security teams from the nearby cities. They systematically began searching the area on either side of the A7 including the Harz Mountains. Klaus and Günther exited the autobahn at Highway 248 taking a northeasterly route through the town of Seesen to Highway 82 and Langelsheim.

"Günther, we need to establish a base from which to work. Look for the first possible lodging."

"How about that place over there on the right, the Gästehaus Mueller?"

"Good, let's do it."

Günther parked the Mercedes out front, and they walked inside for a chat with the owners. Frau Mueller greeted them in the lobby.

"Guten Tag, kann ich Ihnen helfen?"

"Guten Tag, gnädige Frau. Gibt es ein Zimmer frei?" inquired Klaus.

Frau Müller blushed, then automatically replied, *"Ach, ja, ein Doppelzimmer kostet nur eine hundert Mark."*

Klaus replied, *"Gut, wir möchten Ein mit zwei Betten."*

Frau Mueller said, "We still have a two-bed room available."

Klaus retrieved his wallet from his coat pocket and handed her a hundred-mark note. "This should get things started. By chance have you seen an American man and a Russian woman travelling together?"

Frau Mueller paused for a moment, wondering who these slickly dressed men might be. Why were they looking for that nice couple who checked in late last night? She instantly took a dislike to them and responded with a lie.

"No, we haven't seen anyone like that."

What had prompted him to ask her that question? He hadn't planned it. It just leapt out of him. Why had she hesitated in responding? He became instantly suspicious. Of all the places in Germany they could have stayed, could they have actually been here last night? Were they coming back tonight? This hotel would make an excellent home base for the operation, especially since he smelled the scent of the two thieving engineers around. Once they were in their room, he called Dieter on his mobile to report their progress.

"They couldn't have gotten any further north than this. We're watching all the nearby autobahn intersections with cameras and teams, plus we're checking all the secondary roads along the A7. I can sense that they're not far away. In fact, I believe they're very close by."

Chapter 29

THE RIDE ON the narrow gauge railway was the icing on the cake of Hank and Natasha's most enjoyable day since their drive on la Route du Vin d'Alsace a few days before. Steam locomotive No. 997243-1 of the Harzquerbahn with its old-fashioned red carriages pulled out of the Wernigerode train station and into the mountains arriving forty-five minutes later at Drei Annen Hohne, 540 meters up. From there, the train wound its way up the slopes of der Brocken for an hour until reaching the top of the 1,142 meter peak. It was a short walk from the small train station to the summit area with its two domed-topped buildings; red and white painted communications tower, and other assorted structures. Rocks and grass now replaced the thick forest of der Brocken's slopes. Hundreds of people were walking around enjoying the mountain top view. The day was unusually clear for the middle of July. Ordinarily, the summer haze would've obscured the details of the landscape, but they could clearly see the valleys and towns below.

"It feels like we're on top of the world looking down on all of creation."

"You know that song?"

"What song?"

"You know, by the Carpenters. It's too bad about Karen Carpenter dying and all. Anorexia. She died of starvation."

"I did not think that anyone died of starvation in America. It would be impossible with all of the food you have, the supermarkets, and the money. Some people in Russia do die of starvation. Look at Chechnya, and Siberia. Some of our food is polluted with Chernobyl radiation. You don't realize how lucky you are to be an American," Natasha was on her soapbox.

"She starved herself; thought she was too fat although she wasn't in the slightest. It was the disease, a mental problem. She had such a wonderful, deep, low alto voice."

"Maybe you can play the song for me someday."

"I think I might have an LP of it somewhere in my collection back home. I still play the old LP's even though I have CD player. I often hit the Goodwill stores, garage sales, and antique stores looking for them. There's an incredible flea market up in Nappanee, Indiana I often stop at when I go visit my folks. They have more records than you can look at in a day, and all of them for only a dollar each."

"They still make LP records in Russia."

"You've got to be kidding!"

Natasha laughed, "Oh, and we have CD's too!"

"I'm glad to hear that things are up to date in Russia."

"You will have to come for a visit and find out for yourself."

"I think I might like that. You should come to the US. That flea market in Nappanee…I need some help looking through all of those records."

Hank and Natasha sat looking out over the green carpeted land that lay below them. From the corner of his eye Hank spotted a moving object.

"Hey, look down, over there. I think it's a helicopter. Can you see it?"

"Yes, I see it."

"I told you that James Bond had a helicopter coming to take us to safety!" said Hank with a big smile on his face.

"Yes, James Bond. We will get on this helicopter and fly away from all of our troubles and take the generator all the way to Sweden, right?" Natasha fired back with a smile.

"Something like that."

Unbeknownst to Hank and Natasha was the fact that this helicopter was actually looking for them. It was now making a pass through the middle of the Harz Mountains in hopes of spotting the blue Ford.

"This is Energia Three reporting in."

"Go ahead Energia Three. What is the situation?" said Klaus into his mobile phone back in his room at the Gästehaus Mueller.

"Nothing much to report up here on der Brocken. I'm climbing up toward the summit right now. I can see a large group of tourists walking around, but no cars. They take the train up here," reported the pilot of Energia Three.

The helicopter continued its path over the top of the mountain.

"Boy, he's coming in real low. Probably going to land, just like I said. Our escape route, Natasha."

"Uh huh," she replied over the noise of the helicopter's blades and engine.

The helicopter circled around the summit hovering a hundred meters above, but out of the way of the communications tower and buildings.

"Don't waste any more time up there if there aren't any cars," suggested Klaus.

Energia Three responded, "I can see some vans and trucks over behind the tallest domed building. There seems to be a small garage in the shorter building next to it. I think it must be for the crew of the weather radar station. The tourists clearly come here by train. There are way too many of them to have come in these vans."

"All right, head over to the eastern Harz starting in Quedlinburg, Thale, and up toward the Hexentanzplatz near Friedrichsbrunn. That's a big tourist site with lots of parking lots to survey. They may not have gone that far from the autobahn, but I want you to check it out anyway."

"Affirmative. Will report in shortly," said the pilot of Energia Three as he guided the helicopter away from der Brocken off to the northeast.

"Hank, there goes our escape route. What shall we do now?"

"I guess we'll have to use the other half of our round-trip train ticket," he replied throwing up his hands in defeat.

"We might as well use them, since it is such a long walk back to the car."

"You're right, have to get our money's worth, especially considering how much they cost and how tight our budget is, until tomorrow, of course. Don't you think it was kind of strange the way that helicopter just hovered there for a while then took off?"

"It was a little odd. It was as if they pilot was looking at all of us here on the mountain."

"That's how it seemed. Well, he's gone now. Why don't we walk over to the east side? Maybe we can see your house in Russia from here."

"I believe the curvature of the earth will make it very difficult to see it, you know. Even with the air as clear as it is today."

As in Wernigerode that morning, they walked hand in hand around to the summit's east face hoping for a clear view toward Natasha's homeland. With luck and continued good visibility they could possibly see the German-Polish frontier. The conversation rapidly shifted from concern about the helicopter back to popular music and other fanciful topics. With each passing minute their intellectual, emotional and spiritual bonds grew. Minutes grew to an hour as time sailed by. Soon they boarded the train for the ride back to their car in Wernigerode. Little did they know that unwanted visitors awaited them upon their return to Langelsheim.

For now, Hank and Natasha needed this diversion from the immensity of their shared mission: the continuation of Project Atlantis, and the prevention of its recovery by its rightful owners. Their success depended upon their combined intelligence, quick intuitive thinking, and the worthiness of their quest. In spite of the odds that were mounting against them, the angels of good fortune followed them as well.

Chapter 30

THE TRIP DOWN the mountain was rich with vistas of lush green forests and the gentleness of the afternoon sunlight. The angle of the light through the mountain air made the trees look aglow with an extra vibrancy of life and energy. Gradually the mystical world of the summit gave way to the everyday reality of the valley below. Two hours later the train pulled into the station at Wernigerode. Hank's car was an easy ten-minute walk away. They found it just where he had parked it, toward the back of the public lot surrounded on each side by minivans.

"The generator is still safe back here," said Hank breathing a sigh of relief upon inspecting the luggage area of the car.

Natasha, now sitting in the passenger's seat smiled back at him in response, "She is specially protected."

"She? Hmm. Maybe you're right. Keep thinking that way. I guess we'd better get going, it's after five."

"She is a she. She will give warmth and energy to the world."

"Okay, it's a she. You'll get no argument from me. Can you get the map out? I think I need a navigator to get through all those roads we took here."

They headed back to Langelsheim along the same route they had taken earlier in the morning. The same afternoon sun that had graced their ride down der Brocken now glared in their faces as they traveled due west. Traffic was heavy with people returning home from their weekend get-a-way in the mountains. Driving required extra concentration and focus. Half an hour later they rolled down Lange Strasse into Langelsheim. As they approached the Gästehaus Mueller

Hank's eyes suddenly became riveted on the black Mercedes sedan parked out front. Right next to the stairs leading to the front door was the almost familiar face of Klaus Vogel lighting up a cigarette.

"Oh, shit!" Hank blurted out as he altered the left turn he was about to make toward the hotel.

"What's the problem? Oh, I understand."

"Quick, crouch down in your seat and maybe he won't spot us. That looks like the same guy from the restaurant and the car chase back in Frankfurt. I can't believe they found our hotel! Let's just fit in with the locals."

Natasha turned to the right and slouched down as far as her tallish frame would allow. Hank jammed on his sunglasses that he had just taken off when he entered the town. The blue Ford Mondeo station wagon crept along inconspicuously with all the other cars on the road. As Klaus finished lighting his cigarette he looked up from his perch on the stairs and caught a glimpse of the back end of the Ford as it rounded the curve in the road and headed west out of town.

Klaus' internal radar went off as he thought to himself. "Hmm, the color and type of car was correct. Damn it, if I hadn't been fumbling around with this cigarette and had been paying attention I could've made sure. It could have been them!"

He racked his brain for a few seconds between puffs on his cigarette. Then it hit him. The license plate was from Hessen. He could never forget that license plate directly in front of him all through the streets of Höscht. He flicked his cigarette on the ground and ran into the hotel. Günther was sitting at the bar drinking a beer when Klaus grabbed him on the shoulder.

"Günther, it was them! Let's get in the car and go!"

Günther nearly spit his beer all over the bar, but managed to ask, "What! You're joking?"

"Come on, let's go!"

Günther looked at his half-finished beer, then up at Klaus.

"Forget the beer, give me the keys. We can't let them get away!"

Günther mournfully glanced at his beer, tossed Klaus the car keys, grabbed his coat, and followed him out to the car.

The screech of the Mercedes' tires caught the attention of everyone in the neighborhood, including Frau Müller who was in the kitchen preparing the evening meal. From her view out the window she saw the entire scene. First there was Hank and Natasha's car, followed a minute later by sharp movement of the black Mercedes as it entered into the thick flow of traffic. She instinctively whispered a prayer of protection for the nice, handsome couple who had spent the night with them, and made a note to herself to store their luggage for them in the hope that they would return.

"Can you see them behind us?"

"No, but you are right. That was definitely the man we walked by at the Rettershof," agreed Natasha.

"I'll never forget the face of that guy in the car as it approached us in Frankfurt after we took the generator. That's a face you don't forget. A kind of cold, all business sort of face."

Hank kept his eyes on the road. The heavy traffic was flowing along at a good pace. Twists and turns in the two-lane road prevented all but the foolhardy driver from passing slower cars. With the lag time between Hank and Natasha's drive by the hotel, and Klaus' taking the helm of the car, nearly twenty cars now separated them over a space of two kilometers. However, when the road suddenly widened four lanes, Hank decided to take advantage of its extra wideness.

"Hold on!"

Hank down shifted the transmission into fourth gear and floored it around the slower cars in front of him. A yellow Audi A6 that had been tailgating him since Goslar followed suit. The two cars reached speeds of 140 km/h on a road signed for 100 km/h. Other slower cars that had been using the left lane ceded their space to the Ford and Audi and moved over into the more sedate right lane.

"This car's got a lot of pickup for a four-banger."

"How fast are you going?" Natasha was starting to get a little nervous.

"One hundred-forty, but that's in kilometers not miles an hour."

"How comforting to know," she said as she looked back at the front end of the Audi with his light flashing on and off, "I think he wants to pass us."

"Another day perhaps, but not now," Hank said as he glanced at the Audi in his rearview mirror, "He's actually helping to push us along."

At the junction with Highway 248 the road narrowed back to two-lanes. Hank let the Audi pass by. In the meantime, Klaus and Günther had wasted no time in trying to gain ground on them, using the four-lane stretch of road as if they were driving the Daytona 500. However, the fast driving that Hank had engaged in prevented them from gaining no more than a few car lengths. When Hank and Natasha arrived at the A7, they took it northbound. Within a couple minutes Klaus and Günther followed suit.

Klaus flipped out his mobile and with his thumb clumsily punched in some numbers.

"Do you want me to drive?" offered Günther.

"Shut up, Günther, we'd lose too much time changing seats. I can handle this," Klaus was annoyed with the progress of the chase.

"Energia Four, report in."

"*Ja*, this is Energia Four," the pilot responded.

"Proceed to the A7 north, we've spotted the car."

"We cannot help. Our fuel is low and we are returning to Göttingen for more, so has Energia Two."

"Damn it, all right. What about Energia Three?"

"I don't know, sir. They were over the eastern Harz Mountains. I think they may have had to refuel at Madgeburg."

Klaus clicked off the phone as he weaved in and out of the autobahn traffic. He punched in the numbers for Energia Three.

"Energia Three, come in."

"This is Energia Three."

"Where are you now?"

"We're in Magdeburg getting some more fuel. We could find no sign of the car in our search of the eastern Harz."

"Never mind that, how fast can you get in the air and over the A7?"

"We can leave in five minutes, perhaps. But, it will take us at least thirty minutes to reach the A7."

"Get here as soon as you can and call me when you're in position," Klaus clicked off the phone again. "This is not going well, Günther."

A few minutes later his phone rang.

"*Hallo*, Vogel."

"This is the Frankfurt office calling, the blue Ford was just seen by our camera at the junction of the A7 and A39 heading northbound on the A7."

"*Gut, danke.*"

Klaus turned to Günther, "We've got them now!"

Chapter 31

IT WAS EARLY Sunday afternoon in Bloomington, Indiana. Darrell LeBrec had been sitting on the sofa in his living room reading the newspaper waiting for his friend to call. He had stayed home from church that morning to let him know where he had wired the money and he was beginning to get concerned. His wife, Nadine, rubbed him on the shoulders and reassured him, "He'll call, you know Hank, he's real steady."

At 1:19 p.m. the phone rang."

"Hello."

"Will you accept a collect call from a Henry Hudson," said the operator.

"Yes! Hank is that really you?"

"Yeah, Darrell, it's me," came a familiar voice over the phone.

"Where are you? I thought you would call a lot earlier."

"I'm at a pay phone just north of downtown Hildesheim."

"Where's that?"

"Just south of Hannover. I can see a small airport across the street. Hey, I can't talk very long. These guys from Energia are on to us. I don't know how they did it, but they staked out the hotel we stayed in last night, and we didn't even use a credit card. I think we've got to keep moving. Did you send the money?"

"It's there. I found a bank in the suburbs, the Volksbank in Hannover. It's the Buchholz branch at Sutelstrasse 73. I figured you'd want to avoid having to maneuver in downtown Hannover, so I opted for this branch near the autobahn."

"Hold on, Darrell, let me jot this down." He pulled one of his own business cards out of his wallet and began writing.

"What was the bank again?"

"The Volksbank, with a 'V' on number 73 Sutelstrasse. They open up at 8:15 in the morning. Just show them your passport and they'll give you the money in cash. $1,000 adds up to 1,097 euros or 2,147 marks."

"That'll be fine, how can I ever thank you?"

"I'll send you a bill. Just get done what you have to do. The world needs the Atlantis generator. It's exactly what Nick Spencer has been tracking for all these years."

"You may be right, Darrell. Keep the prayers going for us, my friend. It's getting to be quite an ordeal."

"You got it. Call me from Sweden."

"With your help we may actually get there, or get caught trying."

"You won't be caught. You can't!"

"Okay, bye Darrell."

"Bye, Hank."

Hank walked back to the car to tell Natasha the good news.

"The money is all arranged, and is waiting for us up the road in a place called Buchholz."

Natasha, who had been studying the map of Hannover, noticed it right away.

"It is here, on the northeast side of the city. If we stay on this road it will lead right into Buchholz."

Within twenty minutes Highway 6 became Messeschnellweg when they entered the south side of Hannover. Soon they were in the thick of Buchholz.

"Take the turn for Klingerstrasse and go north."

"Klingerstrasse?"

"*Da*, Klingerstrasse, to the left. Go north to Podeleskistrasse and turn right."

Hank exited Messeschnellweg onto Klingerstrasse heading north. After about half a mile they turned onto to Podeleskistrasse.

"Okay, go about another five hundred meters and turn left onto Sutelstrasse."

Sutelstrasse and the Volksbank were easy to find.

"The bank is over there on the left," Natasha pointed in its direction.

"Good. Now we have to find a place to stay tonight. Did you notice that hotel a few blocks back on the other street?"

"Yes, I did, on a smaller street off of Klingerstrasse, the one with the church across from it."

They retraced the route they had taken to the bank and found the Hotel Eilenriede on Guerickstrasse just as they had remembered. They parked the Ford out front and went inside to see about a room. The lobby was walled in windows and decorated with numerous potted and hanging plants. After a couple of minutes the owner, a man in his forties greeted them.

"Kann ich Ihnen helfen?"

Hank looked at Natasha, "Let me try this one," and turned to the owner, *"Bitte, ich möchte ein Zimmer."*

"Yes, sir, you are in luck, we had a cancellation on a double room. It's not easy getting a room this week with the Expo 2000 in town," replied the owner, Herr Schmeltzer.

"Well, I tried to use my German."

"Your German is very good, sir,"

"Danke. Let me try once more. *Wie viel kostet das Zimmer?"*

Herr Schmeltzer smiled.

Natasha smiled. "Hank, your German is improving a lot. Next you will have to learn Russian."

"One language at a time."

"The room costs one hundred thirty-nine marks per night. However, it is only available for tonight."

"That'll be fine," Hank pulled out his wallet and surveyed his cash supply. He had a hundred-mark and a fifty-mark note left. He pulled them out and handed them to Herr Schmeltzer.

"Please sign the guest register while I get your change."

"Sure."

"Here's your change, Mr. Hudson, eleven marks."

"Thank you. Is there a good place around here to eat, something modestly priced?"

"There are several excellent restaurants nearby, but if you're looking for something quick and inexpensive, there is a bratwurst stand around the corner by the supermarket on Buessestrasse. They are open until nine on Sundays."

"Thanks for the tip, Mister...?"

"Michael Schmeltzer, I'm the owner and manager. Here is your key to room number four, just down the hall on the left. The breakfast buffet is included in the price, and is offered in this room over to the right, starting at seven o'clock."

Since their luggage was still at the Gästehaus Mueller, they went straight to their room. Natasha opted for the bed while Hank flopped down in one of the two wicker chairs that decorated the room. After several minutes of gathering their physical, mental, and emotional wind, Hank sat up.

"We've got eleven marks to our name. Are you hungry?

"I have a five -mark coin in my purse, and some smaller change. Here, let me get it for you," as she reached for her purse by the nightstand.

Hank got up from his chair and walked over to Natasha who handed him the coins. He counted it all.

"16.53 marks. I'll go find that bratwurst stand Herr Schmeltzer mentioned. Be back in a few."

Hank left the room and went outside to the car to check on the generator. Satisfied as to its security, he walked down Guerickstrasse for a couple of blocks and then right onto Bussestrasse. The Bratwurst-Wissmann was a free standing fast-food style restaurant across the parking lot from the big supermarket. Its large plate glass window-walls revealed a throng of customers lined up for takeout food, or eating at the stand-up tables. Hank went inside and joined the queue. Bratwurst with a roll and mustard were only four marks. Half-liter bottles of soft drinks were three marks. He had enough for both of them. Now came the moment of truth for Hank, ordering in German. There were two other customers in line ahead of him. While he waited he practiced his lines several times hoping that he wouldn't make a fool of himself. Finally, it was his turn.

"Ich möchte zweimal Bratwurst, und zwei Coke, bitte," Hank said with deliberation.

"Möchten Sie Senf?" asked the older woman employee.

"Uh, *Senf,* sure... *ja, bitte."*

Once the bratwurst, roll, and the added mustard were wrapped up in foil, and the two Cokes were retrieved from the refrigerator, the woman said, *"Vierzehn Mark, bitte."*

"Here," Hank handed her the ten-mark note Herr Schmeltzer had given him in change, plus Natasha's five-mark coin.

"Eine Mark," she said as she handed him his change in the form of a one-mark coin.

"Danke," as he grabbed the wrapped up bratwurst, still warm from being grilled, and the two bottles of Coke. Clutching the food in his arms, he walked the three blocks back to the hotel. Using one of the Coke bottles he knocked on the door of their room.

Natasha had passed the time reading a magazine she had found on a table in the hallway. She opened the door just as Hank's hands and arms let go of dinner. Instinctively she caught one of the Coke bottles with her hands and the open magazine. Hank somehow managed to balance the rest of it.

"Thanks for catching that. I probably should've asked for a bag. Those brats are still hot. My hot hands can attest to that. It's not much, but for fourteen marks, it will keep us whole 'til tomorrow."

"This will be fine, Hank."

"Sorry about no apple strudel, but it was three marks and I only had 2.53 left."

"I can live without apple strudel for a day, can you?"

"I'll try. I really will. Hey, you should've seen me in the restaurant. I ordered the entire meal in German. Not one word of English! I don't think anyone knew I was an American. I'm rather proud of myself."

"Maybe you can try again at the bank tomorrow morning."

"As long you're there to back me up."

"I will be there. Where else would I be?"

Dinner was a fast process. Afterward, they both watched TV, the German language version of the movie, *Volcano*.

Later, Hank remarked, "I didn't know that Tommy Lee Jones could speak German. Even the swear words."

"I do not think that he can speak German, rather the film is dubbed with professional actors. Are there volcanoes in downtown Los Angeles?"

"I've been to downtown LA. They don't have any volcanoes; it's all computer generated special effects."

"I know."

Without their luggage to provide them with pajamas, they decided to sleep in their underwear. Their natural shyness, and the intensity and abruptness with which their relationship had been formed, made them a little apprehensive about doing so. However, there was no sense wrinkling their clothes by sleeping in them. Fifteen minutes after they turned off the lights, they held hands for a while, just as they did earlier that day.

Just before he drifted off to sleep, Hank leaned over Natasha, and kissed her cheek, "Good night."

To which she replied, "Good night, my dear."

Their exhaustion, brought on by the fullness of the day, quickly carried them deep into sleep. An even fuller and longer day lay before them only hours away.

Chapter 32

"THEY MUST HAVE exited the autobahn back at Highway 6. We haven't seen one blue station wagon yet."

"Yes, Günther, thank you so much for stating the obvious."

"According to the map, it runs parallel to the autobahn then goes under it into Hildesheim."

Klaus had pushed his car to the limit in attempting to overtake Hank's, but with no success. He had thought that they would surely drive north on and catching up to them would not be a problem. Now he faced the fact that he had lost them, again. The chronic frustration of the past few days was gnawing at Klaus' nerves. They had turned the car around and were now heading south on the A7. Klaus was deciding whether to get off on at Highway 6 and look around, or regroup back at the hotel. Just then the sound of his mobile phone filled the car.

"*Hallo,* Vogel."

It was the boss. "Have you caught them?"

"They were seen passing through Langelsheim, and then one of our satellite cameras spotted them at the A7-A39 junction. We have determined that they are presently in the Hildesheim area. Günther and I are checking on that lead right now," Klaus had learned to proactively spin bad news for his boss.

"I see. Why aren't the helicopters helping you? With this new information, Hudson and Shakhova should have easily been in your hands by now!"

"There have been unexpected refueling delays with all three helicopters. Energia Three should be in the Hildesheim area within the next twenty minutes, the other two within the hour."

"Klaus, I have decided to personally supervise the search for Hudson and Shakhova. I'm just south of Kassel. Once you've finished searching Hildesheim, meet me at the Mercure Atrium Hotel in Hannover at nine o'clock."

"I see. Making it there by then is going to be difficult. We left our gear over at this little hotel where we set up our base of operations. We'll need to go pick it up."

"Why isn't it with you?"

"We left there in quite a hurry once their car was spotted. Unfortunately, the traffic was so heavy that we lost them until the camera picked them up on the autobahn,"

"Call in the other cars to search Hildesheim while you collect your belongings. I will see you in Hannover at nine. *Verstehst du?*"

"Okay, but our car is the closest to Hildesheim. I would recommend that we begin the search and then return to the hotel once some of the other cars are in the area."

"Agreed, but meet me in Hannover no later than ten. I have an idea how to tighten our net around them."

"Ten it is," Klaus said clicking off his phone.

The Highway 6 exit was coming up in two kilometers. Klaus pulled the Mercedes over into the right lane to get off the autobahn.

"Günther, keep your eyes open for that Ford. Your job depends on finding them."

"My job?"

"Our jobs,"

While Günther surveyed the road ahead, Klaus began calling in his search team to the Hildesheim area. Within an hour Hildesheim was crawling with Energia's best security teams. They found no trace of Hudson and Shakhova.

Chapter 33

MONDAY MORNING AND its impending demands arrived too soon for Hank Hudson and Natasha Shakhova. What ideally should have been a leisurely, relaxed affair was shortly to become an unstoppable rush to transport into friendly hands the greatest technological breakthrough since the discovery of electricity itself. This noble pursuit took precedence over personal relationships. Romantic feelings, now gaining in intensity between them, would have to wait for a quieter, less stressful moment. Natasha awoke to find her left arm pleasantly draped across Hank's shoulder and her body curled up against his back. Rather than leap out of bed into her morning routine, she lay in this position for several minutes looking at him snoring away. She marveled at his strong, well-shaped body for a man of his age. Although his hair had certainly thinned over the years, he wasn't bald. However, beneath his external features lay the most important feature of all, a heart big enough to encompass her and her dreams. No man had ever treated her with such kindness, good humor, and genuine caring — certainly not since Nikolai. Soon she succumbed to her inborn practicality and looked at her watch. 7:15. Time to get up.

"Hank! Are you awake yet?" she jiggled his arm. Yawns through the snores were all that she heard. She gave him a second shake. Now she had him surfacing from his slumber.

"Ahhh, ohh, is it morning already?"

"Yes, Hank. We have to get up. It is already after seven."

"Okay, you go on into the bathroom, like you always do. I'll just lay here a little longer. I had this dream about you and me and a little girl. We were back at my house in Cincinnati, and the girl was going off to school."

While Hank continued to lie on the bed absorbed in the reverie of his dream, Natasha got up and went toward the bathroom. Out of the corner of his right eye Hank caught an image of her tall, slim body covered only by her black undergarments. He thought to himself, "Man, I really must be dreaming."

Hank finally pulled himself up to the edge of the bed and turned on the TV. He flipped through German versions of American cartoons, including Looney Tunes, until he found CNN Europe. Hearing the American English of the newscasters brought a sense of normalcy of what had been an adventure beyond the imagination of even the most right-brained engineer. Who would have thought a week ago that he would be involved in an international theft of a secret industrial machine, and then to smuggle it out of the country with the help of a beautiful woman? His mind flip-flopped between the surrealism of his present reality, and the friendly, homey words coming from the television. Natasha emerged from the bathroom dressed in her clothes from yesterday—a purple blouse and black skirt. With most of her makeup sitting in their room back at the Gästehaus Mueller, she had to make do with the few cosmetics she kept in her purse. The light application of these brought out her natural beauty better than her usual method.

"I am finished in the bathroom if you would like to use it," she said as she sat next to him on the bed putting on her nylons.

"You look nice that way."

"Thank you. How am I different? I am wearing the same clothes."

"It's your makeup. You look better with less makeup."

"You think so? All I have in my purse is some lipstick, eyeliner, and mascara."

"Well, I think it looks good on you."

Hank got up and attended to his bathroom duties. By eight o'clock they were at the breakfast buffet. The room was filled with other hotel guests in town for the Expo 2000. Hank and Natasha managed to find a recently vacated table by a window overlooking the garden in front of the hotel. They ate voraciously, filling themselves well after yesterday's skimpy rations, but also mindful of the time. As soon as they were finished, they checked out of the hotel and drove the several blocks to the Buchholz branch of the Volksbank.

Once in the bank, Natasha assisted by explaining to the teller in German that money had been wired from the US for Hank to pick up. The bank manager was called to the window, and asked to look at Hank's passport, just as Darrell had instructed. Once the manager was satisfied that the transaction was in order, Hank requested an assortment of mostly German marks, along with Danish krone and Swedish krona. By 8:45 they were out the door and back in the car.

Feeling bolstered by an influx of cash, food, and lack of black menacing sedans in the rearview mirror, Hank and Natasha began driving through the surface streets of northeast Hannover unaware that the entire resources of Energia and its CEO, Dieter Schmidt, were closing in on them.

That encirclement had been planned the previous night at the four-star Mercure Atrium Hotel on Karl Wiechert Allee, less than one kilometer from the Hotel Eilenriede. Klaus and Günther arrived late for their appointment with Dieter. The trip back to Langelsheim to pick up their baggage and equipment took longer than expected. Klaus knocked on the door of the suite.

"What took you so long, Klaus? I've been waiting."

"Sorry about that, sir."

"Come on in and let's get working."

They walked over to the large table and sat down. Highway maps and information on Energia's security force and helicopters were scattered across the table.

"I've been thinking about the theft of the E-7 generator, the way it was carried out, and the subsequent transportation of it into northern Germany. Surely Heidel was the one who engineered the heist. He had the inside knowledge of the Höscht laboratory, the layout of the streets, and knew how to dupe those two idiots manning the security station. By the way, Klaus, they are no longer working for us."

"Yes, if it wasn't for those two *Dummkopfs* none of this would have happened."

Dieter continued his analysis, "Hudson and Shakhova could've gone to the Frankfurt airport or train station to make their escape from us, but chose to drive their car north instead, possibly because they were simply pointed in that direction and hadn't a clue where they were going. We know for sure that they spoke with someone at IED in Sweden, most likely with Anders Petersson. Right after that phone call, they stopped using credit cards. The next call from that phone number was to the United States. We have not yet been able to determine with whom they were speaking. The telephone company in the United States has been very uncooperative about releasing the name, saying it is an unlisted number. However, we know the number came from Bloomington, Indiana, which is not far from Hudson's hometown of Cincinnati, Ohio. I'll bet the phone call was a plea for money to be sent, perhaps from a relative or friend. Why else would they be hanging around this area all weekend? They are simply waiting to pick up money wired to them from the US. There's no other possible explanation."

"That's brilliant, sir. What's the plan?"

"Klaus, here's what I want you to do. I want you to put someone in front of every bank in Hannover and Hildesheim. Tomorrow morning when they go to pick up the money we'll easily spot them and retrieve the E-7 and whatever technical papers they have on it. It is also my suspicion that they are heading toward either the Berlin or Hamburg airports, possibly to rendezvous with Petersson. We have to get into their minds for a moment and try to understand them. The last thing they want is to have us breathing down their necks. No matter what kind of altruistic crap Heidel probably tried to fill their minds with, they'll likely want to give up the E-7 and get back to their lives and families in America and Russia. What I want is for them to return it to me and not give it to Anders Petersson. Then we can debrief them in such a manner that they'll begin to see Heidel for the pinhead that he is. Remember, Klaus, they're not spies working for their countries, they're just dull, ordinary power plant engineers. Believe me, I know the type."

Klaus set into motion all the aspects of Dieter's plan. Security personnel were assigned to watch the numerous bank branches in the area and told to be in position by 7:30 the next morning. Overnight, more satellite cameras were installed at all of the autobahn intersections between Hannover and Hildesheim. The holes in Energia's security net were repaired. The trap was set.

"Go back down Sutelstrasse to Podeleskistrasse, but go left instead of right this time," Natasha directed reading the map of Hannover.

"Got it."

"This will take us to the A37 which connects with the A7. It is the fastest way out of the city and to the north."

"To Sweden?"

"Da, to Sweden."

"Before we do, I think we better get some gas. We're down to half a tank. There's a Shell station over there on the right. I'm gonna pull in there."

Back in front of Volksbank's Buchholz branch, Helmut Winkler of Energia's security force called Klaus Vogel with his report.

"*Hallo,* Vogel."

"This is Winkler. I just observed a man and a woman matching the description of the people we're looking for come out of the bank and drive off in a blue Ford station wagon."

"You didn't let them get away, did you?"

"Not at all. I followed them to a gas station only a few blocks away from the bank. I'm parked only a few meters away from them. They appear to be buying fuel for their car, and are so far unaware of my presence."

"Where are you? We'll send more cars over."

"Podeleskistrasse, just east of Sutelstrasse."

"All right, keep observing and reporting on their movements as they happen. However, make sure they do not detect you. When they leave, keep a few car lengths back. I want to personally confront them."

"Yes, I'll do as you say."

As Hank and Natasha returned to their car from the cashier, loaded up with snack and drinks, Hank noticed a black Mercedes parked over to the side of the station. Through the side of his left eye he caught the image of a young, blonde-haired young man on a mobile phone looking up at him.

"Natasha, don't look now, but we're being watched."

"Yes, the Mercedes."

"Yup. I'll bet you one of those new hundred-mark bills that he leaves when we do."

"That would not be a good bet, I think."

As predicted, the man in the Mercedes followed them out of the station and back onto Podeleskistrasse.

"Now what do we do? Can you tell from the map?"

"I am not sure what to tell you. Follow the traffic. Maybe you can lose him in it. The entrance to the A37 should be coming up on the right pretty soon."

"He doesn't seem to be following us very closely, but it is too much of a coincidence that he left when we did. Here comes the entrance to the autobahn, we'll see if he stays with us."

Two other cars now separated the blue Ford from the black Mercedes. All four cars entered the on ramp to the A37.

"He's still with us," observed Hank looking in his rearview mirror.

As they merged onto the right lane of the autobahn, another blue Ford Mondeo station wagon, exactly like theirs, suddenly appeared from behind them in the flow of traffic.

"You're not going to believe this, but it's like looking at ourselves in the rearview mirror."

Natasha looked back. "I see what you mean. The people in the car even look like a little us, a man and a woman. They not only look like us, they look familiar, as if I have seen them before."

"What do I do now? Do I turn onto this highway A2 up here?"

"No, keep going! The A7 is at the next junction."

Helmut Winkler glanced left to check the flow of traffic as he entered the roadway, only to turn back and see two identical blue Ford station wagons a few car lengths ahead. Then, the last of the two merged off the A37 onto the A2. He assumed that it was the correct one. He pulled out his mobile and reported in.

"This is Winkler, the car is now heading eastbound on the A2. Shall I continue to follow it?"

"Yes, continue the surveillance until our helicopters are in position, then we will track it from there."

Klaus turned to Dieter, sitting across the table from him in Dieter's hotel room, and said, "They are ours for the taking."

"Didn't I tell you it would work out this way. No one, but no one fools Dieter Schmidt!" he said clenching his fist.

Meanwhile, Hank and Natasha had reached the junction with the A7.

"Where'd they go?"

Natasha, who had been looking behind, said, "The car behind us got onto the A2 back there, and so did the Mercedes."

"I'll bet the Mercedes thought they were us."

"Let us pray it is so. It was as if God brought that car to help us get away."

"You sure use the word God a lot for an engineer."

"An engineer can believe in God. God is the force for good that cannot be explained rationally, but is still real. God has chosen us to do this work in saving Project Atlantis," Natasha continued her Monday morning sermon.

"Yeah, this whole deal has that kind of otherworldly feel about it, as if we're simply fulfilling some master plan, with a whole lot of luck."

"It was not luck that caused that blue car to appear behind us, it was God's hand."

"You're starting to sound a lot like Darrell."

"Darrell?"

"Our monetary benefactor of this morning."

"Oh."

"He used to be a preacher, now he's a professor of psychology, but there's still a lot of preacher in him. Maybe you'll get to meet him once all of this is over."

"Preacher?"

"Minister, priest, speaker."

"Perhaps you can explain American religion to me sometime."

"I'll try. What do you say we put this buggy in gear and haul ass?"

"Excuse me?"

"Here's what I mean."

Hank pushed down the accelerator and brought the car up to 150 km/h. Traffic was light, and the sun, now shining brightly from the east, illuminated the road before them.

"Energia Three, proceed to the intersection of the A2 and A37 and follow the car east on the A2," Klaus spoke into the two-way radio.

"Acknowledged. We are on our way and will be in position in three minutes," said the pilot of Energia Three.

"Energia Two, shadow Energia Three eastbound above the A2," Klaus added redundancy to the surveillance.

"Günther, let's get to the car and catch them," then Klaus turned to Dieter. "My next call will be the news of our capture of Hudson, Shakhova, and the recovery of the E-7."

"Call me immediately as soon as you have them."

Klaus and Günther retrieved their Mercedes from the hotel-parking garage, and with Günther at the wheel, made haste for the A2.

"Energia Three, where are they now?"

"This is Energia Three, we are passing over Peine. They don't seem to be driving very fast, about 110 km/h. He drives like an American."

"He is an American. Well, that's good, we should be able to make up the distance fairly easily."

Klaus could smell the impending kill. It was time to be done with this job. After about an hour of breakneck driving Klaus and Günther sighted the blue Ford two hundred meters ahead of them. Klaus took out his binoculars and checked their license plate. Sure enough, it was from Hessen.

This was their best look at the car since it slipped by them in Langelsheim. Now it was dead in their sights.

"Can we pull over at the next rest area? I need to go to the bathroom," the occupant of the passenger seat of the blue Ford said to the driver.

"Sure, I think there's one coming up ahead," responded the driver.

The blue Ford put on its turn signal and exited the autobahn into the rest area.

"Günther, they are stopping at the rest area. Here's where we'll make our move."

The black Mercedes slipped into the rest area and parked a few cars behind. Meanwhile, the female passenger got out of the car and headed to the WC. The male driver stayed in the car studying a map.

"This is Klaus, we have them," he said to Dieter in his mobile.

"Where are you?"

"The rest area a few kilometers past the turn off for Wolfsburg."

"Do you have it yet?"

"Not yet, but we will in a few minutes. I can assure you. Shakhova has gone inside the WC. Hudson is still in the car. I will call you back shortly with the news of our success," Klaus clicked off his phone and got out of the car.

The driver of the blue Ford looked up from the map he was studying and suddenly saw a tall well-dressed man in his thirties appear alongside his driver's door. The man knocked on his window indicating that he wanted to talk. The driver dropped down the window.

The tall man said to him, "Excuse me sir, what is your name, please?"

"Steve Richardson, can I help you with something?" Klaus' stomach muscles began to tighten up, "Uh, no, thank you sir. I mistook you for an acquaintance of mine. You look so much like him, I simply had to find out if you were he."

"No problem, I'm sorry I'm not him. I'm sure you would've have a good time visiting." He went back to his map.

"You are an American, aren't you?"

By this time, Steve Richardson decided that chatting with this friendly German fellow was far more interesting than staring at his map. He popped off his seat belt and got out of the car to continue the conversation.

"Yes, my wife, Laurie and I are from Cincinnati. That's in Ohio. Have you heard of Cincinnati before?"

"Actually, yes, I've heard of it."

By this time Laurie Richardson returned from the bathroom.

"Hi, who's your friend here, Steve?"

"I'm sorry, I didn't catch your name."

"My name is Klaus. I'm on business with a colleague. That's Günther in the car over there," Klaus pointed to the Mercedes. "We were on our way to Berlin when I noticed your husband. He bears a remarkable resemblance to an old friend of mine, Karl Geppert."

"Well, that's interesting. We're going to Berlin too. We just finished visiting the Expo back in Hannover, and now we're going to visit my old college friend, Renate Zeumer, in Berlin. She just had a baby girl, you know. We can just hardly wait to see her and her family. She and her husband, Christian, have three children. Are you from Berlin?" Laurie asked.

"No, I'm from Frankfurt."

"Wow, that's a long way from here. We were in Frankfurt on Friday to pick up our rental car. We took the train from Paris to Strasbourg and then up to the Frankfurt airport. You see, we're flying home from Frankfurt next week after we visit with Renate. We thought it was best to get a rental car at the airport. This has been such a wonderful trip. Have you ever been to the United States, Klaus?" Laurie finished outlining their itinerary.

Klaus' eyes drifted from the Richardson's to the blue Ford's luggage compartment. All he saw was conventional luggage through the glass, nothing long and cylindrical like the E-7 generator.

"Yes, I have. I went on holiday to Florida two years ago," answered Klaus with a charm belying his inner turmoil.

"Well, that's nice. Steve and I have been to Florida so many times we can't remember. Can we, Steve?"

"You're right about that."

"Well, you should come to Cincinnati sometime. You'd love it, I'm sure. Cincinnati was mostly settled by Germans, so we have a lot of German food there, like brats and metts," she said invitingly.

"I'm sure I would, Mrs. Richardson. Well, it was nice meeting you. Enjoy the rest of your trip," said Klaus extending his hand to both of them.

"You too," said Steve.

Klaus returned to his car, got in, and closed his eyes.

"Was passiert? Aren't we going to get the generator back?" Günther was puzzled.

Klaus let out a deep breath of utter defeat and stared out the windshield at the Richardsons, who were now getting back in their car to leave.

"Klaus, they are getting away. Has there been a change in the plans?"

Klaus continued to stare out the window. His face was expressionless. The blue Ford backed out of the parking space and proceeded to the on ramp.

"Let them go, Günther. It's not them."

"You mean, that isn't Hudson and Shakhova?"

"That's exactly what I mean. Those are the Richardsons, who are also from Cincinnati, like Hudson. For all I know, they're probably next door neighbors! And get this, they've been all the same places that Hudson and Shakhova have been…Strasbourg, Frankfurt, Hannover. Günther, we followed the wrong damn car!" Klaus' demeanor changed from lifelessness to controlled irritation.

Klaus picked up a sheet of paper with the listings of all his security teams and called Helmut Winkler.

"Winkler, this is Vogel."

"*Ja*, what is it?"

"The blue Ford we followed did not belong to Hudson. You are positive you tracked them from the bank to the gas station, then onto the autobahn?"

"That's correct. However, there was one irregularity I neglected to mention before."

"And what might that be?"

"When I got onto the autobahn I turned my head for just a moment to check the traffic and when I looked back there were two blue Fords ahead of me. I assumed the rear one was Hudson's and followed that one. It made good sense at the time."

"Shit! Why didn't you report the other car as well? We could have sent Energia Two to follow that one. Now they're long gone you stupid idiot! You're fired! Turn in your car back at the Hannover office and go find yourself another job!" yelled Klaus as he clicked off the phone.

Klaus picked up the two-way radio and summoned Energia Three, "Proceed to Hannover immediately for refueling and then await instructions. Energia Two, follow Energia Three back home."

"Are you going to call Herr Schmidt and tell him what happened?" Günther asked the wrong question.

Klaus handed him his mobile and curtly said, "Be my guest."

As Günther started the car to return to Hannover, Klaus' mind drifted into questions of, "Why is this happening to me?" to thoughts of, "This doesn't happen to me." Amidst this self-examination the annoying noise of his phone intervened. He dreaded what was coming next.

Chapter 34

"*H*ALLO, VOGEL."

"I've been waiting for your call. What's going on?"

"We were...misdirected. The car we pursued was not Hudson and Shakhova's, but an American couple on vacation. Their car was identical to theirs."

"*Das ist unmöglich!*"

Klaus covered up the phone and turned to Günther, "He doesn't believe me."

"It was an incredible fluke, but there is still hope, sir. My former underling informed me before I fired him that he had two blue Fords in sight, not one. He followed one and let the other one go on, neglecting to inform me about the latter until a few minutes ago. They must have been in the other car. I have sent the helicopters to base for refueling. We'll have them back up in the air very quickly. I'll be contacting the Frankfurt office about rechecking the satellite cameras in the area of the autobahn junctions around Hannover to see if we can pick up their direction after the last sighting."

Dieter breathed deeply trying to regroup his thoughts after this disappointing report, "Put every available person on this, Klaus. We cannot let them get away!"

"They only have an hour head start. We'll find them."

"I'm counting on you!"

Klaus called the Frankfurt security office; "I want you to check the tapes from the autobahn junctions along the A7 through Hannover."

A few minutes later his mobile rang with some good news. The second blue Ford had entered the A7 north from the A37, and was later observed crossing the junction with the A352. They were heading north!

Klaus quickly called Dieter back, "They are northbound on the A7."

"They must be going to the Hamburg airport. There could be no other explanation. Where is Energia Four?"

"It should be ready to go. I'll dispatch it toward Hamburg immediately."

"Good. Get back here to the hotel and pick me up. I want to be present when we confront Hudson and Shakhova and take back our precious generator."

"At our present speed we should be there in twenty-five minutes." Klaus was guessing.

"I'll be waiting for you in front of the hotel."

Klaus picked up the two-way radio, "Energia Four, proceed to the A7 and go north Hamburg."

The net was extended northward.

"This has really been a really smooth drive so far," said Hank.

"Yes, it has been a good day."

"The land here reminds me of northern Indiana, nice and flat, and full of farms and woods."

"It is much like the trip from Nizhny to Moscow."

"How much farther is it to Denmark?"

"It is at least another two, perhaps three hours. The traffic in Hamburg might delay us a little. We should be coming into the suburbs in a few minutes," she said looking at the map.

High above them at one thousand meters, Energia Four paused while its pilot used his binoculars to confirm his sighting of a blue Ford Mondeo station wagon. Reducing his altitude another two hundred meters he was able to verify that the license plate did indeed belong to the car Henry

Hudson had rented from the Hertz agency at the Frankfurt airport. The pilot picked up his cell phone to report his discovery.

"You are absolutely positive that the license plate numbers match the ones on your sheet?"

"They are the same," confirmed the pilot of Energia Four.

By now Klaus and Günther had picked up Dieter from the hotel and were advancing northbound on the A7 leading a column of black Mercedes sedans like a high-speed funeral procession.

"Continue to follow them and report in at five-minute intervals. It is imperative that you not lose them!" commanded Klaus.

"Do we have anyone left in our Hamburg office who could assist?" Dieter asked from the back seat.

"No, we pulled them all down to Hannover yesterday. Energia Four is our only hope of tracking them at the moment."

"I know the chief director of the Hamburg airport. We may not be able to overtake them on the road, but I can have their flight delayed," boasted Dieter.

A few more minutes passed by before Energia Four reported, "They are now passing through the junction with the A1 but are still northbound on the A7."

"That's in the direction of the airport," said Klaus reviewing the map.

"Just as I predicted."

The column of black sedans began to gain ground quickly.

"What do I do when I get to the next bunch of autobahns?" asked Hank.

"The A261 will merge with the A7, but just keep following signs for the A7. After that, we go a little further until we come to the Elbtunnel."

"The Elbtunnel, what's that?"

"On the map it looks like a tunnel under the Elbe River."

"That sounds interesting. We don't have those back in Cincinnati, just bridges and the Anderson Ferry."

Hank and Natasha continued to negotiate the midday traffic through the southern suburbs of Hamburg blissfully unaware of the danger that lurked above and behind them. Within a matter of minutes they came upon the blue three-mouthed monster and were ingested down its right hand esophagus twenty-seven meters under the Elbe River. For a moment, they were safe from detection by the forces of Energia.

"The Ford has now passed under the Elbtunnel. We can't follow them until they come out the other side," reported Energia Four.

"Okay, get across the river quickly and position yourself so that you can spot them when they exit the tunnel," Klaus hurriedly said.

As ordered, the helicopter crossed the river, positioned itself in front of the tunnel, and hovered about fifty meters above the roadway. Soon the blue Ford emerged from the bowels of the monster.

"Wow, that was cool! That took some smart engineering to put together. It looked like they were building another tunnel over on the left when we drove in."

"I saw it. It is amazing what they have done."

"See that helicopter up there?"

"Yes, I do."

"It looks a lot like that one we saw back on that mountain, der Broken."

"*Der Brocken*. It is identical to it. There's an insignia on its underside. I can just read it. Ener...gia 4."

"Energia 4! Jeezus, that's one of their company's helicopters! They've must have been following us all over the place!"

She looked back after they passed under it and noticed that it moved in their direction.

"You're right. It is them, and they are following us."

"What do we do now? Any ideas?"

Natasha closed her eyes and prayed for an answer.

"I believe that if we keep going straight ahead, everything will be fine. It will all work out well. I can sense it."

"Even with Darth Vader looming overhead?"

"Who is Darth Vader?"

"I'll show you the video someday. It's too hard to explain in all this traffic."

Hank and Natasha, aware that they were being followed, felt a greater urgency to escape the confines of urban Hamburg and cross the border into Denmark. The black Mercedes caravan, now traveling at over 220 km/h was passing the Naturschutzpark Lüneburger Heide and fast approaching the Hamburg metro area. Klaus' mobile phone rang.

"Sir, there is something peculiar going on with the Ford," Energia Four chimed in.

"What?" asked Klaus.

"We observed the vehicle coming out of the tunnel, and have been tracking it from there for several minutes, but it hasn't taken any of the airport exits."

Klaus looked at Dieter, "They're not going to the airport. Energia Four says they're bypassing all the roads to the airport."

"Maybe they're lost and don't know where to exit. Ask them for more details."

Klaus returned to his phone, "Is there anything else you can see?"

"Yes, since the tunnel they've been gaining speed, using the left lane a lot. They don't seem to be behaving like they're looking for an off-ramp. We just passed the exit for Highway 432. I would say that they are heading out of the city."

Klaus looked at Dieter and shook his head; "They've speeded up and are still driving north without any sign of getting off the autobahn."

"They're running for the border!"

"I would agree with that assessment," said Klaus as he returned to his phone. "Energia Four, keep following them out of Hamburg. We are closing in behind you."

"Affirmative, we will continue the surveillance, however, our fuel is below half. We're only going to be able to go as far as Kiel before having to refuel."

"Stick with them as long as you can."

He turned back at Dieter; "We've got a problem. They are low on fuel and have to set down in Kiel."

Dieter leaned forward and tapped Günther on the shoulder, "I believe this car is capable of a few more kilometers per hour. *Schnell!*"

The lead Mercedes increased speed to 240 km/h. The others tried to follow along. Meanwhile, Hank and Natasha were through the northern suburbs of Hamburg and entering the countryside.

"I'm beginning to wish I hadn't drank so much coffee at breakfast."

"I understand. I need to use the toilette too."

"Can you see the helicopter anymore?"

Natasha looked up and out of the passenger side window.

"No, but it may have risen higher."

"There's a rest area coming up in two kilometers, should we chance it?"

Natasha looked ahead, feeling her discomfort, weighing it with their predicament, "If we go quickly."

Hank pulled the car into the rest area.

Klaus' mobile phone rang again.

"Sir, you won't believe this, but they've stopped at a rest area," reported Energia Four.

"And?"

"They're running into the WC. The woman is looking up into the sky…at me. She's pointing at me. Now, the man is motioning her toward the building."

Klaus looked at Dieter, "They know we're on to them."

"Faster, Günther!" commanded Dieter.

"We're going as fast as we can."

"No you're not!"

"What are they doing now?" Klaus returned to his phone.

"Nothing as yet. They're inside the WC. Hold on. The man is coming out and is running toward the car. He's getting in. Here comes the woman, also running. She's in. They're leaving the rest area."

"That was a quick pit stop. Faster than the crew on Andretti's car at the Indy 500."

"I feel much better, too," said Natasha wondering who was Andretti, and what was the Indy 500.

"We've got over half a tank, I think we can make it to Denmark on that."

"We must keep going north."

"Yes, dear."

Hank Hudson now got to drive like many fans of auto racing only dream about driving, as fast as he had guts to drive. The extent of Hank's racing mettle limited him to 160 km/h, or about a hundred miles per hour. They soon breezed through the Dreieck Bordesholm where the A215 veered off toward Kiel. By now, the Energia convoy had cleared the slowdown through the Elbtunnel, and was past Hamburg's northern suburb of Norderstedt gaining distance on the fugitive engineers at the rate of more than one kilometer per minute. It was now a numbers game—a function of distance, speed, and acceleration.

Energia Four called Klaus Vogel to report, "We are now below a quarter of a tank, which is barely enough to get us up to the Kiel airport for refueling. The Ford is still northbound on the A7. Request permission to refuel."

"The helicopter has to refuel, shall I let them go?"

"I really don't like the idea of losing visual contact. We must try to slow them down somehow. Hand me the phone!"

"Energia Four, this is Dieter Schmidt. What I am about to ask you to do is dangerous, but we must attempt to slow down the car you've been tracking. I want you to approach the car from its front. Frighten them into stopping!"

"Yes, sir," said Energia Four.

Suddenly, without warning, the helicopter that they had such difficulty seeing from their car windows now appeared directly in front of them approaching at high speed. Hank instinctively stomped on his brakes, as did the other cars on the road. Chaos ensued in the flow of traffic.

"What the hell does that guy think he's doing? Is he trying to get us killed?"

"I believe it is the second thing you said."

"They think they can scare me, eh? They're only pissing me off!"

Hank shifted his foot from the brake to the accelerator and gave it a push. He soon encountered slower traffic, terrified by the unsafe antics of the villainous chopper. However, in spite of this challenge, he maneuvered through the cars with the expert dexterity of a nine-year-old playing a video game. Soon Energia Four came around for another pass.

"Here we go again!"

Natasha closed her eyes. Hank's reflexes caused his head to duck. The cars in front of him began to scatter toward the middle shoulder and the right lane. As before,

Hank kept his composure and played dodge-em with the other vehicles on the road. His nerves were energized with a newfound strength and confidence. Natasha opened her eyes in time to see the helicopter swerve away from the oncoming traffic and off toward the east. Her eyes followed it until she couldn't see it any more.

"I think he is gone."

"Damn, I was already for another round, how about you?"

"*Nyet*, no more, please."

Hank and Natasha felt a momentary sense of relief now that the helicopter had flown away. Were there more on the way? They had no way of knowing for sure.

Dieter called Energia Four, "Did you do it?"

"Yes, sir, we made two passes at the Ford. I sure hope none of the other drivers on the road could read our serial number. We came in at them at only ten meters above the ground. I'll be in huge trouble with the aviation officials if I'm reported. We're on our way to Kiel now, running on fumes."

"Excellent work, Energia Four. Don't worry about the officials, I know plenty of them personally," bragged Dieter.

Thinking that the strafing runs had slowed down the blue Ford sufficiently, Dieter Schmidt began to relax his fixation on the chase. Although he couldn't see them anymore, he knew where they were heading. All they had to do was overtake them before they crossed the frontier into Denmark. Physics was on his side. At the current rate of gain, they would be able to prevent their flight out of Germany. But, why were they driving to Denmark, he wondered? They would eventually have to get a flight to Sweden or the US perhaps. He began to tighten up again.

"Klaus, you can't drive to Sweden, can you?"

"I don't think so. Don't you have to take a ferry?"

Günther piped up; "I read in *Die Welt* an article about the big bridge the Danes and the Swedes built across the Baltic Sea."

"Yes, the Oresund Bridge. I had been so caught up in the details of the convention I haven't paid much attention to the news. It isn't open yet, is it?" asked Dieter.

"*Ja*, last week. Now you can drive direct to Sweden."

"Not with my E-7 generator, they won't! Step on it, Günther. I'm not paying you to read *Die Welt!*"

For the next forty-five minutes Dieter's cars made up the distance on Hank and Natasha. Since their encounter with Energia Four, Natasha settled her nerves by meticulously studying the map, searching each road for a possible alternative route off the now dreaded autobahn.

"Hank, the exit for Highway 201 is coming up. I want you to take it."

"Why? We're really making good time. We should be in Denmark soon and away from these morons."

"I do not have a good feeling about staying on the autobahn. If we get off of it they will never find us. Highway 201 intersects Highway 76 that would take us all the way to Flensburg. There we can pick up Highway 200 and go across the border."

"Okay, if you say so."

As Natasha directed, Hank followed the route she outlined for him. By the time Dieter's car crossed the exit for Highway 201, Hank and Natasha were past Sleverstedt, just twenty-five kilometers from the border.

"According to my calculations, sir, we should be coming up on them pretty soon."

"Keep your eyes open, Klaus."

When Energia's fleet of Mercedes arrived at the border they saw no blue Fords. What they did see a swarm of white police cars assembled on the Danish side. Meanwhile, Hank and Natasha, having used backroads, negotiated their way through Flensburg, and unceremoniously slipped across the border into Krusa, Denmark. At the first phone booth they called Anders Petersson using the phone card they bought at the Shell station earlier in the morning.

"You've arrived in Denmark, how wonderful. Did you find our welcoming committee?"

"I do not understand, welcoming committee," said Natasha.

"We arranged with the Danish national police to escort you across the country. They should be there," he said with concern.

"There is no one here in this town."

"You're in a town. Oh, I thought you would be coming across the border on the autobahn. Where are you, then?"

"We are in Krusa. According to the map, we are only two kilometers from the autobahn."

"Hold on, a moment," Anders got on another line and spoke with someone. A couple of minutes later he returned to the conversation, "Drive up to the autobahn and get on the on ramp, but wait on the side until you see the police cars. They are coming up from the border to greet you. I better let you go. We'll see you here for dinner!"

Natasha returned to the car, "Let's go. We have friends waiting for us on the autobahn."

Hank started the car and pulled it onto Danish Highway 170, to Highway 8 and the E45.

"Look, those police cars are starting to leave. That seems rather suspicious," Klaus noted to his boss.

"I agree. We haven't seen Hudson and Shakhova's car, but I'll bet they know where it is. Follow them!"

All six black Mercedes started their engines and crossed the border into Denmark closely following a dozen or so white Danish Politi Ford Mondeo sedans. Within a few minutes they crossed the junction with Highway 8.

"That's our cue," said Hank as he put the car in gear and entered the right lane of the autobahn. Soon, four Danish police cars surrounded their car, each officer waving a sign of friendship to Hank and Natasha.

"Can you believe it, look at them. They're waving. Wave back!"

From behind the sea of white Energia's lead car and its occupants saw the blue Ford Mondeo station wagon in all its glory, protected by Denmark's finest. From his seat, Dieter could almost see the white lab coats wrapped around the E-7 generator.

"*Scheiße!*"

"Would you like us to pursue them, sir?"

Just then, two of the police cars slowed down to create an automotive wall between them and the rest of the police convoy. Blue-shirted officers sitting in the rear seats rolled down their windows and drew their guns and pointed them at the approaching cars. Dieter's heart jumped a beat. He knew he was defeated. The chase was over.

"Umm, if we're voting on this, I vote we don't," said Günther.

His face reddened with rage and frustration, Dieter said to Günther, "You may turn around at the next exit and take us back to Germany."

Chapter 35

ONCE THE HORDE of black Mercedes cars hightailed it back toward Germany, the lead police car waived Hank to pull over at the rest area now fast approaching on the right. The car followed them off the autobahn and parked next to them. Several other police cars subsequently arrived outnumbering all the other cars in the parking lot.

"What do we do now?" Hank turned to Natasha.

Just then, a stocky, balding, middle-aged man wearing a police uniform stood up from the bench where he had been sitting and walked up to their car.

"I believe he will have the answer."

Hank rolled down the window to hear what the policeman had to say.

"Good afternoon, you are Mr. Hudson," he leaned through the window, "and you must be Mrs. Shakhova. Welcome to Denmark!"

"Thank you," said Hank and Natasha in unison."

"Allow me to introduce myself, I am Chief Superintendent Armin Lindvig of the Danish National Police. You've no doubt seen many of my other officers in their cars. This is Sergeant Clausen who directed you into this rest area."

Hank shook the hands of Chief Superintendent Lindvig, while Natasha extended her hand to Sergeant Clausen who was standing next to her door.

"We have been directed to extend to you every courtesy, and to escort you across Denmark to your friends in Sweden. Is there anything you require before we begin the drive?"

Hank looked at his watch; it was after two o'clock. "We haven't eaten anything since eight this morning, and our car is low on gas. Can you recommend a good restaurant in the area? My treat," he turned and whispered to Natasha, "It's always smart money to take care of your local police."

"I believe that can be arranged. There is a very good restaurant only a short distance up the road in Aabernraa. You will enjoy it very much. The owner is a good friend of mine. Let me give him a call."

After a couple of minutes on his mobile phone, he spoke to his fellow officers who returned to their cars. He walked up to Hank, still seated in his car.

"Follow me. We'll take you directly to the restaurant."

Aabernraa was a small port town known locally for its busy market. Its short distance from the autobahn made it a convenient place for Hank and Natasha's first Danish meal. To their delight, the restaurant was located within sight of the of Aabernraa Fjord, one of the many bays that filled the hilly Baltic Sea side of Denmark's Jutland peninsula. They followed Superintendent Lindvig and Sergeant Clausen into the old brick building. The restaurant owners greeted everyone with warm hospitality.

"Come on in, I have a table over by the window with a view of the water. Come, this way!"

"Let me introduce you to my old friend, Paul Sorensen, and his wife, Katherina," said the Superintendent.

"Good to meet you. I'm afraid I don't know how to say 'hello' in Danish," confessed Hank.

"Goddag," said Natasha extending her hand in greeting.

"Goddag!" said Paul Sorensen.

"Oh, excuse me, this is Mrs. Natasha Shakhova, and Mr. Henry Hudson. They are my guests for the next few hours, and they are very hungry."

"We are closed until dinner, but I have made a special exception for you. Please feel at home here. The food is coming shortly. What you would like to drink?"

"I'll have coffee," said Hank.

"Two coffees for the sergeant and me," said the Superintendent.

"I would like glass of vodka," said Natasha.

"Vodka?" Hank said with surprise.

"Vodka. It is the same word in Danish, I believe. After all we have been through, I am ready for a glass. Maybe two."

"Bring the lady some vodka," said Hank.

"I have a bottle already chilled in the refrigerator. Three coffees, and one vodka."

Before the drinks arrived, Katherina Sorensen brought out several trays of cold cuts, cheese, fish, and bread.

"We Danes call this kind of meal, *smørrebrød*. You can make your sandwich any way you wish," said the Superintendent.

"*Fru Sorensen, undskyld, taler De engelsk?*" Natasha said to her in Danish.

"*Ja,* I speak a little English."

"Your name, 'Katherina.' It is my daughter's name as well."

"I see. You must miss her. I can see it in your eyes."

"I do. I have not seen her in over two weeks. She is with my mother and sister, but I do want to be back with her very soon."

"Perhaps you can call her. Come with me, you can use our phone."

Katherina Sorensen showed Natasha to their telephone back in the kitchen. After a few minutes she got through to the family flat in Nizhny Novgorod.

"Hello, is that you, Natalya?" Natasha said into the phone.

"*Da*, it's Natalya. Where are you, Natasha? How are you? You were supposed to be home last Friday. They've been calling here from the power plant."

"I'm fine. We are here in Denmark. I'll be home soon, hopefully by the end of the week. Many things have happened in a very short period of time. It's too much to explain right now."

"I'll say. What do you mean by we?"

"Well…I have met a man, Natalya," she looked around to see if anyone was listening, "I think he may be the one we talked about. He is an engineer, just like me."

"Natasha! I don't believe my ears. You and a man? And an engineer no less!"

"What do you mean, me and a man? Of course! His name is Hank Hudson, from US," putting her sister in her place.

"An American! This is incredible! How does he feel about you? I can tell that you're in love with him. It just screams through your voice."

"Stop it, Natalya! He's not a highly emotional person. Engineers tend not to be like that. However, I am certain that he likes me. He calls me 'dear' sometimes, and has talked of my coming to see him in America. Yes, he feels the same way about me."

"*Khorosho!* I can stop worrying about you growing old all by yourself now that you have this Hank Hudson to take care of you. When's the wedding date?"

"Natalya! We only met this past week. It is not right to discuss marriage so quickly. We are just getting to know each other—how we think, our likes and dislikes, our tastes in music, food, literature, culture. This takes time you know."

"What other things have you been doing to get acquainted with each other?"

"That, sister, is none of your business! Everything in its right time."

"Uh-huh, so you're still getting acquainted in that way"

"Is Katerina there?"

"Yes, here she is"

"Hi, Kat. How are you? I miss you so."

"I'm fine, Momma. Aunt Natalya and I have been having a great time together. We went to the movies yesterday."

"That sounds good. How are your violin lessons coming along?"

"I practice an hour every day. I've had three lessons with Mr. Stratsky. When are you coming home, Momma?"

"Very soon. There are some things I must do before I can come. I've met a new friend from America. His name is Hank."

"That's a funny name."

"He's a funny person. I think you will like him very much."

"Here's Aunt Natalya. Good-bye."

"Good-bye," said Natasha with tears welling up in her eyes.

"Don't worry about Katerina. She's doing fine. Just do whatever it is you have to do. Call me when you get back to the plant, and I'll bring her home to you."

"*Spasibo,* Natalya." said Natasha as she hung up the phone.

Her glass of vodka was waiting for her when she returned to the table. She wiped a tear from her left eye and sat down.

"Are you okay? You look sad."

"Thank you, I will be all right. I talked with my little girl," she said to everyone.

"You have a daughter. That's nice. Do you and your husband have any other children, may I ask?" said the Superintendent.

Natasha gathered herself and responded, "I have no other children. Katerina is my only child. My husband died several years ago."

"I apologize for prying. My condolences for your loss."

With that, Natasha drank the entire glass of vodka straight down and looked out the window at the sea. Other than the recent dashes across the waterways of France and Germany, this was the first opportunity she'd had to sit and stare at water. Her mind drifted back two weeks ago to her long chat with Natalya on the Chkalov Staircase. Would she be able to put the past behind her and take hold of the future and all of its possibilities?

"Earth to Natasha!" beamed in Hank's message with a wave of his hand.

Natasha shook her head, and smiled at him. He smiled back, and took her hand in his. She felt his loving support.

"I was informed by my supervisors not to ask specifically why you needed our help at the German border. However, can you satisfy my curiosity as to why those cars were following after you?" asked Superintendent Lindvig.

"Well, if you were the German police you'd probably have us locked up in jail rather than wining and dining us in this fine establishment."

"Now you've aroused my curiosity even more. Why would anyone want to put a nice looking couple like you in jail?"

For the next hour Hank and Natasha told them a tale of intrigue, suspense, danger, and adventure. Superintendent Lindvig and Sergeant Clausen sat riveted to their seats. Finally, the Superintendent's curiosity was satiated.

"Isn't it unbelievable that this company was going to destroy a device that could solve the entire energy crisis?"

"That's right. Crazy, isn't it? That's why we had to steal the generator, otherwise it would have been lost for good."

"And those cars that followed us from the border were looking for you, to take back the generator and dismantle it.

I'm afraid to think what they would have done with you. They must be evil people."

"God protected us the whole way," Natasha spoke up.

"I suppose it was God that called me to your aid. I'm flattered. Speaking of God and his plan, we must get going now," said the Superintendent turning to his friend, Paul, "The food was great as usual."

"How much is the bill? Remember, it's my treat," inquired Hank.

"Oh, Mr. Hudson. There is no charge. I'd give up ten lunch bills to hear a story like you have told," said Paul Sorensen.

"Thank you, *tak,* whatever you say," fumbled Hank.

"*Selv tak.*"

Everyone said their good-byes to the Sorensens. Then suddenly, almost out of nowhere, the armada of police cars reassembled, escorted Hank and Natasha to a nearby gas station, and then whisked them back to the E45.

The trip to Sweden breezed by without a hitch. The convoy quickly picked up the pace north to Kolding where they connected with the E20 east. In less than an hour they traveled the length of Funen Island across the Great Belt Link Bridge at Nyborg. An hour and a half later the convoy passed through Copenhagen and across the newly opened Oresund Bridge to Malmo, Sweden. As they passed over each of the great bridges connecting Scandinavia with the rest of continental Europe, the engineer in Hank and Natasha marveled at their construction.

"Check out the height on that suspension bridge, will you?" said Hank.

"Just think about it," said Natasha, "You can drive from as far as Istanbul or Madrid all the way to Stockholm or Oslo."

"They are impressive bridges. Like the cathedral in Strasbourg, it all goes to prove that where there's a will, there's a way. They found a way to do it."

Upon their arrival in Malmo, they thanked Chief Superintendent Lindvig and Sergeant Clausen for their assistance in crossing Denmark. A couple of Swedish police cars picked them up for the half-hour drive north to the IDEON Research Park at Lund. As they drove into the parking lot Anders Petersson was there to greet them. Hank, Natasha, and Project Atlantis were safe at last. Anders and two of his workers from IED helped Hank remove the E-7 generator from the rear cargo area of the Ford.

"I'm amazed at its compactness and light weight."

"It's not very big, but it sure cranks out a lot of juice."

"She is quite a marvelous machine," added Natasha.

"She?" asked Anders.

"We failed to mention, the E-7 is a she. Don't ever call it a he or you'll answer to her!" said Hank nodding toward Natasha.

"I'll remember to call it she from now on. Let's get...her into the lab. I've a million questions to ask you about how she works."

A smorgasbord dinner along with plenty of Swedish aquavit drink and beer was brought into the lab to expedite the debriefing process. For the next several hours Hank and Natasha shared the technical papers on the E-7 generator and Project Atlantis that Franz Heidel had given them. They attempted to explain the theory of how the crystal interacted with the earth's magnetic field to create an electrical current, and how the xenon gas helped to modulate the current.

"This is utterly fascinating. We've tried to produce such a device here at IED, but we needed more research and time. As much as I abhor the behavior of Dieter Schmidt and his company, one must admire and respect the incredible strides they've made here. Your explanation of the process is so simple, so obvious, yet light years ahead of our present day science."

"Hey, we're only the delivery service," explained Hank, "Franz Heidel is the guy you really need to thank. This is his baby."

"Thanks to you, the delivery was made. I hate to think what would've happened if Energia's security department had actually caught you. They're notorious in our business. I had a visit a few years ago from Klaus Vogel. He subversively attempted to coerce me into selling IED to Energia. But, I'm not easily intimidated."

"Klaus Vogel, who's he?" asked Hank.

"Dieter Schmidt's hatchet man, his head of security. I have no doubt that he was hot on your tail the whole time you were trying to get out of Germany."

"Well, I sure don't want to ever see another helicopter through my windshield, nor another black Mercedes in my rearview mirror. We were real lucky they didn't catch us."

"Klaus Vogel could never catch us, even with his helicopters and big cars. We were always divinely protected. I am convinced that the Project Atlantis is a gift from God to humanity. Even if an evil man helped to create it, then tried to destroy it. God's will was for it to survive. Hank and I were chosen to do this. We had no choice but to bring it to you, Dr. Petersson."

"Please, call me, Anders. Your courage is to be admired. It took a lot of bravery and self-sacrifice to do what you did. Your combined engineering skill and experience was certainly crucial to your agreeing to take the generator in the first place. You could understand Franz Heidel technically speaking; otherwise you would've dismissed him as an imbecile. Perhaps there has been a greater design in the flow of events."

"You're welcome. We only did what anybody would have in the same circumstances. But, as I was trying to tell you earlier, Franz Heidel is the real hero. I've never seen anyone with as much guts as he has. Not only did his team build this thing, he broke ranks with his company and engineered the plan to steal it, right down to the last detail. If he hadn't driven that ambulance into the street at the last minute, I think we probably would've met Klaus Vogel," explained Hank.

"Perhaps we should invite Mr. Heidel here to IED. The creator of the generator should be united with his creation. His presence would certainly speed up the process in getting this miracle machine to work right."

"I have his sister's phone number back in Germany. I presume that he is with her. Her name is Gerta Bauer," offered Natasha.

"I'm sure he's looking for a new job now," added Hank.

"That's good. Natasha, if you could give me his sister's phone number we'll contact him right away. In the meantime, I'll bet you're both pretty tired from all the activity today. I have an extra room at my apartment you can use if you like, but it only has one bed. Or, we can get you your own hotel rooms."

Hank looked at Natasha for guidance. Her gentle tap on his knee and her beaming face was all the guidance he needed.

"You know, we've been in a lot of hotel rooms lately, a nice room in a home would suit us fine, and save a little money. We'll come with you."

Once Hank and Natasha were in their room at Anders Petersson's apartment, they wasted no time shedding the clothes they had worn for the last two days, got into bed together, and wrapped their arms around each other as the Scandinavian summer sun slipped below the horizon.

Where would this lead? They didn't know. They didn't care. They were safe, and they were together. They could finally relax. They were one.

Chapter 36

Monday EVENING FOR Dieter Schmidt was far less celebratory when contrasted with the party going on in Sweden. He sat back in his hotel suite in Hannover filled with rage and frustration. If a can of gasoline had been placed in the room it would've spontaneously ignited. Yet, at the same time, total helplessness consumed his psyche. Despite his single-minded determination to capture the elusive American and Russian engineers, and recover his E-7 generator, he had completely failed. With no leads to investigate, no trail to follow, he sent Klaus back to Frankfurt.

He surmised that by now they were certainly with Anders Petersson and his bunch. No other outcome could have been worse than to have the ultimate alternative energy technology fall into the hands of one of the leading alternative energy companies. Bad luck was neither an excuse nor an option for him. He was used to getting his way, and had evolved an organization to ensure he achieved his intended goals. How could they have slipped through his elaborate and extensive net of manpower, machinery, and technology? These two engineers must either be very smart or just plain lucky.

Although the E-7 was merely a prototype, it worked. He'd seen its last test himself over at the Höchst lab. During that test he knew that if it ever went into production it would change the world forever, and rein in his vast energy empire. For a moment he felt his life crumbling into oblivion before him. In an effort to dominate the world's energy production he would soon be dominated and reduced by the very machine he had helped to create. In a matter of only a couple of years the world would be liberated from its dependency and reliance upon conventional fuels and power systems. It didn't seem right that energy should become virtually free.

He proceeded to polish off an entire bottle of Jägermeister and fell into a drunken sleep.

Chapter 37

THE TUESDAY MORNING sky mysteriously hung over southern Sweden. A cold front had drifted in from the north blanketing the land in a layer of cool mist. The muted light of the sun softly illumined the upstairs bedroom of Anders Petersson's apartment. As usual, Natasha awoke before Hank. He lay on the bed asleep facing her. She observed the definition of his face — the occasional wrinkles, the shape of his eyes, nose, and mouth. It was the same kind face she first saw back at the restaurant in Strasbourg a week ago. Had it been only a week since they had met? Was this really happening to her?

Several days ago she had been in another world, another life. Her job at the power plant, Katerina, Natalya, and Mama felt different to her somehow. Her memories of Papa, Anatoly, Nikolai, and Alexei became like ghosts passing into another dimension. Her life in Russia now seemed dreamlike, fading fast into the background of her mind. But, where was her life leading if not back to Russia? Where was her relationship with Hank headed? Had God sent him to her to create a new life, or were they brought together for an even higher purpose? Was it by accident or providence? These thoughts consumed her as she continued to study the contour of his face.

There had been an instant recognition of one another, an unforced rapport and an understanding that was natural and genuine. They were opposites in many ways, yet their shared values, insights, and dreams of a better world, not to mention their jobs, made them highly compatible. Last night had been a complete coupling of energy, chemistry, and passion. She couldn't remember having ever made love with such intensity and desire. No wonder he was still sacked out, snoring away. For a moment, she basked in her feelings of love and appreciation for him. Could their relationship have a storybook ending, or was it all simply too good to be true? One thing was for certain; she was a changed person for having met Henry Hudson. Did he feel the same for Natasha Shakhova?

There was a knock at the door. Although it was delivered most gently, the noise jarred her from her contemplation. She instinctively pulled the covers over her naked body and replied, "Yes, who is it?"

"It's Anders. I was just checking on the two of you. How did you sleep?"

"Very well, thank you."

When you're up and dressed, come downstairs for some fresh coffee and breakfast. I've got an idea I need to share with you."

"All right, we will be there soon."

She returned to Hank's face, his eyes still shut, seemingly oblivious to her gaze. She dove back into her world of wonderment and leaned over and kissed him on the lips, not expecting a response. However, to her surprise, he instantly drew her into his arms and passionately returned her advance. She didn't resist. When their lips parted she said, "How long have you been awake?"

"Oh, since Anders sounded reveille."

"What?"

"The knock on the door."

"You are very sneaky," she said as she took great pleasure in knocking Hank across the head with her pillow, laughing all the while. He returned the favor.

Natasha got out of bed and wrapped herself in one of the towels lying on the dresser. Her fair, trim, and tall body didn't go unnoticed through Hank's groggy vision. He especially noticed her beautiful brunette hair draped across her shoulders.

"See you in a few minutes, my darling," she said as went down the hall to the bathroom for a lengthy shower. Hank fell back into his bed wondering if he was dreaming.

Yikes! Could this be the woman he had been hoping to find someday? Could this really work? God, he hoped so.

Chapter 38

HANK AND NATASHA came into the dining area of Anders Petersson's home aglow. Although they were dressed in the dirty, wrinkled clothes they had worn for the past two days, they shone.

"How about a good cup of Swedish coffee to get you two started?"

With that question Hank was taken back to his grandmother, Naomi, a full-blooded Swede. She used to make coffee so strong a spoon could stand straight up in it. Nothing could get you going in the morning better than a cup of Grandma Hudson's Java. He could never forget the abundant assortment of coffee grounds that sank to the bottom of the cup. He snapped out of his reminiscence and responded, "Sure, love some."

"And you, Natasha?"

"Yes, please."

Once they were all seated with coffee in hand Anders began his pitch, "I've been pondering our situation and awoke early this morning with an idea. Given what you two have been through, you'll surely think I'm out of my mind. I've talked with my colleagues, Sven Solberg and Bjorn Johansson, and they concur. Project Atlantis is bigger than we all are. Its ramifications for the world once it can be put into production are staggering. In a way, it will be as big as the splitting of the atom. In September 1997, the City of Lund adopted Agenda 21. Have you heard of it before?"

"No, can't say I have," said Hank.

"I am not familiar with Agenda 21," answered Natasha.

"It was an international program developed at a UN conference on the environment held in Rio de Janeiro in

1992. Agenda 21, meaning twenty-first century, is about sustainable development of the environment. Sweden is a signatory to Agenda 21, but it's usually up to the local community to decide how to implement its objectives. Here in Lund we are quite serious about it. Goals have been set to reduce carbon dioxide emissions, energy consumption, and waste products. Farming is to be done as ecologically as possible. Recycling of waste and the use of renewable resources is also a part of the plan. Almost everyone is involved in the process."

"So, Project Atlantis helps to fulfill Agenda 21?" asked Hank.

"Precisely, and not just for us here in Sweden, but for the entire world. It may seem idealistic to imagine a world with an abundant, environmentally clean source of energy. The reduction of carbon dioxide alone would be phenomenal. But, what impresses me the most about the possibilities of Project Atlantis is that no person or country would be wholly dependent upon other persons or countries for their energy needs. It's no wonder that Dieter Schmidt wanted to squelch this technology. When you took it away from him, he did everything in his power to get it back, to bury it. He knew he would lose control of his vast energy empire if he didn't. In the end he will witness the reduction of his company's size."

"You mentioned that you had an idea to share with us," reminded Natasha.

"Here's where I'm going with all of this. If we're going to handle Project Atlantis correctly, we must do so honorably and justly."

"Which means?" asked Hank.

"It means that we must include Energia in its first public demonstration. And not only that, they must have a part in producing it as well. After all, it's their machine."

Hank and Natasha sat in stunned silence, speechless.

Finally Hank finally piped up, "How in God's green earth do you propose to do that?"

"I don't have all the details worked out, but if it is the right thing to do, a way will surely be shown to us. I have a good friend in the Riksdag, an old college classmate, Henrik Ottosson, who I feel can help us with the politics. But first, we will need to ensure your security with regard to Energia, and immunity from larceny prosecution from the German authorities. I think once they hear what Dieter Schmidt was planning to do with the generator, or not do, shall we say, they'll be amenable. We'll also need Project Atlantis' chief engineer who helped you, Franz Heiden, I think you said his name was?"

"Franz Heidel. You remember that I have his sister's phone number upstairs in my purse?" said Natasha.

"Yes, his expertise and familiarity with the project are vital. If all goes well, he may not have to give up his job with Energia. They'll have to hire him back, with a raise I'm sure, that is if we don't hire him ourselves! So, may I ask, what do you think of this harebrained scheme?"

Hank and Natasha looked at each other, then agreed with a nod of their heads. They were too exhausted, too wrapped up in each other to respond otherwise.

"Good! I hoped you would see the appropriateness of the idea. If you could bring me that phone number, Natasha, we could give him a call right now and see if he could fly up here, hopefully today. The Copenhagen airport is very convenient for us since they opened the Oresund Bridge. Is there anything you two need right now?"

"Now that you mention it, we could sure use a ride to a department store or mall. We've been in these clothes for days, and our luggage is back in Germany," requested Hank.

"I think that can be arranged," said Anders.

After a few phone calls, Anders turned to Hank and Natasha, "My secretary, Johanna will take you to some stores here in town where you can pick up some clothes.

Afterward, we'll meet for lunch at the Restaurant IDEON in the park."

"Sounds good to me," said Hank.

"Me too," said Natasha.

Chapter 39

By LATE THURSDAY morning Dieter Schmidt was back in his office at Energia headquarters in Frankfurt. From his perch on the sixtieth floor of the Messeturm, he stared out the window down upon the city below pondering his predicament. Hudson, Shakhova, and the E-7 had been beyond his grasp for two days. He suspected that those Swedes from IED were probably sheltering them, or worse, they could have just as easily flown to the US where Hudson's company and friends would have certainly helped them. What were they brewing? Either way, he was ruined. Was there some way he could have averted this dreadful and final outcome, or have foreseen the circumstances that made it possible for Hudson and Shakhova to escape? He lamented his security staff's ineptness in the face of such amateurish opponents. What a bunch of bumbling idiots, *Dummkopfs!* They had not failed him in far more difficult situations. Klaus had especially let him down. Even given all his prior training with the Stasi in the former East Germany, he proved to be unreliable. Why had this assignment been different than all the others?

The phone rang. Gretchen informed him, "Herr Schmidt, it's the Chancellor on line two for you."

"The chancellor of what?" he snapped out of his melancholy reverie.

"He's calling from Berlin."

"Thank you, Gretchen."

Dieter wondered what this could be about. It wasn't election time. He cleared his throat and punched line two, *"Guten Morgen, Herr Chancellor,* what can I do for you today? Do you need more money for your party's bank account?"

"Dieter, we need to talk, in person. Can you come to Berlin?"

"Was gibts? You sound mysterious, Gerhard."

"Please come, Dieter, as soon as possible, preferably today."

"What's the rush? Today isn't very good for me."

"I can't talk about it over the phone, other than to say it has to do with something you are missing."

Dieter felt a tightening in his stomach, "You have my attention. Hold on a moment."

He called Gretchen on the intercom, "When is the next train leaving for Berlin?"

"Just a moment, sir. There's a 13:15 train from the Frankfurt Hauptbahnhof that arrives in Berlin Zoological Garten station at 17:19. Would you like me to book you on it?

"Yes, for two of us."

Dieter returned to the phone, "I'll be up this evening."

"Good. I'll see you for dinner at my house."

Dieter hung up the phone, bewildered. How did the Chancellor find out about Project Atlantis? Who told him? Even though the last two days had been living hell for him, he wondered how he was going to survive the four-hour train ride to Berlin wondering exactly what the Chancellor knew. As powerful and mighty as he was as the President and CEO of the largest energy company of the world, he now felt powerless to halt the unrelenting flow of events. He summoned Klaus into his office to share the news of his phone call with the Chancellor and their upcoming afternoon excursion.

The day before, Franz Heidel finally came out of hiding from his sister Gerta's house in Fischbach. Anders Petersson had called to ask if he would come to Sweden and help unveil Project Atlantis to the world. Gerta had given him a ride to the Frankfurt Flughafen where a ticket to Copenhagen was waiting for him at the Lufthansa desk.

Since his arrival in Lund, his thorough knowledge of the generator's unique functioning proved to be invaluable. What would have taken weeks now only took hours. Hank and Natasha assisted him along with the rest of IED's engineers. By Thursday afternoon they were ready for a test. Just as it had performed at Energia's lab in Germany, Project Atlantis did not disappoint. The crystal generator was activated and fine-tuned to the earth's magnetic field. Electrical power became instantly available without any fuel being consumed. By God it really did work! The excitement of the test flew through the entire IDEON complex. The genie was creeping out of the bottle.

Chapter 40

THURSDAY EVENING, DIETER and Klaus arrived for dinner at the Chancellor's residence in an upscale section of Berlin.

"Come on in, Dieter. I'm very pleased you came today. And this man with you is?"

"Klaus Vogel, our head of security. I felt that he should be present since you said something of ours was missing."

"*Selbst verständlich.* Good to meet you Herr Vogel."

"The pleasure is mine," said Klaus, as he shook hands with the Chancellor.

"Come in and sit down. Can I get you something to drink? I've got some excellent American whiskey."

"No thanks, Gerhard. I'm not in the mood for celebrating."

"None for me, danke," said Klaus.

"Just the same, I think you're going to need one, Dieter," insisted the Chancellor as he poured two glasses, one for each of them.

"Let me speak plainly. I received a call from my counterpart in Sweden, asking me to grant immunity from prosecution to one of your former employees, a Dr. Franz Heidel."

He looked at a piece of paper on the table next to him, "And also to a couple of his *Ausländer* friends, a Herr Henry Hudson and a Frau Natasha Shakhova. Apparently they made off with some of your property last Saturday. Is that true, Dieter?"

"Go on," nodded Dieter.

"It seems that Herr Hudson and Frau Shakhova have some pretty influential and powerful friends in Sweden.

They're going to get their immunity, as will Dr. Heidel. I need a promise from you that you and Herr Vogel here will cease bothering them. Agreed?"

"Agreed."

"Now, this item they stole from you is not some simple coffee maker, but, as I understand it, a device that can produce electrical energy virtually out of thin air. They've told me that you were going to destroy it. Can this possibly be true?"

"Well, not necessarily. We were merely reassigning some of the staff from that little project to other more important ones."

"Don't bullshit me, Dieter! Remember that I'm a politician. I can smell someone trying to deceive me, and I smell that now!"

Dieter smiled, and returned the look, "It was only a prototype, and not a very reliable one."

"Evidently, your device is not as unreliable as you claim. According to the Swedes it's producing electricity as we are now speaking. In fact, it's powering a computer at a laboratory in Lund, Sweden. Come over here to this desk and look at the screen on the computer. One of your Swedish colleagues has something to share with you."

Anders Petersson appeared on the screen and began speaking, *"Guten Abend.* I want to offer you a deal, Herr Schmidt. As you now know, we are in possession of your Project Atlantis E-7 generator, and have as our guest its creator, Dr. Heidel. I believe you two are acquainted."

Franz Heidel, adorned in his traditional white lab coat, turned from a control panel in the background and joined Anders Petersson in front of the mini-cam. Dieter's face boiled with fury at the sight of his former employee.

"Dr. Heidel has been extremely helpful in our tests on the generator. Right now it's producing 19.27 kW of power at 240 volts with only a .05% fluctuation in the current flow. I must congratulate you and Dr. Heidel in producing what will certainly become a whole new way of life for the citizens of our planet."

Dieter turned and looked up at the Chancellor and said, "Do I really have to listen to any more of this?"

"You have no choice!" said the Chancellor in a commanding tone pointing at the screen.

"Dr. Petersson, what kind of deal are you offering? I can't imagine that you would need anything from Energia or from me. You've got the generator, and I doubt that you're just going to simply hand it back to me. My own government doesn't appear to be doing anything to retrieve it," said Dieter as he threw a vexed glance at the Chancellor.

"Oh, Herr Schmidt, don't be so combative. You once offered me a deal to buy my company, and now I'm finally responding to your offer. Without the wealth, strength and resources of Energia, Project Atlantis would simply not have happened. You are its natural parent, in a manner of speaking. My company is small by comparison, and although we're one of the top companies in the alternative energy field, we're not appropriately equipped to raise this child on our own. I am proposing a joint effort between Energia and IED to develop and market the Project Atlantis technology. The rest of the R&D would be done here in Lund, while the mass production, marketing, and licensing agreements would be handled by your worldwide organization. Herr Schmidt, let's go into business together! We Swedes are not such a bad people to work with."

Dieter sat quietly attempting to digest the words he had just heard. He could hardly contain himself.

"That's a very generous offer, Dieter. He doesn't have to make it. Dr. Petersson appears to be a decent and principled man, and from what I can observe, he's giving you your company back. I am sure there are dozens of other companies he'd rather do business with. You don't want him talking with General Electric, do you? Your reply to him is 'Yes,'" urged the Chancellor.

"All right, Dr. Petersson, let's do business."

"Please, call me Anders. Let's meet here next Tuesday for a public demonstration of our generator and the announcement of our joint venture. How does ten o'clock sound?"

"Fine."

Dieter got up from the desk and walked back toward Klaus and the Chancellor.

"How could you have sat on this, Dieter? It makes no sense to me at all. You create the most incredible device that the world has ever known and you simply decide to discard it like a dirty old rag!"

Dieter responded by throwing up his hands, "Blame it on my Soviet upbringing if you must find a reason. Innovation was not our strong suit. You see, control and power always took precedence. We initiated Project Atlantis as much to prove to ourselves that it couldn't be done, so that we would have nothing to fear from the Anders Petersson's of the world. We called it Atlantis because we assumed it would fail and return to the world of myth and fable, just like Atlantis. But, it actually did work, and if it were produced, then all that I've spent building the last thirty years would have been erased. I didn't want to be erased, damn it!" Dieter began to sweat profusely, his face flushed.

"Dieter, I am extremely disappointed in you. The unveiling of your Project Atlantis could have been Germany's finest hour — to bring virtually free energy to the world. This could have helped us redeem ourselves for all the atrocities of the past. Now we have to share the glory with the Swedes. How humiliating for our country!"

Both men silently sat there for a moment allowing the Chancellor's last remarks to linger in the air.

"I've got to tell you something, Dieter, this proposal of cutting you into the deal was totally Anders Petersson's idea. I had nothing to do with it. They could've gone it alone and left us out entirely. We should count our blessings that he's not a politician like me, nor a ruthless bastard like you."

Chapter 41

IT WAS FRIDAY morning at the Petersson apartment. Anders knocked on the door of Hank and Natasha's room, "Are you awake yet? I've got some good news."

Through the door he could hear the rustling of sheets followed by a groggy female voice, "Yes, Anders, come on in."

Anders came in and said, *"God morgon."*

Natasha was sitting up on the bed in her brand new pajamas. Hank was snoring away beside her.

"God morgon, Anders." Then she nudged Hank, "It's Anders. Wake up!"

"Huh, yawnnn," said Hank as he gained consciousness.

"Good morning, Hank."

"Morning, Anders. Man, I slept like a rock." Both Anders and Natasha looked at each other and shrugged their shoulders.

"I've got fantastic news. The Swedish and German governments have agreed to the plan. You're both free from the larceny charges, and are welcome back in Germany whenever you wish.

"That's great news, Anders. Now I can pick up our luggage and return that rental car without being tossed in the slammer."

"Thank you very much for helping us, and letting us stay here in your home," added Natasha.

"I am honored to have the rescuers of Project Atlantis staying with me. None of this would have been possible without you."

"Anytime," said Hank.

"I've got some fresh coffee brewing and a box of pastries waiting for you downstairs. In the meantime, I've got to get into the office. There is much work to be done in preparation for next Tuesday's debut of the generator, and the announcement of our joint venture agreement with Energia."

"You're really going to work with that whacko?"

"That whacko, as you say, will be coming here on Monday to sign the preliminary papers to start our new enterprise. Dieter Schmidt may be a real scoundrel, but he's also a good business man. We actually need him as much as he needs us."

"Hey, man, it's your call. But, after what we've been through the last several days, we could do without Dieter Schmidt in our lives."

"Truly, I understand your feelings. Hopefully you can tolerate his presence here for a short while. Also, our press conference will include some real big shots including the Prime Minister of Sweden, The Crown Prince, the Chancellor of Germany, and both of your country's ambassadors to Sweden. Well, I've got to go. Come on over to the lab if you like, or do some sightseeing in town."

With that, Anders left the room. Natasha, still supporting herself with her arms, released her props, dropped back into the bed, and snuggled up next to Hank. He slipped his arms around her shoulders.

"Now what do we do?"

"I was wondering the same thing."

"I think if we want to stay employed somewhere we'd better spend a little time over at the lab. I don't think there's going to be the need for anymore large, monstrous power plants."

"I was thinking of us, Hank. What are we to do?"

"Hmm, good question. How would you like come to America?"

"I was hoping you would say that."

"I was also thinking that maybe I should visit, where are you from again, Nizhna Novgrod?"

"Nizhny Novgorod."

"Yeah, Nizhny Novgorod. That's a mouthful. I would like to meet your family, especially your mother."

"My mother? She does not speak any English, you know."

"It doesn't matter, I just have to meet the woman who gave birth to you, raised you, and helped to make you who you are. She must be one hell of a person to have done such a terrific job."

"And?"

"Since your father isn't around to speak with, I guess I'll have to talk with her and fumble through whatever you Russians say when you're asking to marry their daughter."

"Hank, you are sure about that?"

"I may be a plodding, methodical, cautious engineer, but I know a good thing when I see it, and you're it!"

Hank took her into his arms and kissed her, repeatedly. They never made it downstairs to enjoy the coffee while it was still fresh.

The following Tuesday morning at 11:00 a.m., while the world watched on CNN, and with all parties in attendance, the Project Atlantis generator was turned on, just as it had been two times before. But, this third time was the charm. With the flick of a switch the stage lit up with an array of lights that encircled it, and illuminated a message board that read: "The people who walked in darkness have seen a great light. Those who dwelt in the land of the shadow of death, upon them a light has shined."

On Wednesday, Natasha flew from Copenhagen back to St. Petersburg and was reunited with Katerina, and her job at the Baltic Regional Power Plant. Hank drove back to Frankfurt for his flight home to Cincinnati. On the way he stopped at the Gästehaus Mueller and picked up his and Natasha's luggage. In his rapidly improving German he told

Herr and Frau Mueller the whole story over a bottle of wine and a hearty German meal, including apple strudel.

Chapter 42

THREE MONTHS LATER, back on Lake Pomme de Terre in the Missouri Ozarks, Hank's fishing woes continued. Since he began fishing several hours ago he had landed only two little crappie. Together they were barely big enough to make a small sandwich. He threw them back wondering if he had caught the same fish twice.

"When is my luck going to change? I know there are bigger fish in here!"

"I think our luck is pretty good. It's really not luck but fate, destiny, Providence, don't you agree, my dear."

"Pass me the night crawlers, will you? They're right under your seat."

Natasha leaned down to pick them up causing the boat to tilt slightly to the left, and then the boat rolled back to center as she handed the container to Hank.

"Thanks, or, umm...*spasibo.*"

"You're welcome."

"So, what did you think of Cincinnati? It's a pretty nice city, don't you think?"

"It's very nice, what's not to like? Cincinnati has everything anyone could want."

"Yeah, and the view of the Ohio River from the back porch, that's the best."

"Almost, but I can understand your point of view since you haven't seen a real river like my Volga from the top of the Kremlin wall."

"All right, I give up, the Ohio River isn't the Volga, but it will have to do now that we'll both be working for OVP. I just knew those hotshots in the corporate office would leap at the chance to get in on the ground floor with IED and Energia."

"When we go to Russia next week for Natalya and Yuri's wedding I'll personally show you the Volga."

"I'd like that. Don't forget, I've got something to ask your mother when I'm there."

"Yes, my dear, you do."

At that moment, the ear-splitting sound of Hank's satellite pager went off. Hank looked at the phone number on the small screen.

"It's the office calling. Should I call back?"

"You should. It could be important."

"Your right, it could be," he said until another pulse sounded, "Nah!" said Hank as he flung the pager into the lake.

A moment later Hank's bait casting rod jerked strongly downward. He quickly grabbed the rod and attempted to pull in the catch. The fish ignored his actions and began to pull the boat away from the shallow shoreline out into deeper water.

"You have hooked a very large fish, Hank!"

"Kind of looks that way, doesn't it? With the force this one's exerting, this one's got to be a muskie, a real big one!"

"How big do they grow?"

"Oh, about seventy-five pounds, and five feet long."

"That's huge!"

"No kidding."

Hank's grip on the pole intensified as the fish continued to fight back.

"You know that part in the movie, *Jaws*, where Roy Scheider says to Robert Shaw, 'You're gonna need a bigger boat?'"

"*Da.*"

"This is one of those times."

Epilogue

VICTOR HUGO WROTE, "Nothing in the world is as strong as an idea whose time has come."

With tons of pollutants spewing into the environment each day from power plants all over the world, maybe it's time for a new way to be found to produce electricity. We can continue to drill for oil, mine coal, dam our rivers, and fan the fires of the atom, or, we can be open to the possibility of something greater, like a Project Atlantis, to emerge from the depths of humanity's creative potential.

About the Author

ALDEN STUDEBAKER IS an author and minister. He is the author of *Wisdom for a Lifetime in the 21st Century – How to Get the Bible Off the Shelf and Into Your Hands,* a Bible handbook for progressive minded Christians. He is also the author of *The Fault,* a novel set in the world of seismology, and the comedic book, *Hoosieritis – The Contagious Condition That Is Indiana.* He has a degree in religion from Western Michigan University.

Made in the USA
Columbia, SC
27 September 2020